Being Polite
TO HITLER

Being Polite

TO HITLER

A NOVEL

ROBB FORMAN DEW

Little, Brown and Company

NEW YORK   BOSTON   LONDON

Copyright © 2011 by Robb Forman Dew

Little, Brown and Company
Hachette Book Group
237 Park Avenue, New York, NY 10017
www.hachettebookgroup.com

First Edition: January 2011

Little, Brown and Company is a division of Hachette Book Group, Inc.
The Little, Brown name and logo are trademarks of Hachette Book Group, Inc.

Chapters one and two were previously published, in very different form, in the winter 2009 issue of *The Kenyon Review,* for the 75th anniversary of that review, which was founded by the author's grandfather John Crowe Ransom.

The characters and events in this book are fictitious.
Any similarity to real persons, living or dead, is coincidental and
not intended by the author.

Library of Congress Cataloging-in-Publication Data
Dew, Robb Forman.
    Being polite to Hitler : a novel / by Robb Forman Dew. — 1st ed.
        p. cm.
    ISBN 978-0-316-88950-6
    1. American life post–WW II — Fiction.   2. Universal implications of domestic life — Fiction.   3. Ohio — Fiction.   4. Evolution of a family — Fiction.   I. Title.
    PS3554.E9288B45 2010
    813'.54 — dc22   2010012794

10 9 8 7 6 5 4 3 2 1

RRD–IN

Printed in the United States of America

Especially for Emily O'Rourke

And for
Matthew Freeman

With gratitude and admiration. I love you both.

Also for Pamela Marshall,
who knows exactly what I mean to say

Being Polite

TO HITLER

Chapter One

AGNES SCOFIELD didn't know—nor would she have cared—that at precisely the moment she gave up her pretense of disinterest and lost touch altogether with her common sense, the Mississippi River reached its lowest level in history farther south in Memphis, Tennessee. As did the Kokosing River, right there in Washburn, Ohio, on the Monday afternoon of October 5, 1953, as it made its sluggish progress past the industries that had grown up along its banks.

Since early spring a drought had overspread most of the country, extracting energy from every source available and causing extreme reactions on the part of all manner of plant and animal species. Locally, however, no one in Washburn gave much thought to the communal stress caused by the prolonged and extreme heat and the lack of rain. It would be unseemly, in October, to complain about heat and light when generally the weather at that time of year would be shifting toward fall and the short, gray days and the often painful cold of winter.

On Saturday, October 3, the Brooklyn Dodgers had tied the Yankees at two games each in the 1953 World Series, but she had listened to game five on Sunday afternoon with her youngest son, Howard, and Sam Holloway, who had dropped by with tomatoes from his garden and stayed on to hear the game. It had been a blowout: eleven to seven Yankees, but Agnes remained optimistic, and Sam pretended to believe there was still hope, because he hated seeing Agnes disappointed. Having grown up in southern Louisiana, where football reigned, Sam had never known any woman—any *family*—as passionate about baseball as was Agnes Scofield and the assorted lot of people who were more or less related to her. Any one of them could generally be found at her house during a game—just stopping by briefly to catch the score or settled for an afternoon or evening on the wide back porch, where two radios were set to different stations if both the Cleveland Indians and the Cincinnati Reds happened to have games scheduled at the same time.

Sam himself had slowly been converted from the adrenaline surge of an LSU football game on Saturday nights to the subtle and sometimes excruciating tension and obsessive statistic keeping of the game of baseball. In fact, it was Sam's idea to set up Agnes's schoolroom with some of the trappings of a genuine ballpark so that she and her third-grade students could listen to game six.

He went to some lengths to make arrangements for Agnes's class to listen to that sixth game, which was broadcast live at noon on Monday. He brought his radio from home, tuned it to the right station, and left it centered on her desk in her classroom at Jesser Grammar School. At lunchtime, instead of filing into the cafeteria after "big recess," her third-grade students returned to the classroom for what Agnes had explained to them would be an "afternoon at the ballpark." Sam had called in a favor from the Eola Arms Hotel, where he conducted a lot of business, and two of their kitchen staff set up a buffet table at the back of the room from which Agnes served potato salad, baked beans, and hot dogs from a chafing dish. She dressed the hot dogs with each child's choice of condiments as he or she filed past one by one.

As Mr. Byerly, head of the Eola Arms crew, directed the clearing away—including the buffet table itself and other assorted equipment—Agnes invited him and his two helpers to stay and listen to the game as well, but Mr. Byerly said he knew he wouldn't be able to stand it with the Yankees likely to win the series again.

As the game progressed inning by inning, Agnes passed out twenty-eight boxes of Cracker Jacks and, in the seventh inning, twenty-eight bags of Tom's Toasted Peanuts. The hotel had also provided Coca-Cola, root beer, and Nehi grape and orange soda, all bought out of Sam's own pocket, Agnes imagined, but set up for her in an ice-filled tub by the Eola Arms crew.

Some of her students didn't know what this particular event was all about; they weren't sure what the World Series consisted of, especially the girls, but no one had any complaints. Sharon Kuhlman, for instance, who was eight years old, didn't discover that the World Series was not always a game between the New York Yankees and the Brooklyn Dodgers until her first year of college in Bennington, Vermont. She had made a point in her life, as soon as she was old enough to realize she had a choice, of ignoring athletics altogether as an anti-intellectual pursuit. But in her first year away at an all-women's school, she fell in love with a boy from Williams College, thirty miles south of Bennington, who happened to be on the college's baseball team. His major, though, was art history, which, in Sharon's view, made his interest in sports endearing.

But in Sharon's third-grade classroom during the sixth game of the World Series in 1953, she pretended enthusiasm when any of her classmates cheered. Otherwise she simply enjoyed the freedom to color or paint or read any of the books Mrs. Scofield provided in low bookcases at the back of the classroom.

As the game wound on, though, and the excitement of unlimited Coca-Cola and the inevitably disappointing Cracker Jack prizes wore off, Mrs. Scofield resorted to busying those students less self-sufficient than Sharon Kuhlman with a jigsaw puzzle she had spread out on a card table. She encouraged freehand drawing and watercolor painting, and she even agreed to the paper-airplane-folding-and-distance competition. But the children's sweaty hands smudged their artistic efforts and wilted and grubbied the crisp upturned wings of their white paper planes. An air of petulance hung in the classroom as the heat intensified throughout the afternoon inside the unshaded, wedding-cake-white-embellished but otherwise dark redbrick box of Jesser Grammar School. And, as the Yankees' Billy Martin got hit after hit, Agnes, too, grew disconsolate, although she believed she was successful in not showing her disappointment.

By the time the game ended, the Yankees had clinched the series, beating the Dodgers four games to two for their fifth consecutive World Series win. Ricky Johnson and Adrian McConnell—who were best friends but each a passionate fan of those separate opposing teams—erupted from their desks into a shoving match in the aisle. The confrontation escalated into punches thrown and furious name-calling. Agnes came from behind her desk and stooped to separate the boys. Ricky was red-faced with heat and despair, and Adrian was also overheated but fervently triumphant.

Agnes grabbed the backs of their sweat-dampened collars as if they were rabbits, and pulled them apart, but just at that moment Adrian sprang backwards, and his head slammed against Agnes's temple. She exhaled a sharp "Ah!" of surprise and put her hand to her head, and each boy immediately subsided into his desk across the aisle from the other. They were still so mad at each other, though, and horrified by Mrs. Scofield's dismay, that they dissolved into tears, as did Agnes Scofield herself, to the consternation of her dumbstruck students.

The classroom became unnaturally quiet as Mrs. Scofield continued to speak to Ricky and Adrian without any quaver of crying in her voice, but with tears running freely down her face. As she spoke, she stroked a gentle circle with the tips of her fingers over the side of her head that had collided with Adrian McConnell's. "...and you both know better! You both...Being a good sport about losing—and winning, too..." She wasn't aware that she was crying, but her voice floated away without resonating in her own mind as the pain of the collision briefly blossomed across her forehead and the bridge of her nose and shockingly deep behind her eyes and along her cheekbones.

She paused midsentence and briefly closed her eyes until the pain subsided a bit, and then she carried on, carefully looking out the window so the children wouldn't notice her distress. She aimed her gaze above her students' heads at the dry playground, but she found no consolation there. The jungle gym glinted white in the appalling glare, and the swings baked in the sun just beyond the shade of the single, ancient walnut tree, under which the girls played jacks at recess. "...learning how to lose is part of growing up," she said. But she knew what she was saying was nonsense; it was only ever possible to pretend not to mind losing: Losing was always terrible.

Agnes's head hurt; her lips were chapped and dry, and yet the nape of her neck was damp and her collar clammy with perspiration. "And learning to win without *bragging*—especially if you're a Yankees fan"—her own voice suddenly broke tearfully—"and your best friend's team loses to them for the second year in a row..." Ricky and Adrian were all attention, as was the rest of the class, and the steady throbbing of her head as well as her own bitter disappointment hit Agnes like a ton of bricks, transforming the brief welling-up of tears into a genuine sob, which was interrupted by the final bell. She was able to pull herself together while the children gathered their things and fell into place in the separate girls' or boys' line, departing in opposite directions in relatively good order.

As the summer of 1953 had dwindled toward autumn across much of the United States—in Milwaukee, Chicago, Cleveland, Indianapolis, and Washington, DC—the unusually dry, hot weather, which had first manifested itself in June, held fast, and anyone whose livelihood depended solely upon agriculture became edgy and preoccupied by the relentlessly sunny days. Small farmers were worried, of course, but not

nearly so anxious as the major national and international bro-
kerage houses, newly invested in the booming postwar food-
processing industry, pesticide manufacturing, and grain and
sugar importing and exporting. That a prolonged arid season
had stalled over much of the United States and part of Canada
was of interest worldwide, and a change in the weather was
hoped for by powerful industrialists, major and minor bureau-
crats, and a variety of businessmen all over the world.

Residents of the stricken areas were far less aware of the
consequences of the drought, even though most endured a
mild variation of grief as the climate continued to confound
their expectations. But who could complain about the daz-
zlingly clear skies and weekend after weekend of being able to
go fishing, or swimming, or golfing? What a boon it was to
busy mothers that, day after day, their children could play outside from morning till night.

Gardeners, however, from Indiana to Washington State
were at liberty to bemoan the dry pods of overlarge pole
beans, the stunted corn. And, too, anyone whose household
relied upon a private well was free to complain about having
to abandon watering the arduously cultivated but frivolous
flower beds in order to save the tomato plants and melons.

Late in September and into early October, the crop damage from the drought had already been done, but, still, the
peculiarly dry, hot, windy weather didn't abate. Day after day
an unarticulated discontent grew even among people who
had no stake at all in agriculture, commercial or otherwise.
Even people who never set foot in a garden grew short-
tempered and uneasy, although it remained the case that the
general edginess wasn't recognized collectively. Most people
blamed their disquiet, if any, on issues particular to their own

lives, and certainly those tensions were at a peak under the persistently bright, sunny, rainless skies.

Agnes, in her deserted third-grade classroom, collected the children's artwork, picked up the paper airplanes, and straightened the desks into neat rows; she leaned out the window to clap the erasers clean in a cloud of chalk and then returned them to the shelf beneath the blackboard. She boxed up and put away the jigsaw puzzle and folded the card table. She straightened the room by rote, all the while thinking how much she hated the Yankees, hated Billy Martin and his shoddy life ... Mickey Mantle, with his pugnacious but smarmy boy-next-door expression that didn't quite disguise what Agnes believed to be an underlying nastiness. She pegged him as a slyly disguised bully. She didn't even have a kind thought for Yogi Berra, too cute by half. It simply wasn't fair ... and what sort of parents would allow their son to be a Yankees fan?

She sat down again at her desk, in a sudden clutch of panicky breathlessness. It was a sensation she had recently begun to notice with fair regularity, and she sat very straight with the heel of her hand against her chest, imagining she would feel the odd flutter beneath her palm, imagining she could quiet it with applied pressure. She concentrated on slowing her breathing, and although she could not, after all, find any rushing pulse beneath her hand, that unnerving internal quaking did begin to ease, and her breathing became less ragged.

She slumped once more against the back of her chair and took a deep breath, which turned into a sigh as she exhaled. It was only October and all at once she was assailed by the fact of all the many long days remaining in the school year. She glanced out the windows, again, in the idle hope of a mitigating distraction, but the arid landscape offered her nothing more than a visual manifestation of persistence under duress.

She never wanted to teach another day in her life! That realization finally eclipsed her disappointment over the ball game, overshadowed the throbbing pain in her temple, and came full into her mind, at precisely the moment regional waterways reached their shallowest levels of the century. Of course, Agnes had no idea of that fact, and perhaps it had nothing at all to do with her own bottoming-out.

Once the notion of being free of her teaching responsibilities solidified, however, she recognized the inflexibility of it. But she also had to take into account the fact that she was just over fifty years old and couldn't possibly afford to retire, and her eyes filled with tears once again, which embarrassed her even though she was all by herself.

Julian Brightman, the documentary filmmaker, viewed the long, dry spell of weather as a godsend; he hadn't had to postpone filming for a single day since he had arrived in Washburn in mid-June. But the heat did make it hard to sleep in his third-floor hotel room. The temperature rarely dropped below ninety degrees all night, and for weeks now he had slept in only three- or four-hour intervals of tossing and turning, rotating his pillow when one side was damp with sweat. Each morning, he awoke feeling unrested and dissatisfied until he raised the shade and the brilliant, flat, white light streamed through the window of the Eola Arms Hotel. And each morning, the early traffic of cars and delivery trucks and pedestrians on and around Monument Square, directly across from the hotel, filled him with unexpected and expansive elation.

On that same first Monday in October, Julian gazed out at

the people of Washburn taking up their various everyday lives on a day when it was unlikely that any devastating surprises would be visited upon their tidy, bustling community. Of course, he knew that they had no idea of the luxury they enjoyed, which made them doubly fortunate. Mr. Brightman wasn't a petty man; he didn't begrudge these luckiest people on earth their safety, their freedom to engage in ordinary pursuits. What he did feel toward the people of Washburn that morning was a tender beneficence as he stood at his window, planning the day's filming. He would make a record of these people moving about with unself-conscious ease, walking along the sidewalk or sitting down on a bench to read a newspaper without the slightest hesitation. The very fact of their existence seemed to him to be the bedrock of any hopefulness left in the world.

In the hotel's shadowy dining room Julian sat gazing out at the light reflected off the automobiles, a newspaper stand, a metal awning, and it seemed to him that the fearlessness of everyday life in the United States made Americans glisten with well-being. He was determined to illustrate their conscientiousness, as well, their industry; he wanted to illuminate their good-natured diligence, which he admired with a nearly familial and entirely sentimental indulgence, as he sat sipping his coffee. For a moment he was so intoxicated with affection for every single citizen of Washburn that it was as if he had suddenly fallen head over heels in love. He hurriedly finished his breakfast, all the while looking forward to the day's work, during which he and his assistant, Franklin Cramer, would film an example of a day in the life of an ordinary American doctor.

Julian had already completed *The Town,* and *The Businessman,* and had begun filming *The Doctor* in mid-August. If everything continued to go smoothly, he expected that by the end of November he would be finished with the final three films, *The School, The Working Man,* and *Growth and Progress*—for which he already had bits of footage. So far, Dr. Edwin Caldwell, a retired physician who was cast in the leading role of *The Doctor,* was proving to be the easiest to work with of all the townspeople who had agreed to participate as characters in the films, essentially, of course, merely playing themselves.

As a very young boy, Julian had been that unusually gratifying child who was truly mesmerized by the tales told by the missionaries who visited and spoke at his father's Presbyterian church in Titusville, Pennsylvania. Eventually he followed in their footsteps, more or less, giving up his studies at the Union Theological Seminary in order to travel and record the actualities of the world. In 1932 he returned from Russia with remarkable film footage of the day-to-day life of the people of the Soviet Union, and he launched a secular, educational lecture tour of his own.

He was invited to speak at Rotary clubs and Masonic lodges and other civic associations all across the country, to ladies' garden clubs, and at small libraries as well as a few charitable organizations attempting to serve the population of immigrants fleeing Stalin. It was among the latter group that his film of village life in rural Russia produced consternation, although Julian was never aware of the occasional emotional havoc that often befell certain members of his audience. The film put forth at face value the legitimacy of his representation of the Russian sites to which he had been given free access: charming locales with market shelves fully stocked, abundance in every household, earnest delight on every peasant's rough-hewn face.

He had made that film while in the constant company of

his Russian guides; otherwise he wouldn't have been able to get around the country at all, nor would he have understood much that was said. Generally, as he traveled across the United States, any foreigners in his audience chose merely to be politely noncommittal. In Chicago, however, Professor Vladimir Ipatieff and his wife, who were recent émigrés from Moscow, attended a presentation of Julian's film, and they remained in their seats while the lights came up and the audience slowly took its leave. Professor Ipatieff proclaimed Julian's tidy, hourlong presentation criminally fatuous. He said so in his own language and quite loudly to his wife, who sat next to him silently, her eyes filled with tears.

They both were stunned and exhausted by the realization of the extent to which the situation of their native country—where their four grown children remained—was misunderstood. The professor was bitterly angry and loud-voiced and his wife was grief-stricken, but Julian, who had mastered only a smattering of Russian, couldn't follow their rapid speech and assumed they were grappling with homesickness brought about by scenes so familiar to them. He nodded in recognition and directed an inclusive, knowing, and vaguely conspiratorial smile in their direction as he packed away the projector.

But in 1939 Julian interrupted his vacation in Switzerland for a brief foray to Poland, with the intention of filming behind the lines of a country that would soon be under siege by the Germans. When he arrived in Warsaw, however, he discovered that not only had the Polish government fled the city but so had all the foreign correspondents. He found, as well, that there were no battle lines as far as the citizens of Poland were concerned; the Nazis were waging war upon the civilians.

One day he stopped his borrowed car on the outskirts of Warsaw, where he had unexpectedly come upon a bucolic scene of women working industriously in the fields of a distant farmhouse. He parked beneath the spreading, intertwined branches of enormous old trees and set up his camera on the road so he could film at a distance without interrupting them as the women bent steadily to their task, their skirts pulled back to front between their legs and tucked into their waistbands for efficiency and to fashion two hammock-like aprons for holding whatever they were harvesting. They didn't even interrupt their work to glance his way when their children spotted him and pointed and exclaimed. They made a pastoral tableau with their kerchiefs tied over their hair, and with the youngest children hanging on their skirts. In fact, as he had them in focus he tried to remember where he had seen a painting similar to the scene he was recording.

Out of nowhere, though, two German planes appeared, and as soon as the women heard the engines, they flung themselves to the ground, dragging their children facedown in the dirt as well, in an attempt not to be noticed. The planes homed in on the small farmhouse nearly two hundred yards away, and Julian's lens followed their path over the gently rolling terrain until they disappeared over the horizon, leaving behind them only the space where the farmhouse had been. Smoke and dust billowed outward and then gathered into a single rising stream of smoke snaking into the otherwise warm and pleasant air.

Only later did Julian realize that he must have heard the explosion, must have seen what had happened, because it was all there on film, but in the moment he had existed only as a mechanism without human sensibility, operating the camera.

After a wait of perhaps three minutes the women were up and digging once more, and Julian continued filming. But the planes came skimming into view very nearly at ground level and strafed the field, killing two women on the spot, and leaving a woman and child wounded.

The first time he saw that film he wondered how it was that the Germans had not noticed him; clearly he had not understood what was happening, had not had the presence of mind to fall flat himself. As that footage emerged in the darkroom, where he was locked into the inescapable intimacy of being the agent of its existence, he had begun to tremble with shock and was overtaken by a peculiar fury at those women who had arisen too soon, who had died for no reason at all, right before his eyes.

He had six thousand feet of sixteen-millimeter film left from his Scandinavian vacation, and he set about documenting the devastation of Poland as it happened. He was a man of such optimism that he was often rendered foolishly gullible, but Julian had never lacked courage or outrage, and the footage he brought back was inarguably significant. In fact, the film led to—among other things—his being asked by Nelson Rockefeller, head of the Office of Inter-American Affairs, to come up with a proposal for the series of films on which he was now at work.

After a good deal of travel and research, Julian methodically narrowed his search for the small city or town most representative of ordinary life in the United States during what he characterized as the prosperous and serene aftermath of World War II. He wanted an economy that was dependent on both industry and agriculture, and a town that was a pleasant enough place but also one of no particular consequence or extraordinary beauty. He had eventually settled on the state of Ohio, and then winnowed his selection further to the central part of the state, and finally had chosen Washburn, Ohio, as the best place to document and explain the lives of regular Americans to the children of Poland and France, Brazil and Paraguay, Norway, Denmark, Sweden, Spain, and Portugal.

Eventually, in fact, the sound track of Julian Brightman's film shot in Washburn, Ohio, was translated into forty languages. Generations of schoolchildren from Europe, Latin America, Polynesia, and many other parts of the world—later in their lives, whenever they thought of the United States— were assailed by those examples chosen by Julian Brightman to illustrate the customs of his country. Only seventeen years after those films were made, in fact, when news and images of the Woodstock festival flashed around the world, those now-grown children were hard-pressed to reconcile the muddy hysteria in Upstate New York with Julian Brightman's sunny, crisply clean Washburn, Ohio. Perhaps the terrible climate and endless rain of New York State had fostered the kind of hopelessness that eventually resulted in drunkenness, drug-taking, and rebellion.

And Julian Brightman, too, in spite of the remarkable footage of Poland he had brought home in 1939, would think of the series of films he made in Washburn, Ohio, as his greatest legacy. The idea that he might have had any part in facilitating greater understanding among nations was more than a little gratifying to him, given his early exposure to missionary zeal.

Dwight and Trudy Claytor and their daughters, Amelia and Martha, shared a handsome, rambling, three-story house with Trudy's parents, Robert and Lily Butler, halfway around the square from the Eola Arms Hotel, in the section of town still known as Scofields—or, occasionally, as "Snow Fields" by newcomers who misheard the original designation. The Claytor-Butler household together with Agnes Scofield's house right next door were the last vestiges of Washburn's original residential area. There was a handsome third house on the property, but it had long ago been ceded to the town by the late George Scofield and was occupied by the Mid-Ohio Civil War Museum, which housed George's lifetime collection of Civil War memorabilia, as well as an apartment for the curator.

Those three houses and their various outbuildings sat on nearly ten acres, all told, but they fronted on a relatively shallow crescent of lawn across the street from Monument Square. At one time the property had marked the northernmost edge of Washburn, but by 1953 the houses and outbuildings sat stolidly in the very center of town, where there were no longer any families with young children living nearby.

Trudy Claytor planned to help her mother, Lily Butler, give a dinner party at Scofields that Monday evening in October, and after breakfast Trudy decided to give herself a permanent. As soon as her older daughter, Amelia, had gone off to school, Trudy shooed Martha outside, warning her not to cross the street but encouraging her to watch the filming going on in Monument Square.

Martha was a grave little girl, very responsible, and for a while she looked on from her front yard at the activity in the square. After five minutes or so, though, she became increasingly immersed in a project she had idly begun, and the reason she was out in her front yard—where she rarely played—slipped her mind. She became entirely absorbed in creating a whole city, whose highways and byways she was tunneling as best she could into the dry, cracked earth beneath the old trees along the drive, using a short, stout stick she had picked up. She was so engrossed in what she was doing that she forgot all about the filmmaking going on across the street.

Julian Brightman was satisfied with the interior scene he had filmed earlier that morning of Dr. Caldwell ostensibly making a house call on a patient, played by Mrs. Caldwell, who had lain draped with a blanket on the sofa in her living room while her husband checked her pulse and listened through his stethoscope to her heart and lungs. But Julian wanted to exemplify an idea of the busy-ness of the average doctor's day. He entreated Dr. Caldwell, who was a tall, distinguished-looking man with flaring dark eyebrows and a sweeping crest of white hair, to cross the square again with more of an air of urgency. Mr. Brightman asked the doctor to try to appear to be hurried, if he wouldn't mind doing the scene once again, and Dr. Caldwell was perfectly amenable, even ad-libbing a nice little piece of business of glancing at his pocket watch as he once more strode briskly through the east gate of the square and along the central path.

It was just then, however, on what, in fact, *was* an ordinary workday in October of 1953, that Martha Claytor became conscious for the first time in her life of the shrieking blare of what happened to be the Scofield Engine Manufacturing Company's noon whistle, which through all the company's various incarnations had bleated one long, loud, breathy note every weekday for over forty years. Undoubtedly Martha had heard it almost every day of her life, but she had failed to incorporate it into the context of the regular pattern of her existence. That Monday noon, when at last the sound permeated her consciousness, she had not one other thought in her head than that it was a siren foretelling the end of the world.

Her sudden perception of the blast of that warning whistle was as startling as if an electric current had temporarily galvanized her. For a moment she didn't move, and then she looked straight up into the terrifying sky from which the bomb would fall, from which, in fact, she expected to see the sinister and sleekly gray-finned object closing in fast upon her. But the overarching canopy of leaves along the drive was undisturbed by turmoil of any sort—not even ruffled by a light breeze—and Martha was further disoriented and briefly dizzy. The high, streaky clouds rushed eastward far overhead, and Martha sprang up from the ground and stood gazing up into the scudding distance, not even aware that she herself had let loose a long shriek of anguish, a continual wail of horrified aloneness, despair, and resignation, uncommon among children who live in a country that's not under siege.

Dr. Caldwell broke into a run as he headed toward her to see what had happened, and her mother, Trudy, raced from her bedroom when she heard Martha's keening, elongated cry. Every ounce of Trudy's adrenaline propelled her down the stairs and out of the rarely used front door without even considering that her head bristled with pink rubber rollers and white endpapers, that the sulfurous neutralizing lotion of her Toni Home Perm trickled down the back of her neck in milky rivulets, unblotted. She stooped to her daughter's height and shook her rather fiercely to break through the spell of Martha's loudly transfixed terror.

"Martha! What is it? Martha! Martha! Hush! For heaven's sake! Tell me what's the matter!"

Dr. Caldwell, too, was bending over Martha, inspecting first one hand and then the other, using his handkerchief to wipe them clean. It seemed likely to him that she had cut or hurt her hands while she was playing in the dirt. Julian Brightman simply moved closer and continued filming.

When Martha's attention was finally caught by the intervention of adults, she instantly went quiet—as abruptly as if she were a record from which someone had lifted the needle. There was the doctor, earnestly inspecting her hands, and at the same time, she recognized her mother's expression of worried alarm but also her air of embarrassed irritation. Martha's imagination evaporated; her mind was swept clean of the details of her morning's work, and she looked without interest at the dusty ground, which a moment earlier had been a real world teeming with life and possibilities. Gone, too, was her terrified expectation of impending obliteration. All around there was concern directed her way, but, if nothing else had convinced her, the slight note of impatience she detected in the voices of the people stooping over her was certainly proof enough that the world was not coming to an end.

"What is it? What? What happened?" her mother continued to ask.

"Were you stung by something?" Dr. Caldwell asked the little girl, since he hadn't found any sign of injury. "A bee? A wasp? The queens nest in this mossy ground."

"I heard the siren," Martha said in a shy mumble.

But Dr. Caldwell and Trudy Butler were so accustomed to the sound that they hadn't even noticed the noon whistle, and they merely gazed at Martha blankly. Martha didn't have enough practice—or the presence of mind—to gather the facts retrospectively and explain herself to her mother, much less to the strangers gathered around her. Her expression was unrevealing, although she remained shocked and pale.

Trudy wasn't comforting. She had been so frightened by the nature of her daughter's screaming that when Martha finally calmed down and Trudy assured Dr. Caldwell—had assured the filmmaker, as well, after he had asked her to smile, please—that everything was all right, her adrenaline resolved into nausea. She was sickened with relief and embarrassment while she assured the few people who had gathered within hearing distance that her daughter was often carried away by this or that thing she had imagined. "She even has an imaginary playmate. Did Dilly tell you something, Martha?" she asked, turning again to her daughter, who seemed not even to have heard the question.

Trudy continued. "Dilly—her 'friend'—sometimes Dilly tells Martha horrible stories…oh, really terrible things," Trudy explained over her shoulder to Julian Brightman, who murmured his understanding, smiled, and nodded, and gently urged Dr. Caldwell back in the direction of the square, while Trudy hurried Martha into the house.

The fact was that after the Second World War, even those children like little Martha Claytor, who had not yet been born before the end of the war, understood that, one way or another, they were very likely doomed. One August morning in 1945 the American B-29 bomber *Enola Gay,* piloted by Paul Tibbets and named for his mother, dropped a nine-thousand-seven-hundred-pound uranium bomb on the Japanese city of Hiroshima. The bomb decimated an area a little over four square miles in less than one minute. Three days later, on August 9, a second bomber, *Bock's Car,* took off from the Pacific island of Tinian, carrying a ten-thousand-pound plutonium implosion bomb. *Bock's Car*'s primary objective was the ancient Japanese city of Kokura, but it was obscured by heavy ground haze and smoke, and the plane was short of fuel. The pilot, Charles Sweeney, turned to the secondary target, which happened to be the city of Nagasaki.

Over time, whatever deeper, complex consequences that first salvo of the atomic age may have had on the townspeople of Washburn, it was an event that cleaved the relatively fortunate childhoods of its youngest inhabitants into segments: They enjoyed long spells of an assumption of security in the world, broken now and then by bouts of temporarily inconsolable terror.

In fact, in America of the 1950s there was not a single community that didn't harbor an unacknowledged dread and anticipation of some sort of retribution for having perpetrated an act of aggression previously unmatched by any other country. Simultaneously, however, each one of those communities took a certain civic pride in believing itself to be at least the fourth or fifth target of destruction in order of importance to the Soviet enemy. And, too, those separate American towns and cities were inescapably proud of their country's rawboned ingenuity, which had finally brought an end to the Second World War.

Certainly there were fewer casualties in Hiroshima and Nagasaki than had been caused elsewhere through the use of conventional warfare, and in the aftermath of those bombings, opinions often differed bitterly—among former friends, within families—on the necessity of such immediate, seemingly effortless, mass destruction. But whatever judgment any individual eventually arrived at, the whole world was stupefied as it came to grips with the fact that the utter decimation of those two targets resulted in no loss at all of American blood and treasure. It was that point, that curiously inglorious sticking point, that stripped the previously naive, abundant, generous-seeming, supposedly good-intentioned young country of its virginity. Twice a bomb was released—first "Little Boy" over Hiroshima and then "Fat Man" over Nagasaki—and the single plane that delivered the bomb—along with its two-plane escort—banked sharply to avoid the concussion, and within forty-five seconds an entire city was turned into a boiling firestorm rising in a turbulence so brilliant it was as bright as the sun. And not a single American life was lost.

It was a scenario difficult even to imagine, although it was impossible not to try to grasp the consequences of such concentrated, lethal power. In the month of August 1945, the United States tied a bright red sash around the waist of her slightly dingy white dress, tucked a red hibiscus behind her ear, and joined ranks with Great Britain and the other old tarts of Europe.

And, of course, in this case, too, as is usual with any successful act of aggression, it was the perpetrator who was most terrified of suffering a similar fate.

Martha Claytor didn't know anything about the bombing of Japan; she was born two years after the event, but she was imbued with the enormity of the devastation that could be wrought in the world. That particular noonday, she had been helpless against the sudden notion of that horror let loose upon herself, and the dreadful knowledge that she would be pulverized on the spot where she stood, before ever again seeing her mother or her father, her dog, her cats, her sister. She couldn't think of anything worse than that; nothing else she had yet imagined had ever made her so thoroughly desolate.

Chapter Two

A T THE SAME MOMENT Martha Claytor was expecting the world as she knew it to be blown to smithereens, her maternal grandmother, Lily Butler, was also thinking about the atomic bomb, among other things, including the hapless Brooklyn Dodgers and whether or not the two Bundt cakes Agnes Scofield had made and brought over the day before for this evening's party would serve everyone. They would have to, Lily decided. Agnes's Dr. Bird Cake was dense and so rich that Lily would simply adjust the proportions to suit the company. And, if she could convince Robert, the oppressive heat offered the perfect excuse not to set up a bar but to serve iced tea instead.

Lily was a practiced hostess, and earlier in her marriage—earlier in her life in general—she had taken a good deal of satisfaction in her ability to seamlessly manage any number of guests throughout an evening, beginning with cocktails, proceeding through dinner, and, finally, a general regrouping after supper, with fresh drinks and various tidbits spaced out over hours of conversation. Tonight's meal would be casual, laid out as a buffet following a reading at Harcourt Lees College by two former students of Robert's who were also the guests of honor.

But Lily's usually efficient contentment with the job at hand had been displaced by a fairly gloomy anticipation of the hours ahead. These past few years it seemed to Lily that whenever the family gathered for a meal, cocktails went on forever, right through dinner, in fact, with her daughter and her nephews replenishing their drinks and bringing them to the table. Sam Holloway always brought wine to suit the meal, but Lily had once heard her nephew Claytor Scofield decline a glass in the same endearing, self-mocking manner that invariably reminded Lily of his father, Warren. Claytor had always possessed his father's charm, but when Lily overheard Claytor's exchange with Sam it gave her pause. "I believe I'll stick to whiskey, Sam," Claytor said. "It works so much faster."

Lily was out in the garden first thing in the morning, still in her nightgown and robe, in order to cut flowers before the heat built up, although it seemed to her that the temperature had never cooled down, and she let the cut stems rest in cool water in hopes that they would recover from the stress of the dry, hot weather. When she had brought them inside, all but the hydrangeas had looked like flowers tentatively sketched in pencil, a fragile representation of their full-fledged selves, and she was glad to find that by the time she dressed, had her breakfast, and checked them again, the daisies had perked up, the few creamy roses had recovered from their look of imminent bruising, and the gladiolas and lilies had plumped out to their waxy Crayola voluptuousness. She arranged a centerpiece of mixed flowers, but each one white, interspersed with spikes of park-bench-green leaves from the lilac bushes.

Arranging the table was a pleasure to Lily, a reward for giving a party, and she sat down in the dining room under the ceiling fan to cool off. It was a beautiful room, still, and she hadn't changed anything at all about it since it had first been furnished by her mother before Lily was even born. She didn't intend to use a tablecloth this evening, and the flowers were very pretty against the dark wood of the long table. She was genuinely pleased with the production, but Lily very nearly dreaded the play itself.

Just after breakfast she put a turkey in the oven and then spent the morning finishing what she could of the evening's dinner preparations. She could almost have assembled this meal in her sleep, since she was serving what she thought of as the Charleston menu. Years and years earlier, when she had been a guest of a friend from Mount Holyoke at a debutante ball in Charleston, South Carolina, Lily had first come upon this sumptuous cold supper. It had been far more extensive and exotic than this evening's version would be, but essentially the meal depended upon a ham at one end of the table and a turkey at the other. Lily supposed she had relied upon that same menu at least twice a year during her married life—she must have put variations of this same menu on the table for as many as eighty separate occasions, perhaps even more times than that.

She was counting on forty-some-odd guests, but you never knew with this sort of open-ended invitation, and she put water on to boil and set about peeling, hollowing, draining, and stuffing a few more than fifty tomatoes, having selected like-size, firm specimens from the two baskets Robert had brought in from the garden. Agnes had provided dessert; Sam Holloway had found beaten biscuits for her somewhere in Columbus to serve with the ham—he had come by and had coffee with the Butlers that morning, dropping off five bakery boxes of twenty biscuits each, and he had also brought enough peach chutney for Lily to use as a condiment with the turkey as well as the ham.

"Phyllis DeHaven loads me up with at least two jars every time she can catch me after a broadcast. They won't be here, will they? The DeHavens?" Sam looked to Lily, who shook her head in confirmation. "Well, it probably wouldn't make any difference. She'd probably be flattered, anyway. So! Here you go." He lined up six pint jars of Phyllis DeHaven's carefully labeled and dated peach chutney in the pantry off the kitchen so it wouldn't be in Lily's way until she needed it.

When Sam Holloway had first settled in Washburn after the war, he had accepted a tentative job offer from Phyllis DeHaven's husband, Clifford, its permanent status dependent upon the success of the enterprise at hand. The two of them, along with Phyllis's help and that of various other members of the DeHaven family, had founded WBRN—the first local radio station. By now, of course, these six years later, Sam had so many other irons in the fire that he only kept a hand in now and then at the station, which was a modest, squat building sited on the highest ground of Dr. DeHaven's farm. Even so, Sam had become regionally famous for his annual hour-and-a-half broadcast he still performed every Christmas Eve, and the DeHavens remained his close friends, as did pretty much everyone else who got to know Sam at all.

"It's the best chutney I've ever tasted," he told Lily. "I think it's got cardamom in it. Phyllis won't say. Well . . . and she won't *not* say, which isn't like her. Agnes wanted the recipe. Generally Phyllis is a generous person. . . . She just changes the subject, though. I don't know where she'd find cardamom, anyway. But there's only so much chutney one man can eat in a lifetime." It occurred to Lily after Sam left that the DeHavens might, in fact, turn up at dinner that evening if they attended the reading, but no one was ever offended by anything Sam did.

At noon Lily tuned the radio on the back porch to the sixth game of the World Series, with the volume set high enough that she could hear it in the kitchen through the open window, but when it began to look like the Dodgers would lose, she simply turned off her hearing aid so she wouldn't have to listen to the Yankees win. She finished up about 1:30, arranging the tomatoes on trays and covering them with dampened, wrung-out tea towels before refrigerating them.

Generally Lily fell into a state of serene contemplation as she tied up the loose ends of preparations for whatever occasion she had planned, but today, in her self-imposed silence, she was sorely irritated when she somehow cut her finger as she wrestled the large serving platters, which she had decided not to use after all, back into their storage place beneath other seldom-used pieces of kitchenware: the unassembled meat grinder with its exposed blade, four heavy, graduated, earthenware mixing bowls that were a chore to haul out for use but were heavy enough that she counted on them to stay in place as she mixed a batter.

She made a mental note to herself to have a tall divided cabinet—dedicated solely to storing baking sheets, broiler pans, and large trays—installed in the kitchen of the new house she and Robert were building eight miles or so away in nearby Enfield, within walking distance of Harcourt Lees

College. She was uncharacteristically annoyed when she realized she had gotten a streak of blood on the breast pocket of her shirtwaist. Usually Lily didn't care two sticks about her wardrobe or these inevitable little annoyances of everyday life.

Anyone catching a glimpse of Lily that morning—an unremarkable but pleasant-looking woman, neatly white-haired, trim, older but not yet *old,* and busy in her kitchen—wouldn't have thought twice about her absorption in and seeming preoccupation with any bits of domestic business. She would be virtually invisible to her own husband, her own daughter, as she moved predictably through the party preparations. Nothing in her appearance was particularly noteworthy or eccentric, and her role in Robert's and Trudy's lives was familiar. So familiar, in fact, that they would never be likely to come across her and stop still in their tracks, suddenly reminded that there's no such thing as an ordinary person anywhere in the world—a bit of knowledge worth hanging on to when observing your wife or mother in her own kitchen. Not that anyone who knew her would have thought of Lily as ordinary, in any case.

But certainly upon reflection Robert Butler wouldn't have been at all surprised had he known the unlikely ponderings running through his wife's head. Possibly Trudy, who was still young, had not yet come to the inevitable conclusion that the profound and the mundane are joined at the hip, and each one is dependent upon the human ability to recognize the other.

Lily gave the impression of concentration on nothing more than the supper she would serve that evening; her efficiency in her kitchen indicated a complacent familiarity, and she was humming and singing a song that had been running through her head:

"He'll bring to me a big bouquet of roses...
Da da da da...
The ones that broke my heart..."

She had never been able to carry a tune, but now that she couldn't hear herself, she was no longer inhibited about the pleasure she took in singing now and then. But even with all that domestic busy-ness, the nooks and crannies of her mind were filled with an undertow of knowledge that—were she to speak it aloud—would challenge the most ardent optimist in the world. Would send people fleeing from her company, Lily sometimes thought.

She had concluded at some time in her life—possibly during the war, but in retrospect she was unable to pinpoint it precisely; it had not been a sudden epiphany—but she had come to grips with the fact that if she allowed herself always to consider everything she knew...well, she doubted if she would even bother to get out of bed in the morning. Sometime after she became a wife and then a parent, after she slowly gathered the idea that no one she loved was immune from the perils of the earth...At some point she finally realized that *all* of the things that are always true are always true *all* of the time.

She no longer felt the need to remind herself that while she prepared a fairly sumptuous buffet dinner in Washburn, Ohio, somewhere else a person was weeping with the misery of hunger. She had long ago recognized that her good fortune was not due to any particular merit on her part, but it was a bit of knowledge she initially surrendered to begrudgingly because it diminished any moment of pure joy. On the other hand, she had discovered that, oddly enough, that very idea often mitigated what might otherwise be overwhelming despair. The sweeping recognition of human community was humbling, even diminishing to one's sense of self, but it made it damned near impossible to take oneself too seriously for very long. Whatever the grief, whatever the injury.

Lily believed, too, that anyone who failed to recognize that singularly human reality was a person afflicted with a naive grandiosity, egocentricity, and a lack of empathy so encompassing that it made that person a hazard to bystanders and civilians.

In fact, Lily's concerns and desires and random thoughts in the hot, bright kitchen as she absentmindedly sang aloud while wiping down the counters and setting things to rights were inescapably encumbered with the entire sweep of her life: everything she knew, everything she remembered, and even the expectations she projected into the future. This morning in particular, however, she happened to be wondering who was the actual person who had come up with the name and illustration of the Doomsday Clock. Earlier over coffee, when she turned to the second section of the morning paper, she'd been startled by the picture of that iconic, stylized, fourth-quarter clock face beneath the headline TWO MINUTES TO MIDNIGHT! RISING THREAT OF NUCLEAR WAR.

Originally that clock had been set at seven minutes until midnight, although Lily hadn't known that until she skimmed the article. It had been reset two years later to three minutes following the USSR's test of its first atomic bomb. Now it had been reset again, after the Soviet Union's successful test in August of a hydrogen bomb. The image bothered Lily for a number of reasons but primarily because the illustration of the clock was marked only at five-minute intervals, which, in her opinion, made a one-minute difference far too subtle. But too subtle for what? Certainly Lily understood that the idea was to heighten awareness, that some sort of call to action was implied. But what was expected, for instance, of *her?* She bristled at being manipulated into feeling responsible for the apparently inevitable use of the atom bomb.

All through the day she remained a little unnerved by that oddly chilling illustration, but, at the same time, she reminded herself to soak the bloodstained pocket of her dress in cold water, and she decided not to turn her hearing aid back on to see if the Yankees' good luck had changed and the Dodgers had surged ahead. The chances of that were so slim that she didn't want to know the outcome just now. And along with the other various thoughts that came and went, she continued counting down the things she still needed to do before any guests arrived. For the most part, though, the strategy of serving dinner was only a minor theme intermingled with more resonant concerns running through her head.

In fact, though, Lily wouldn't have been in the least surprised to find out that Martyl Langsdorf—an artist, and the woman who had hastily drawn that illustration of the Dooms-day Clock years earlier at the request of her husband, the atomic scientist Alexander Langsdorf—was, at that very moment, feeling aggrieved in the face of conjuring up a meal to serve unexpected guests. Her husband had telephoned her just after lunch to let her know that a young professor of architecture and his wife were visiting the University of Chicago and were eager to see the Langsdorfs' new home. Alex seemed not to have considered the fact that they were still in the process of moving into the house, which had been designed and owned by the architect R. Paul Schweikher.

Packing boxes of the Langsdorfs' belongings were stacked unopened along the hallway, and they were using a card table in the dining room while they waited for the rest of their furniture to be delivered. But Alexander had encouraged the visiting couple to feel free to come see the house that very evening. "And I think it would be nice to offer them some supper," he added.

Martyl closed up her studio for the day and looked into her kitchen cupboards. Alex had the car, and it was too late to call in a grocery order for delivery that afternoon. There was nothing for it, she decided, but to use canned salmon for salmon cakes. And accompany them with grilled tomatoes. She could make a cucumber salad, she thought, and snip a little fresh dill over it in order to pass the meal off as vaguely Scandinavian. But she was exasperated by her husband's oblivious courtesy to perfect strangers.

In Washburn, Ohio, at the very same time, Lily Butler was only anticipating her own exasperation. Her darkening mood coalesced around her hope that any topics of conversation that were particularly incendiary—subjects of great consequence, no doubt, but that also drew forth furiously divergent opinions—could be avoided that evening so she would have time to catch up with Robert Lowell and Peter Taylor, since she would miss their reading in the afternoon.

Lily found a bandage for her finger, took the turkey out of the oven, put the ham in to bake, removed her apron, and left the kitchen. She didn't remember that the radio on the back porch was still loudly broadcasting the baseball game across the grounds of the three houses and assorted outbuildings that made up the Scofields compound.

Lily's hearing had begun to decline in her late fifties, and at sixty-five she depended entirely on a hearing aid, with the receiver affixed to her brassiere and concealed beneath her blouse. It was a nuisance, but Lily remained undaunted, and only people who knew her very well realized that she was almost completely deaf. There were occasions when she was called upon to explain, of course.

Only a few weeks after she had been fitted with the hearing aid, for instance, she had been at the Lazarus department store in Columbus and had decided to call Robert and let him know she would be late getting home. She located the phone booths next to the elevators, but as she was placing the call she was interrupted by a young sailor in uniform, who tapped her on the shoulder, exaggeratedly shaking his head in discouragement and gesticulating determinedly in an effort to tell her something.

At first Lily thought he was indicating that the phone was out of order. He didn't speak a word to her aloud, however, and therefore Lily concluded that he must not be able to speak at all. Or perhaps he didn't speak English. He wasn't unattractive, but he did have a swarthy, simian face that could well be foreign. She fell into the reflexive courtesy of a similar pantomime, pointing first to herself, then to the phone, then to him, and raising her eyebrows in mute inquiry. She thought perhaps he was indicating his need to use the phone, although there was an empty booth next to her own.

He continued to shake his head and finally placed a phantom phone call, picking up an imaginary handset, holding it to his ear, dialing an invisible number. For a moment Lily was perplexed, trying to imagine what he intended, until finally she realized he thought she had no idea how to operate a telephone.

Lily had left the door of the booth ajar because it was stuffy inside, and, as she had done ever since being fitted with her hearing aid, she held the telephone upside down, with the hearing end of the handset against her cleavage instead of at her ear so she could listen through the hearing aid's receiver. She smiled at the worried sailor and pointed to her ear and shook her own head vigorously and then unbuttoned her blouse to point to the rectangular playing-card-size black receiver, although it wasn't until later that she realized that she had continued not to speak out loud. Neither had the young sailor ever said a word.

He backed away a step or two, flustered and flushed with embarrassment, pointing to himself and then putting his hand over his heart, to indicate an apology, exaggeratedly turning his mouth down at the corners in dismay, although Lily had thought him kind to be concerned. She wasn't particularly self-conscious, and was rarely embarrassed, just as she wasn't that afternoon in the Lazarus department store. Nevertheless, she was careful from then on to close a telephone booth door no matter how hot it was inside.

And there was an aspect of her deafness that she found useful. After finishing in the kitchen she purposely left her hearing aid turned off and retreated up the back stairs and down the hall to her room, where she slipped out of her scuffed black pumps and settled comfortably on the chaise longue in the bay window to work on Mr. Lewis's crossword puzzle in *The Nation* magazine.

She and Robert, as well as their daughter, Trudy, and Trudy's husband, Dwight, with whose family she and Robert shared the house—and Agnes Scofield, too, who lived just next door—were stumped by an eighteen-letter phrase: "6, 6, 6, A bird's eye view of the nursery." Robert had toyed with the idea that it might be some sort of allusion to the newly popular Birds Eye Frosted Foods, or perhaps something about Poe's raven, and Lily turned those ideas over in her head:

> ...But the silence was unbroken,
> And the stillness gave no token,
> And the only word there spoken was the
> Whispered word, Lenore...something, something...
> Merely this, and nothing more.

Never more Lenore? Nursery...No, that was seven letters. *Lenore...window...birdie?* All of those had six letters. Well, nothing there, she thought.

*Birds Eye Frosted Food? Lima beans. Jack and the Beanstalk... frozen beans...cold beans...Peter, Peter, Pumpkin Eater...*Who was it? *Peas and honey. Winnie the Pooh? Mother Goose?*

> I eat my peas with honey
> I've done it all my life.
> It makes the peas taste funny
> But it holds them on my knife.

Eatmypeaswithhoney was eighteen letters. *Frozenpeasandhoney*, too. But neither phrase worked, anyway, or even made sense.

Lily let the puzzle lie in her lap, no longer looking at the pattern of it, hoping the answer would pop into her head once she stopped trying to force it. She ran through the plan for dinner once again, thinking that she might have stuffed the tomatoes too soon. Perhaps she should tip them one by one very carefully over the sink to drain any juice that had accumulated beneath their cream-cheese-and-minced-vegetable filling.

With her hearing aid turned off, Lily hadn't heard either the noon whistle from Scofields & Company or the racket of her granddaughter Martha Claytor's dismay, and she remained unaware of the commotion in her own front yard. With the sheer drapes drawn against the heat and glare, she wasn't even aware of the filming going on across the street. Her attention wandered from the crossword puzzle to plans for the new house, and then to the logistics of a trip to Columbus to select a chair for the new living room and also to buy a winter coat, until her head rested laxly on the cushioned chaise and she nodded off in the dappled heat of her shady bedroom.

After dinner most of the guests took their leave, and the rest of the company moved again into the long parlor across the hall from the dining room, gradually separating into two groups. Robert was at the far end of the room, having restocked the makeshift bar he had hastily set up on Lily's late mother's wheeled tea cart.

"I think Cal would imagine we weren't serving liquor on his account. He might see it as some sort of judgment of him. And Peter might think the same thing," Robert had protested when Lily brought up her idea of offering nothing more than iced tea because of the heat. "Either one of them might see it as a rebuke — might think we disapproved of them, I mean," Robert had gone on to explain. But Lily hadn't been thinking of Robert Lowell or Peter Taylor; she was fond of both of them, and, after all, Cal Lowell had lived with them for an entire year while he was a student at Harcourt Lees. But she couldn't waste the energy to worry deeply about them, just as she had abandoned her share of responsibility for nuclear war. Her concerns all around were closer to home.

Robert had gone heavy on the water and tonic and club soda in the first round of drinks he'd mixed before dinner, but in the stifling heat, guests quickly returned for refills. The ice-filled glass pitcher of translucently amber, cold, thirst-quenching iced tea and crushed mint, as well as the small plate of quartered lemons, hadn't fared well throughout the evening — the tea grew cloudy as the ice melted, and the lemons showed a slight, dry curl by the time the guests returned to the room after dinner. In her capacity as adjunct hostess, Lily's daughter, Trudy, removed them to the kitchen and also collected, emptied, and replaced ashtrays. Robert refilled the ice bucket and left it to the remaining guests — all of them old friends — to take it upon themselves to mix their own drinks.

He became involved in an earnest conversation with William Empson and Red Warren and his wife, Eleanor Clark, as well as a brilliant young visiting clergyman, Tyler Caskey. The previous Friday a number of writers, editors, and contributors had arrived at Harcourt Lees College for a series of strategic discussions about the future of the *Harcourt Lees Review*. Robert and Lily's supper party marked the unofficial culmination of the weekend's event. Lily cared very much about the *Review* on Robert's behalf, but she was worn out from the effort of providing dinner for so many people while trying to make it seem to be no trouble at all, and she didn't join those guests chatting with Robert around the fireplace at the far end of the room.

She sat down on the small Victorian sofa her mother had always occupied when she had retreated to the front room to read, which was set into a shallow alcove among the bookcases. It gave Lily the advantage of being nominally present among the younger crowd but also of not seeming to intrude on them. And, in fact, she had turned off her hearing aid. Her daughter and son-in-law, Trudy and Dwight Claytor, along with Sam Holloway, and Lily's nephews—Agnes's two sons, Howard and Claytor Scofield—had gravitated to the sofas and chairs arranged to take advantage of a cross breeze with open windows on either side. Claytor's wife, Lavinia, settled herself on the carpet, leaning back for support against her husband's knees, and Cal Lowell and Peter Taylor pulled up chairs as well. But not a breath of air moved through the room, and Lily sat among them, more or less, and let her mind wander.

Agnes Scofield had considered begging off the night's dinner invitation after the day she'd had, and because of the terrible heat, but in the end it seemed easier to go than to offer an explanation that was bound to encourage persuasion otherwise. She simply couldn't say that she was tired from the school day, and that the heat made her miserable, without someone trying to convince her she was mistaken.

Over the years she had discovered she should never reveal to anyone the fact that she would rather endure a blizzard than a heat wave; she had listened to too many reproachful lectures about that particularly outlandish—downright *selfish*—preference on her part in the face of the opposite desires of everybody else!

Only Sam had ever leapt to agree with her at supper one

night. "Until you've spent a summer in southern Louisiana, you don't even begin to know how lucky you are if you never have to do it again," he had said. "When I enlisted I thought I'd hate the cold. Especially flying at high altitudes. But it turned out to be about the only thing I didn't mind about the war." In that moment no one sitting around the table had offered a defense of hot weather.

In Agnes's experience, however, no one ever hesitated to remind *her* that everyone—the farmers, the elderly, the ill, gardeners of every stripe, the *children,* for goodness' sake, all of them housebound by snow—yearned all year for those summer months and all the long, warm, sunny days of leisure.

If only, Agnes thought, her wishes *could* change the temperature at any given time, she wouldn't hesitate for a minute. She would even sacrifice the happiness of all those heat-loving children and housebound invalids in the blink of an eye! Once she realized that people took the weather personally, however, she kept her opinion of it to herself. But, truly, given the choice, she would choose winter over summer; she would choose fall over spring. She was pretty thoroughly miserable in the stifling room, and she had a sharp headache along with a bruise on her temple where her head had collided with Adrian McConnell's earlier in the day. But, aside from any of those conditions, she had been filled for days with an unspecified dread of this gathering that she had thus far refrained from pinning down.

She glanced around the room in search of whatever conversation would require the least of her, and she recognized the posture Lily fell into whenever she didn't have her hearing aid turned on—a relaxed but faux attentiveness, with her expression pleasantly fixed. Agnes joined Lily on the small sofa, and the two of them sat comfortably in relieved non-communication.

Agnes had thought the awful heat surely would discourage anything more than cursory conversation after dinner, and that the guests wouldn't be inclined to linger, but it seemed that the weather was having the opposite effect. She was halfheartedly listening to the conversation going on among her children and other various guests when she realized that the group was more or less embracing the heat, thirstily refilling drinks in which the ice cubes had scarcely had a chance to melt. The men had abandoned their jackets before dinner, and now they shed their ties and rolled up their sleeves. Lavinia pulled her heavy hair back from her face and cinched it at the nape of her neck with a rubber band; Trudy untucked and unbuttoned the tail ends of her sleeveless blouse and tied them in a jaunty, dog-eared knot beneath her breasts, creating a cooler, midriff-baring outfit. Agnes couldn't escape the uneasiness that misted across the span of her attention when she realized that her children's evening was just beginning. Trudy and Dwight had set up a less extensive bar closer to hand, on the fold-down inlaid table that generally stood flat-faced against the wall. Agnes thought they had already had more than enough to drink.

In case he might need a dinner party to edit into one of his films, Julian Brightman had filmed some footage before supper, and Agnes saw with dismay that he was about to join her and Lily in their peaceful nook. It was already too late to pick up and leave by the time she spotted him coming her way, and he pulled a small slipper chair close to her side of the little brocade sofa. Agnes had the dismal idea that he believed the courtesy of keeping her company was incumbent upon him, since she was the only unaccompanied woman in the room.

"Do you mind if I join you, Mrs. Scofield?" he asked, and Agnes smiled pleasantly enough.

"Of course not," she said. "I'm not staying much longer, though. I think the heat is catching up with me," she said. The close air wasn't a languid, heavy presence, like the climate she remembered from when she was a child and had visited her cousins in Mississippi. She hadn't liked that, either, but it did have a soft, romantic, nostalgic quality about it once she had become accustomed to the rotten-egg odor from the paper mill that saturated the city of Natchez.

In Washburn, Ohio, on the other hand, the towering chimneys of the factories that had grown up along the Kokosing River sent those fumes high into the sky, where they were carried east by the prevailing winds. The crackling dry, hot air of Washburn smelled like freshly ironed shirts, and Agnes felt as though she were being turned to Melba Toast in a slow oven. Any curiosity, any energy or animation, had evaporated, leaving behind only a flat, dry, gingerbread man of herself. And, in fact, the yearning she had *not* to make small talk with Julian Brightman was as powerful as thirst to someone gravely dehydrated.

"In this part of the world you have such bounty," Mr. Brightman said. "The wonderful supper tonight! An entire ham and also a turkey! Such lucky people to live in this place. Beautiful! Clear and warm. Always, it's sunny weather," Mr. Brightman enthused while nearby, Claytor's wife and Dwight seemed to be disagreeing good-naturedly about something.

"The truth is, Dwight," Lavinia was saying, "if you want to dance... Well! *Any* of the Big Bands—"

"Oh, no!" Dwight interrupted, "that's all over... That's

gone as far as it can! Become derivative. That era's come and gone, Lavinia..."

But Agnes was distracted once more by Mr. Brightman, who leaned closer to her in a conspiratorial posture. "You have a very handsome family, Mrs. Scofield. They take after you. Although I would never have thought you were their mother. Maybe their sister. Very good for my camera. So healthy. So American."

"Well, thank you," Agnes said, but she was irritated by the flattery, which she was too tired to counter, and also by Julian Brightman's assumption of... well... of a defined *friendship*—a familiarity of any kind between them.

Agnes had never thought of herself as pretty, although over the years she discovered that other people often did. But it was the Scofields' looks—tall and rangy, with dark eyes and light hair—that Agnes had coveted for her children. And they all looked exactly like Warren. Even Dwight—who was her brother, not Warren's son—looked so much like a Scofield that he and Claytor were often mistaken for twins.

"As a matter of fact," Agnes corrected Julian Brightman, "they all take after their father. You know, though, I'm not sure I understand what you mean. How do you see them as so *American* exactly?" Agnes asked. She had been nonplussed the few times she had fallen into conversation with Julian Brightman. It turned out that he was only from Pennsylvania, after all, even though he took on the manner of a worldly-wise foreigner. He certainly wasn't a handsome man, although very few people gave his looks much thought one way or another. Anyone who met him was distracted by his manner. He spoke with an ordinary American accent—perhaps a bit flatter through the vowels than an Ohioan—but his comments were so oddly

constructed that Agnes wondered if English was his first language. He seemed to be speaking from an earlier century, far
more baroque than the present one. Anyone from Washburn
who chatted with him was left feeling foolishly uncertain of
the intentions behind his words; did he intend irony, sarcasm, or
was he genuinely as fulsome in his admiration for the citizens
and town of Washburn as he continued to say he was?

"You Americans are so *generous!*" he said, perplexing her
once again. "Industrious! But most of all it's that you're optimistic. That always impresses me very much. Everyone's still
full of all sorts of big ideas. High hopes," he said. "I think it's
what makes Americans such attractive people. It's delightful to
be among people who are still romantic. It makes me happy
to see them. Nothing like how it is now in Europe."

"*Ah!* Yes. I see," Agnes murmured, simply to end the conversation. His conclusions seemed to her absurdly broad, but
also not at all interesting just now. She didn't have the wherewithal this evening to pretend curiosity, to draw him out into
a further explanation. Agnes was so impatient to go home that
her attention was absorbed by waiting for an opportunity to
make her farewells and cross the lawn to her own quiet house.
In fact, as the conversation among the younger guests seemed
about to deepen, Agnes edged forward, gathering herself
together to rise and take her leave, but she was stopped when
Trudy's voice rose above the rest in an angry complaint.

"Oh, of *course* you think Artie Shaw's a genius," Trudy suddenly said overloudly to Dwight, who was sitting right beside
her. She spoke in a sharp-edged, urgent rush that drew the
attention of everyone at either end of the room. "He *must* be
a genius! He's such a genius he's even disgusted by the gull-
ibility of his own fans. '*Morons,*' he calls them. I *do* know,

Dwight—I *do* know he's good! But please spare me the whole idea of his creative suffering. . . . Oh! I'll tell you what! It's the same way you have the idea that *Tender Is the Night* is sentimental! You never understand that *Hemingway's* whole thing . . . it's not Fitzgerald but *Hemingway*. . . . How can you not see that *he's* the sentimentalist! I know!"—she held up her hand to forestall Dwight's reply—"sometimes he's brilliant . . . but *Dwight!*

"Oh, *Lord,* Dwight!" Trudy said, her voice running down into a breathless rush. "How in the *world* did the two of us ever end up married to each other?"

Trudy had meant that last to be a rhetorical question; she meant to point out that since she and Dwight *were* married to each other, they could safely indulge in and overcome their disagreements. She had intended it to come off as a bit of teasing. But she, too, had had too much to drink; each word she spoke was carefully articulated; her tone plaintive with genuine dismay, and silence fell over the group for a long moment. Even the guests who were out of earshot at the far end of the room turned in Trudy's direction, although they didn't know what had happened. Only Lily Scofield, who hadn't heard what was said, and Julian Brightman were oblivious to the ominous tension reverberating through the air.

Mr. Brightman—whose mother, in fact, was Swedish and rarely spoke English at home—took the opportunity of silence to whisper conspiratorially to Agnes, with quenched delight in his voice like an air bubble rising through water, "You see! In America even the pretty young women have so many ideas . . ."

But Agnes was grappling with the surprise of having her unease justified, of hearing something spoken aloud that might hang in the air forever, words said that—even if rein-terpreted or eventually retracted—would nevertheless remain between Dwight and Trudy. Agnes waved her hand abruptly at Julian Brightman, hushing him perfunctorily. She both did and did not want to hear what might be said next by the group in general, and she prickled all over with sudden ten-sion, as though she had been strolling along and had found all at once that she was standing on the edge of a cliff.

No one is more attuned to the emotional climate of a particular moment than the eldest child of an alcoholic, and among all the roles that Agnes inhabited simultaneously, it was that earliest aspect of her life that more than anything else had shaped her sensibility. Agnes's perceptions were honed to a nearly unbearable discernment. She became slightly breathless sitting in the long room unable to exert any control over the situation.

Finally Howard Scofield, Agnes's youngest son, spoke up. "Well, let's see," he said lightly, breaking into that long pause as if he hadn't noticed it, "since Dwight's determined to bomb Japan, and since he's already got Artie Shaw, the Dodgers, and Hemingway...and since Clay's got Benny Goodman, Faulkner, and the Yankees...and *not* dropping the bomb... well! I guess I'll have to take Harry James, maybe, and... maybe Mark Twain? I'm sticking with the Indians, too. Clay's already got the Yankees, and I don't care about the Dodgers... I don't know about Japan....Nothing's good about it, but first I see it one way and then the other....Okay! I'm just going to stay neutral on the bomb. What about you, Trudy?" But Trudy was angry, and she ignored the lifeline he'd thrown her. Howard skipped quickly over her silence. "All right. It's your turn, Lavinia."

Peter Taylor and Robert Lowell, as well as Sam Holloway, had concluded that this debate was a family dispute of long standing, and they only occasionally offered a suggestion or asked a question. "Could you have more than one author? More books? Could you give up music and take along Shakespeare, for instance?" Cal asked, but he wasn't insistent, and no one responded.

"Oh, no, Howard! Wait!" Lavinia said. "I need to think. . . . When did you take Faulkner, Clay? Umm, well . . . *first* of all, Howie, what in the world? I don't think you'd last two days on a desert island with Mark Twain. There's *too much* of him, but also there's not enough! No real women at all. And not Hemingway—good Lord! And, really, Claytor, not Faulkner, either. Just think about a life of reading nothing but Faulkner day after day after day. Year after year! And I'm Southern, but of course women . . . It's boring when the writer doesn't have any idea. . . . But, Howie, think about it! There you are in the middle of the ocean. All by yourself! You don't know if you'll ever see human beings again, and you want to be there with Tom Sawyer? I guess that's better than Moby Dick. Ah! Or especially that—oh—that book . . . *Giants in the Earth*? *Giants of the Earth*? . . . Rolwart? Rolwag?

"When I was at St. Anne's I thought it would kill me! And if you want to *dance* . . . have fun . . . *all* of you've got it wrong, you know," she went on, consciously or not defusing the charged atmosphere, simply speaking without particular conviction. "It's odd. All this—these desert island decisions. I mean, solitude's something we're always saying we want a little of. I guess *a little* is the key, though. But you've all really and truly got to choose Glenn Miller and Margaret Mitchell. Though I know that not a single one of you'll have the cour-

age to admit it," she mused, the trailing vowels of her Southern accent having slowed the burgeoning intensity.

"Glenn Miller? Lavinia! Glenn Miller's not even in the
contest—" Dwight began to protest, once more, but Lavinia
held the floor and overrode him.

"No, Dwight! All of you have this twisted around! Claytor," she said, turning toward her husband, "you've got it really
mixed up! You can't root for the *Yankees*, have Faulkner—Ah!
You know? What about Tolstoy?" Lavinia interrupted herself,
pausing for a moment. "That would be better than Margaret
Mitchell, and his women are better than her men. And, well,
really they're better than her women, too. There's plenty of
him to read. Or does it have to be American? But anyhow,
Claytor, you can't be so *appalled* at using the bomb and *also* be
a Yankees—"

"You see!" Dwight interrupted. "*That's* what I can't make
sense of, Clay," and his voice, too, was saturated with the particular, scarcely perceptible, sly tone of inebriation, which
Agnes recognized at once, and which indicated the possibility
of danger. "How in God's name can you prefer Benny Goodman to Artie Shaw, root for the New York *Yankees,* and still
think we shouldn't have bombed Hiroshima? Don't you see
how that doesn't follow? You don't want responsibility for the
use of power—"

Despite herself Agnes spoke over the general chorus of
protest or agreement that arose from the group at large in
response to Dwight's and Claytor's differing opinions. She
planted her feet firmly on the floor, leaning forward to make
herself heard. "Wait just a minute, Dwight! Wait! What are you
talking about? Claytor's not a *Yankees* fan! That's just ridiculous!
He's...none of us...Scofields are *always* for the underdog! You

know what your father used to say!" But the group merely looked surprised and turned blankly in her direction.

It annoyed Agnes even more to have to remind them. "Oh! Warren used to say that rooting for the underdog was the curse of fighting your way to the top of the ladder." No one responded, though, and she rushed on in exasperation. "For goodness' sake! You all remember that!" She was met with polite but quizzical attention, and she waved her hand dismissively. "It's not important.... Oh, well! I think he meant that if you've pulled yourself up by your own bootstraps, or something like that. Loyalty to ... well, I guess to whoever's climbing the ladder behind you. Because you'd understand what they faced, you see."

No one seemed enlightened, and she brushed it aside. "It was just one of those sayings your father had. It's not important. And he was only teasing. You know! In that way Warren had that was also a way of saying *exactly* what he meant..."

But neither Claytor nor Dwight—and particularly not Howard—had any clear memory of Warren Scofield with which they could match this sudden notion Agnes resurrected. Warren Scofield had died when the older two were ten and eleven years old respectively, and Howard had just barely turned three. And, in fact, Dwight himself was always, *always* aware that he was not really Warren Scofield's son— not a blood relation of Warren's at all. He was only Agnes's youngest brother, raised as though he were their child. He didn't feel entitled to this familial memory of Warren Scofield, who was the person Dwight had admired—and still did—more than anyone else in his life so far.

"Why do you *care,* Mother?" he said, turning Agnes's way. "What possible difference does it make to you which *baseball* team Clay likes? Of all the things in the world there are to worry about…" He was loudly exasperated but not quite dismissive enough to be considered openly rude; he could have been teasing Agnes in an overly familiar pretense of condescension.

And Agnes couldn't reply. Her own disjointed childhood had bred in her the desire that the children she brought up would have an instinctive knowledge of their solid footing on the earth. She had intended to convey to the children of her household a proprietary, safely connected *Scofieldness,* although she only realized it this very moment, and in retrospect. She had never formed any precise plan — hadn't at the time even recognized her own intention or desire.

But what on earth possessed these people for whom she had been the best parent she could manage to be, for whom she had tried so hard to pretend wisdom, to mime adulthood — oh, Lord! Those children! Why weren't they safe by now? What were they doing? They rushed along through their lives, discarding the days like so many pieces of bad fish. It amazed her that they hadn't absorbed the idea — through all the time they spent growing up — of taking *care,* of guardedly harboring… Well! Why were they so careless of their own contentment? Why *weren't* they willing to be happy all the time?

"We didn't *have* to drop the bomb," Claytor went on, back to one of the subjects about which he and Dwight increasingly disagreed. "Why not an *example!* What could have been more persuasive? Why not have given the Japanese the *chance* to surrender?" Claytor demanded. "Let them *see* what we could do… Blow up an island somewhere… But America's whole goddamned war machine was drunk on… the thrill of it! Once you've got that bomb! Their sudden power—"

"For God's sake, Clay! Spare me that argument again." Dwight's voice enlarged above the others, not in volume, but with a slight pitch of disdain, of sarcasm, a note that put paid to any idea of his own vulnerability, and Agnes heard the equally recognizable defensive tone of Claytor's opposition bloom forth, but also she could hear the lengthening slipperiness and long sibilances infusing their words as they cautiously navigated their syntax to avoid slurring their speech.

She knew the elegant articulation of men who drink but never seem drunk. It was a subtle change of pitch that Agnes had learned to detect over the course of her whole life: her father and her father-in-law, and even Warren now and then, were able to set her teeth on edge with dread, propelling her into a state of such heightened and defensive attention that she could hear her own pulse pounding in her ears, and, this evening, an odd breathlessness. She didn't realize that Julian Brightman was speaking to her, or even that the conversation she had interrupted had picked up once again.

"I *did* like *Gone with the Wind*," Trudy agreed with Lavinia, and in an amiable tone of voice. "Mother and I kept stealing it from each other until Daddy bought us a second copy," she said. "But I didn't *approve* of myself for liking it." And at last she achieved the light note she had meant to inject earlier. There was a general murmur of relieved amusement, and the conversation lost its divisive urgency.

"You might be right about that," Lavinia replied to someone, "but I'm sticking with Glenn Miller. You're right, though. Mark Twain wouldn't have bombed Japan...and probably not even Hemingway would. But I'd bet you Margaret Mitchell would've dropped the bombs herself. Okay. Okay. I *do* think you all make fools of yourselves *not* reading *Gone with the*

Wind. Then you'll heap praise on some pretentious, god-awful, self-indulgent mess of a book.... I'll take...uhmm, maybe Edith Wharton."

Robert Lowell leaned around Trudy to ask Lavinia if she thought he ought to read *Gone with the Wind,* and, when she said that of course he should—"It's a book with a terrific story! It's not like someone's trying to make you eat liver and onions! It's irresistible. Just the first line: 'Scarlett O'Hara was not beautiful, but men seldom realized it'"—Cal nodded and furrowed his brow. He bowed his huge tousled head in apparent consternation, as though he were struggling to comprehend the language being spoken.

Lily had only been absently watching when suddenly she could see that heated opinions had been put forth and debated. It was what she'd been dreading all day, and she was glad that she had literally tuned it out by turning off her hearing aid. It was clear to her, though, that whatever the argument had been, it had resolved itself for the time being, and amiable enough conversation had resumed, not only among the group with whom Trudy sat, but at the far end of the room, where Robert and Red Warren and a few others had seated themselves with drinks in hand. Lily realized that she could tactfully withdraw.

She clicked on the receiver of her hearing aid, which was never particularly helpful in a large room, and made the rounds to say good night, making sure that the guests from out of town knew they were to join her and Robert for breakfast. Just as she was about to slip away into the hallway, however, the answer to the crossword puzzle hit her, and she turned back in her husband's direction.

"Robert?" she said, over what sounded to her like nothing

more than a buzzing swell of indistinguishable voices. He didn't hear her. "Say! Robert!" She raised her voice, forgetting, as always, that in a crowded place she was unable to gauge its volume, and he turned her way, as did a good many of the other guests.

"I've got it!" she said. "*Goosey goosey gander!* It fits. 'A bird's eye view of the nursery.'" And her husband's face was briefly animated with comprehension. He had been toying with the idea of putting a crossword puzzle in the *Harcourt Lees Review* in an attempt to increase circulation, and he turned to explain to the others.

"That's Mr. Lewis's puzzle," he said to Red and Eleanor. "He's pretty good, I think, but no match for Lily." He glanced back in his wife's direction, but she was gone, having hurried upstairs to fill in those last eighteen blank squares.

Chapter Three

WHEN LILY SAID good night and went upstairs, some of the company noted the time and took their leave as well, which detained Agnes where she sat in the little alcove with Julian Brightman hovering at her shoulder. She didn't want to interfere while Robert Butler and Trudy saw guests to the door. Agnes knew that she might feel compelled to stay and help with that duty, and she didn't think she could summon the required niceties, the tiny conspiracy of graciousness required between guests and their host or hostess that enables them to part ways at the door.

It was nothing; Agnes had done it without giving it a thought perhaps more than a thousand times, standing with Warren as they said good night to guests of their own, or ushering parents out of her classroom after Parents Night conferences. She had been socially adept even in her teens, when she stepped in for her mother as hostess during the earliest years of her father's political career.

But tonight her headache intensified, the pain gathering

into one sharp point just at her temple, and as the conversation picked up when the first wave of guests were gone, she was briefly aware of sudden and ferocious nausea and light-headedness.

Just as Julian Brightman turned to resume his conversation with Agnes Scofield, she slumped against the sofa and began sliding silkily off the slippery brocade couch, bending at the knees, folding accordion-style toward the floor. He threw his arms around her, catching her around the waist before she hit the ground.

Julian stood up as he slowly pulled Agnes back to the bench of the sofa, although he didn't dare release her. He was at the wrong angle to be able to arrange her comfortably on the cushions; he could only keep her from once more tumbling forward. "Dr. Scofield," he said, not overloudly but with enough determination that Claytor heard him, although the rest of the group were so involved in their debate, they were unaware that anything was wrong for several more minutes. Little by little, though, conversation quieted at each end of the room. Whatever discussions were going on came to a whispery, rustling halt by the time Claytor had his medical bag open at his feet and his stethoscope around his neck, and was frowning slightly as he tried to determine what had happened to his mother.

Finally he glanced at the group with whom he had been sitting, with an expression he was unaware he possessed but which was a look of indrawn, no-nonsense concentration. His voice was courteous but brisk with authority, and he spoke with an expectation of being listened to. "Dwight, why don't you get the car?" he said. "I want to get Mother over to the hospital."

Agnes had opened her eyes lazily for a moment, while Claytor was trying to assess her condition, but she showed no sign of recognition, nor of alarm, and no evidence, either, of being in pain; she only had an unworried, faraway expression of disengagement until her eyes closed once more, her head lolling loosely against the back of the little sofa, her saliva leaving a faint damp mark against the faded brocade.

"I'm parked just outside under the porte cochere," Sam Holloway said, and with his usual efficiency he was already out the door and had the car ready to go as soon as Claytor carried his mother through the side entrance. He hadn't considered calling an ambulance even though it might have been more comfortable for his mother. He remained convinced—since his internship in Baltimore—that an ambulance flying through stoplights, blasting through traffic signs with the driver suddenly shot through with adrenaline, elevated all at once in importance, glorified by the sound of his siren—Claytor was certain that the ambulance trip alone posed far more danger to the lives of stricken patients than did whatever other catastrophe had befallen them.

Dr. Scofield couldn't attend his own mother, of course, once he'd settled her in a room at Mercy General Hospital. He called Milton Bass, who was one of the few other doctors in town whom Claytor considered genuinely topflight, but Milt wasn't home. The nurses on duty were more than capable of keeping an eye on Agnes, but Claytor made himself as comfortable as possible in a chair beside her bed and settled in. He had early rounds in the morning, anyway. The nurses checked in now and then. They brought him pillows and a light blanket. He was popular among them; he held them in high esteem; he was unfailingly curious about and interested in their lives, and he joked with them on an equal footing. Also, there was simply no question that he was very good-looking, and that's always endearing unless it's nullified by arrogance or vanity.

Howard Scofield drove Lavinia home to Cardinal Hills so that Claytor would have the car in the morning. Lavinia watched from her front steps while Howard drove the baby-sitter, Kathy Morrison, past the two houses that separated the Scofield and Morrison homes, but when the Morrisons' porch light switched off, Lavinia waited a moment until she was sure Howie could see her under her own porch light, waved her thanks, and went inside.

Out in the Cardinal Hills development almost none of the residents bothered to lock the doors of their efficient, single-story houses, especially in the hot weather, when all of the windows were open, anyway. But in order to increase the draw of the attic fan, Lavinia had gone through her house closing all the interior doors except the ones to her daughters' shared room and to her and Claytor's bedroom.

When she looked in on Mary Alcorn and Julia, the ging-ham curtains at their open windows rippled straight out into the room nearly perpendicular to the walls. With all other sources of air cut off, the attic fan created far more than a breeze; a steady wind rushed through the two bedrooms, and although the air drawn in from outside was no cooler than the air it displaced, just its movement provided a little relief.

Lavinia stripped off all her clothes down to her white slip, dropping them where she stood, and lay down with only the top sheet pulled over her, which she shrugged off sometime during the night. She awoke Tuesday morning already run-ning late. She had forgotten to set the alarm; Clay generally set the clock each night. She grabbed an old housecoat, snapping it down the front as she hurried to get Mary Alcorn up and dressed.

In the already suffocating heat of the new house, so easy to keep warm in the winter with its low ceilings, Lavinia's younger daughter, Julia, was still sound asleep, comalike, with her hair damp and plastered to her head, her arms and legs sprawled so that no one part of her touched any other part of her, but even so, she was sheened with perspiration. Lavinia knew the near impossibility of waking her up. And, in any case, Julia was only in the first grade; Lavinia didn't think it would make any difference if she missed a day of school.

As it was, it took nearly five minutes to fully waken Mary Alcorn, who was ten, and on whose account Lavinia had meant to be up earlier. Mary Alcorn's class was in charge of making decorations for the upcoming Jesser Grammar School Halloween Carnival, and she would be beside herself if she missed a day of school.

Even after Mary Alcorn got up and out of bed, she only operated in a state of semiconsciousness, perfectly amenable to her mother's directions but following them in a bumbling haze until the edges of her day came into focus halfway through slowly eating a bowl of Pep, which generally drew some bit of exasperation from her mother.

"Good grief! How can you eat that?" her mother might say, but Lavinia didn't pay any attention to her daughter's breakfast that particular hot Tuesday morning. There weren't any Wheaties in the house, and Mary Alcorn was stuck with Pep, which—right out of the box—tasted to her like liquid vitamins smelled, so she waited patiently while the papery Pep cereal flakes absorbed the creamy milk and became a limp, salty-sweet, slightly crunchy mush. She was ready for school just in time to join Bobby Gillman, who lived just next door, and Kathy Morrison, and the two Bankston boys, who lived farther down the lane, all of whom were already out front waiting for the school bus.

There was no point in awakening Julia, and Lavinia was so hot, the house so stuffy, that after the school bus pulled away, she slipped off her housecoat—printed with whimsical, anthropomorphized, long-faded coffeepots, toasters, and smiling fried eggs—and splashed her face and neck and shoulders with cool water from the kitchen sink. She lit a cigarette and wandered through the house still in her nylon slip, feeling slightly more comfortable as she finally stood damply at the open window of the living room, gazing out at the golf course, just waiting for some movement of the air.

It was too hot to drink her coffee; the first few sips had sent a rush of heat to her face and she felt sweat dampen the nape of her neck. Nevertheless she stood where she was, holding her cup and saucer in one hand, her cigarette in the other, looking out the window and expecting to be overtaken by that click of ignition that followed that first cup of coffee every morning.

More than five years earlier, when she had only been pregnant with Julia, just after Sam Holloway had shown her and Claytor the blueprints of Sam's own favorite floor plan for one of the houses going up in the Cardinal Hills development on the outskirts of Washburn, Lavinia and Clay had bought the second lot on Fairway Lane, where that particular house was to be built. Neither she nor Clay had ever said so to each other, but each was pleased with the idea of living on a *lane*. They did discuss the fact that the street had homes on one side only, was a dead end, and ran prettily along the north side of the fairway extending from the first tee of the Cardinal Club golf course. The lot upon which their house was to be built was a neat patch of shade-dappled green grass—a perfect size, easy to maintain and yet with plenty of room for children to play.

But buying the property had been a battle. Clay refused to take advantage of the GI Bill's loan policy because he hadn't served overseas, and the harshest argument they had had until then came down to Lavinia's feeling that it was *she* who paid the price for Claytor's sense of honor. "It's fine for you, but here I am all day living in your mother's house. You can't imagine...I take a thermos of coffee up to our bedroom! And Mary Alcorn..."

"Mary Alcorn's perfectly happy in this house! For God's sake! What's wrong with you? My mother's at school till late afternoon. It's my decision, anyway, Lavinia. I don't want to hear any more about it."

It was an argument Lavinia and Clay had in private, but any domestic disagreement filters through its entire household, and when Agnes caught Claytor alone on the porch, she tried to explain how hard it would be for any woman with a child to live in another woman's house. "I've done it myself, Clay. Your father never realized, either...It's hard to explain it to a man. After all, Claytor, Lavinia's first husband was *killed*.... She's had a whole life before this."

"Mama, Phillip Alcorn was killed in a car wreck on base in Killeen, Texas! It's sad. It's even tragic. But it's not in the same league as being killed under fire. Think about Dwight and Sam in the Air Force! I treated a lot of men who survived. The flyers...they had terrible burns. They're the ones who need help from the government—"

"I don't see your point," Agnes interrupted. "*Anyone* in the war could end up dead one way or another! Lavinia's first husband is just as dead as anyone else who didn't survive. Dwight lived through the war, and so did Sam, and so did you. *All* of you did what you were assigned to do..." But then Agnes let the matter drop. She was confounded by her own son and especially by her daughter-in-law, who couldn't be counted on ever to behave as Agnes would have expected. She sympathized, though, with the predicament Lavinia was in. Agnes remembered how it felt to live on pins and needles all the time, trying not to disturb the baffling, long-established environment and collective sensibility of another woman's household.

But Dwight admired Claytor's decision not to make use of a government loan, and he said so. "I hope I'd have had the sense...the *integrity*. To do the same thing, I mean," Dwight said one Sunday night when the whole family had gathered at Agnes's for supper. "I hope I could hang on to my principles the way you do," he added, helping himself to one of the toasted and quartered Cheese Dreams Agnes had run under the broiler at the last minute, since it had occurred to her that her grandchildren might be suspicious of the chicken timbale she had made to stretch her budget.

She had baked the chicken in a pretty ring mold that, when inverted, produced a scalloped design on the custard. Agnes had filled the center with buttered noodles and surrounded it with carrots and even a sprinkle of parsley on a celebratory whim at the thought of the whole family gathering for dinner. When she put the platter of sandwiches down on the table near the children, though, nearly everyone matter-of-factly picked one up, and Agnes faced a week of chicken timbale served sliced and reheated, or cold on tomatoes, or simply just a wedge cut from the ring, put on a plate, and eaten while she stood at the kitchen sink watching the two cardinals who nested in a bush right outside the window.

During that same dinner, though, Sam Holloway split the difference between Lavinia and Claytor and put the matter of the GI Bill's loan into a manageable perspective, so that it was something they all could take hold of without burning their fingers. "You might have put too fine a point on those principles, Clay. After all, you gave up what are generally supposed to be the 'most *productive* years of your life.'" Sam had a way of mimicking a commonplace assumption in an officious manner that made the statement seem a little silly. He adopted a conspiracy of sorts that bound him and the person to whom he was speaking in an allegiance against whatever pompous fools had put the original phrase together. He paused for a bite of carrots but held the floor by raising his free hand in a flat-palmed gesture to stop anyone else from taking hold of the conversation. Sam had fallen in with this voluble group the first day he stepped off the bus from Columbus, just after the war, and he had learned early on that in any discussion among them he could not be shy about holding on to whatever control he had.

"Claytor, I'll tell you! If I were you," he said, relaxing into his own casual intonation, "I'd at least look into what's available. No one's going to make you eat the whole pie. But I think it would be worth taking a look just to find out what kinds might be available by the slice."

With a little help from a small government loan, Clay and Lavinia had moved out of Agnes's big, rambling house in the middle of town into their own small home in the serene neighborhood of Fairway Lane during the summer of 1950. By 1953, the neighborhood had grown to sixteen houses and no longer had a raw aspect of newness about it, which was due in large part to the fact that Sam Holloway and Will Dameron, who had invested jointly in the development, had gone to extra expense to make sure that the old trees remained. They had decided to absorb the cost of not clear-cutting the land, which would have lessened the expense of putting in the infrastructure, would have made the roads much easier to establish: straight asphalt lines in a grid pattern, which company policy advised.

In fact, Sam had balked at using all seven of the floor plans and designs offered by Cardinal Homes, and Will had bowed to his decision. Sam couldn't imagine why someone in Ohio would want the stucco, half-timbered Tudor Ranch or, for that matter, the rather squared-off Modern. He stuck with Mid-Century Cottage, Cape Cod, Southern Veranda, and a few Country Brick, which made use of artfully distressed half bricks as a facing on the house, as if those bricks had been discovered tumbled down around an old country manse that had at one time been painted, then stripped, and had grown age-worn. The technique softened the institutional red of a brick house, with flecks of cream, black, gray, and a chalky white. But those brick-faced houses were on the high end of what people were willing to pay.

After Cardinal Hills' initial success, Sam and Will began to pass the cost of building on wooded acreage along to the buyer, because, although Sam swore that the old trees made all the difference in the world, the development was established enough now that it was no longer in danger of looking like a Monopoly board. "And Will, it's not like we're depriving anyone of a choice," Sam said. "People might want to save a little money and choose their own plants. They might want a maple, for instance, instead of an oak." The houses they built on what had already been gently rolling, treeless meadowland were a good bit less expensive, but the wooded lots sold first. "You should see all those houses in New Jersey and Cleveland with their one same-size single tree looking pitiful in every front yard," he had said to Will Dameron, as they made further plans.

Had Lavinia known that it might have been obliterated, the hundred-year-old maple tree that shaded 2 Fairway Lane would certainly have been much appreciated. But on that hot October morning, after the school bus had picked up Mary Alcorn, Lavinia looked right past that tree without giving it a thought. She didn't have much of anything on her mind and was biding her time until Julia woke up on her own.

Since Claytor had the car, she and her next-door neighbor Lacey Gillman would probably take their younger children to swim at the Cardinal Club pool, although Lacey would let her daughter, Melanie, stay in the water for only ten or fifteen minutes at a time because of her fear that swimming pools were a likely source for the spread of polio. In fact, the polio epidemic pretty much guaranteed that they would have the pool entirely to themselves.

Lavinia's mother-in-law worried about Mary Alcorn and Julia swimming at the Cardinal Club pool, and, in fact, since the club pool was privately owned and didn't fall under municipal regulations, it was the only pool anywhere in Washburn not drained and shut down in an effort to curtail the mysterious spread of poliomyelitis. Not that Agnes had ever broached the subject as a complaint to Lavinia. Agnes had asked Clay early in the summer and occasionally thereafter—as if she had forgotten she had brought it up before — if he thought it was really a good idea to expose his daughters to whatever might be spreading the virus. After all, his mother reminded him, polio seemed to prey mostly on children, and the consequences were so often grim.

Lavinia was always right there in the room, too, whenever Agnes Scofield brought it up, and Lavinia was also there when Clay inevitably replied that the whole business of closing the library and the playgrounds and the pools to protect the children of Washburn from contracting polio was a case of hysteria. Not only that, he said, it would only drive those children to swim in local, fetid ponds or, even worse, in those dangerous spots where the Kokosing River pooled and swirled with deceptive placidity.

"Summertime is always dangerous. . . . All by itself summertime's the biggest danger there is to children. Drowning, insect bites, bicycles, roller skates, picnics and food poisoning, ear infections, broken bones! And then, when it gets too hot — too hot for too long — those children have no place to go. . . . Well, *then* they've got to watch out for their parents' bad tempers." He added that in his opinion the actions of the city council had increased the health hazard that the summer months always were to children everywhere.

Lavinia wasn't the sort of mother who second-guessed an opinion that made her life easier, or at least made it more tolerable during the long, hot days of the summer — by now the early fall — of 1953. In truth, Lavinia really wasn't a woman who worried very much one way or another about her children, not because she didn't love them but because she had never viscerally incorporated the idea that she was largely responsible for their physical safety. But, on the other hand, she was instinctively on the side of children—hers and any others—just in general.

Not once, for instance, had Lavinia seen one of her children about to take a fall and experienced the sensation herself. She could watch without flinching as the girls came flying down the lane on roller skates. Whenever she and Claytor took Mary Alcorn and Julia out to Hiawatha Park, Lavinia urged her daughters to join her for a ride on the Ferris wheel and the wooden roller coaster that clattered over its own spindly hills, even while Claytor stood by considering the structure and suggesting that they wait until he met the man who had built it before they bought their tickets.

Lavinia loved her children without sentimentality, but also without an empathetic engagement, and she had no idea that there were other sorts of maternal connections. In fact, whenever she witnessed cautious parents discouraging their children from some sort of adventure, she was irritated on behalf of those overprotected children.

The first summer Claytor and Lavinia had spent on Fairway Lane, an FAO Schwarz truck, dispatched from a warehouse in Hoboken, New Jersey, but essentially coming straight from the FAO Schwarz store on Fifth Avenue in New York, had arrived at their house, carefully backing into the narrow drive. Out had come a trampoline, a Bongo Board, a pogo stick, a One Man Band, a tournament-size Ping-Pong table, a badminton and a croquet set, and a tetherball pole with a leather ball. Lavinia had ordered monkey bars, a self-propelled spinning merry-go-round, rope swings as well as rope ladders, to be suspended from beams installed between the old trees left in place by Sam Holloway's crew, and eight pairs of good-quality, adjustable ball-bearing roller skates with extra keys, so a number of children on Fairway

Lane could skate at the same time instead of arguing over and taking turns using Mary Alcorn's and Julia's good skates.

"Good Lord, Lavinia. These are expensive! These roller skates...why in the world would you buy *eight* pairs?" Claytor had protested when she had consulted him about it, although he, too, was intrigued when Lavinia showed him various marked pages in the FAO Schwarz catalog.

"Well, Claytor! I was going to order *seventeen* pairs! But that just *was* too expensive. But that's how many children live on Fairway Lane. But then I thought that *two* children could take turns.... And not everyone is likely to be outside at the same time, anyway. You've seen what happens when Julia or Mary Alcorn wants to skate. None of the other children on the lane has a decent pair of skates. Their parents just buy those cheap ones at the hardware store that fall apart after one afternoon. So Mary Alcorn always ends up in tears because she agrees to switch skates, and then *those* break! People are so stingy when it comes to their children! How much would it hurt the Gillmans to buy their children a decent pair of skates? I hate it when people skimp when they don't need to. Lacey Gillman always buys RC Cola to save a few cents, so all the children end up over here drinking Coca-Cola. And that cheap peanut butter! That tuna fish that tastes like aluminum."

Lavinia knew pretty much what everyone on Fairway Lane had for dinner most nights, because nearly everyone on the street placed a daily grocery order at Stafford's Grocery Store for afternoon delivery, and Lavinia's house was the second stop on the street. She generally went out to meet the panel truck and help carry in the boxes and bags marked *Scofield*. She couldn't help but notice the boxes marked for her various neighbors as well. She knew, for instance, that the

Gillmans bought the cheaper brands of everything: soap, shampoo, soft drinks, coffee, and so forth. And for some reason it simply annoyed her no end, the same way their failure to buy their daughter a decent pair of skates was none of her business but nevertheless made her angry.

"I mean, Claytor, they spend a lot of money for the things *they* want. That set of Early American furniture. You wouldn't believe the price.... And it's just ugly. And after all, Claytor, you're a *doctor!* Why should we buy badly made swing sets that turn to rust in no time? But *Schwarz!* These will last for years," she said, dismissing his complaint.

And when Claytor thumbed through the catalog he found it nearly as seductive as Lavinia had. Who would have thought toys like this were even available? He was caught up in admiration for them as well as feeling a vicarious acquisitiveness. Imagine having a merry-go-round in your own yard if you were a little girl. What child wouldn't be thrilled to discover these remarkable toys? And he *did* make a good living for the first time in his life, although there were loans still to be paid off.

But in the back of his mind there was the image of his mother painstakingly clipping coupons from the newspaper, and bargaining with the carpenter, or working out a payment plan with McCann's that they never offered anyone else for coal delivery. He had found it humiliating when Aunt Lily dropped off her old magazines so that his mother could clip coupons from those, as well. Humiliated, too, when he discovered that Lily and Robert Butler had sold their green Chrysler to his mother for a dollar, instead of trading it in when they bought a new car. Certainly he didn't blame his mother for his own embarrassment, but he had hated the idea of being a poor relation, particularly to his cousin Trudy, whose teenaged approval he had sought to the same degree he had wanted Dwight to admire him.

Claytor was mortified, too, when in one of their rare arguments during their late teens Dwight had blurted out the fact that Agnes divided among all four of the children the money that her own and Dwight's father sent each year for Dwight's expenses and education. "Why *else* would I spend my summer cleaning windshields and handing out steak knives? Always smelling like gasoline?" Of course Dwight had apologized later, and often thereafter, entreating Claytor not ever to let Agnes know he had seemed to begrudge such a thing. And Claytor believed that Dwight *didn't* begrudge a shared penny of that money, but it was too late for Claytor to *un*-know the fact that he was receiving it.

At the end of that summer, having supplied well over a hundred glasses of water to very thirsty children, Lavinia also had an ice-water fountain installed in the garage. Scarcely a blade of grass had survived the constant traffic through the Scofields' front yard, but there was nothing to be done about that until the children were older.

"Dear God," Dwight had commented when he and Trudy and their girls were visiting, "this is a lawsuit waiting to happen." But Lavinia noticed that Dwight's own daughter Amelia and Mary Alcorn were racing each other up and down the twelve-foot-long rope ladders. Little Julia and her cousin Martha Claytor were sitting on the trampoline where they were involved in what appeared to be a complicated imaginary tea party.

Claytor Scofield had first been introduced to Lavinia Alcorn by mutual friends, at a party on base, where he and she ended up talking for hours, even as the other guests departed and the lights were dimmed. They had a tentative connection through Dwight Claytor, although Lavinia had never met him. But Dwight had been a friend of Lavinia's first husband, and just that tenuous thread had moved Lavinia and Claytor past the first inevitable awkwardness of a new introduction. He dropped by to see her the next day just on the spur of the moment, but she wasn't at home when he found her apartment. Her housemate popped her head out of an upper window and told him Lavinia was most likely at the playground with the baby.

He wandered around the compound until he found her outside, in the common area of newly planted lawn enclosed by the equally new and stark Married Officers' Housing, although since Lavinia had been widowed for over six months, she was expected to make other arrangements by the end of the year. She had told Clay the night before that the most reasonable thing for her to do was to move home to Charlottesville, Virginia, where her mother lived alone in the house that had been in the Witherspoon family forever, and which had plenty of room.

Until Claytor said her name, Lavinia was so caught up in the book she was reading that she didn't realize he was even in the vicinity. He had come upon her where she was half lying inside a portable wooden playpen. Her elbow was cocked on the pink printed plastic mat, her head propped on her hand, and her heavy brown hair fell around her face in a dark parenthesis, obscuring her profile as Clay approached. Her little girl, dressed in a diaper and a sturdy camisole, was sitting down in the sandbox nearby, working with flushed intensity to fill — or to empty — a bright yellow bucket half full of sand.

"Oh! Clay! I didn't know you were coming by," Lavinia said when she glanced up at his greeting. She sat up and closed her book with the heavy-lidded expression of someone coming out of a dream. It took a moment to make the transition from nineteenth-century Russia to twentieth-century Fort Hood, just outside Killeen, Texas. She straightened her skirt and blouse, which were rumpled and slightly twisted, and rose to her feet. Her daughter's attention had been caught, too, and Mary left her shovel and pail behind her as she made her way back to the playpen, rattling the bars from the outside. "Ma ma ma ma," she clamored crankily, wanting to climb in with her mother. Claytor was clearly baffled as he gave Lavinia a hand to help her climb over the relatively low enclosure.

"Oh, you see... Of course, this is *Mary's* playpen. Well, she's really too big for it now. But if I sit on the grass where Mary can get to me," Lavinia said, "then she only wants my book more than anything else," she explained. And at the time, Clay had considered Lavinia's casual caretaking to be a wonderful idea as opposed to the worried eye his mother had kept on him and his siblings, although over the years since then, he had grown less and less enchanted by Lavinia's lack of anxiety on behalf of Mary Alcorn and now their daughter, Julia. Even so, the little girls were fine, and it never crossed his mind to fill the gap by worrying about them himself.

In 1945, he had found everything about Lavinia Alcorn fascinating. Lavinia was not pretty, exactly, like the girls he had known all the time he was growing up, but she was striking and often beautiful and was the most interesting woman he had ever met. There was nothing flirtatious about her, no little pretenses or innuendos. He would never think to describe her as *sweet* or *cute*. Even after talking to her for only an evening, though, he didn't think she was unkind, but neither would he have described her as *nice*. All those terms conjured up for him a certain kind of conventionally pretty girl who would get married, join the garden club and the Junior League, and contribute to her community.

There was nothing at all wrong with that, and it wasn't that Lavinia *wouldn't* do any of those things, but she made no effort to define herself on any terms at all. She went straight ahead at a subject, saying whatever she thought, was never sentimental, and she had an ironic sense of humor—what Clay thought of, in fact, as a Scofield sense of humor, which he rarely came across outside his own family. Meeting Lavinia Alcorn seemed to him then a miracle of coincidence and good luck.

In 1953, on the outskirts of Washburn, Ohio, in the relatively new neighborhood of Fairway Lane, Lavinia Witherspoon Alcorn Scofield wasn't thinking of anything in particular while she gazed out the window, waiting for her younger daughter to wake up. She came to attention, though, when she caught a movement among the trees on the far side of the golf course. At first she thought it was a dog emerging from the woods, but when she leaned against the screen to look more closely, she realized it was a fairly large red fox, cautiously crossing the open green swath of the unwooded golf course. A sandy-brown vixen and four kits followed him at a distance. The vixen had brought her offspring to drink at the water hazard across the way and was watching the male before deciding if there was a threat to the kits.

Lavinia watched while the male and the kits drank, and finally the vixen bent her head to drink after the others had finished. Suddenly, though, her tail stiffened and she cocked her ears forward, raising her head. Her ears twitched as she lifted her nose slowly into the many layers and currents of the atmosphere that kept her informed, and her attention came to rest directly on Lavinia. The male went still and alert himself, but he watched the vixen instead of searching out the source of her alarm.

Lavinia straightened abruptly, away from the screen, startled by what seemed to be the challenge of that animal's steady consideration. Surely the fox couldn't see her, she thought, from such a distance and as she stood inside her unlighted house. But the sense Lavinia had of communion between herself and the animal was unnerving. The babies were thirsty, which presumably slaked any natural wariness of humans on the mother's part, and Lavinia found it impossible to look away until the animal resumed drinking and then moved off, with her four kits following right behind and the red fox bringing up the rear.

Such bold behavior both intrigued Lavinia and filled her with unease. It was behavior for which Lavinia herself lacked an instinct, and which she considered to be an affront to her own natural impulses. In fact, the huddled readiness of the animal, the muscles drawn taut suddenly, when she had sensed danger and coiled herself like a spring ready to attack anything at all that might be a menace to her young, reminded Lavinia a little bit of her mother-in-law.

Lavinia had noticed a similar expression cross Agnes Scofield's face once or twice, when she was anxious. When, for instance, Dwight and Claytor fell into yet another disagreement, or had too much to drink. Or when Betts lit another cigarette, or took one from Agnes's pack stashed in the kitchen drawer. But so far that apprehension hadn't been aimed Lavinia's way, and, besides, Agnes had never seemed particularly judgmental of Lavinia one way or another. The two of them got along well enough. Lavinia thought Agnes resembled a beautiful cow, with her wide cheekbones and hollow cheeks, and her huge round eyes and long lashes.

In fact, Lavinia had been truly startled by the loveliness of cows when she first became aware of it, and she was surprised she had never heard anyone remark upon it. She hadn't grown up in an agricultural area of Virginia, and she had first begun noticing cows on the long drive from Texas to Ohio when she and Claytor and Mary Alcorn relocated to Washburn. The heat had been oppressive, and Lavinia had leaned her head into the rush of air at the window through much of the trip, eye to eye with various domestic animals — sheep, pigs, cows, and even goats, bored and gazing at the passing car from behind a fence.

She would never have guessed it would be the cows that captured her attention. Their large but finely sculpted heads and serene expressions as they bent over their fences, grazing the long grasses in a roadside ditch, could stun her with their look of velvety soulfulness, with their expression of quiet rapture. Lavinia eventually concluded that just like Agnes's own looks, however, the beauty of cows was not aggressive and therefore often went unnoticed. But, because it was surprising, it was also more compelling.

Lavinia didn't dislike her mother-in-law, but the two of them hadn't found much common ground, really. And in any case, as far as other people were concerned, Lavinia was fairly incurious. While she waited for Julia to wake up, wishing Claytor would come home with the car, Lavinia hoped Agnes was all right, of course, but at the moment Lavinia's concern was framed as the question of what she should say to her husband if the news of his mother turned out not to be good.

Lavinia was not *un*interested in other people if information was volunteered, but she rarely asked a personal question. It would have surprised her to learn that she seemed aloof and sometimes unfriendly, when, in fact, she was often intimidated by the easy conversations going on around her. She sometimes felt uncomfortably isolated in a crowd, but the fact was, Lavinia had no instinct or talent at all for incidental friendships or small talk. She didn't understand that an exchange of information about the weather, say, was a way to begin the negotiation of an acquaintance, that it was a hesitant testing of the waters.

Since Claytor was never effusively complimentary of his mother, nor openly nostalgic about growing up at Scofields—except where his father was concerned—Lavinia wasn't backed into any manner of defensive jealousy. In fact, Lavinia thought that all of Agnes's children were curiously—and not favorably—inflexible in their own ideas about their mother. All but Howard, who was warmly and openly fond of everyone he knew, as far as Lavinia could tell. But since everyone in all of Washburn appeared to like him, Howard's extensive goodwill and affection were perfectly reasonable.

Lavinia didn't care much for Trudy, whose opinions were unyielding and who was unpredictably snappish with her brisk, sharp jaw and pointed chin. She was imperious with her crisp certainties, whipping through the fabric of life at Scofields like a basting needle efficiently flashing through a muslin mock-up without great care, at least not the sort of care Lavinia had seen Agnes take before she made a single cut in the expensive fabric for the eventual perfected garment.

And Dwight Claytor had proved to be a constant disappointment to Lavinia Scofield, because she had been led to believe from Claytor's description that Dwight was everything fine in a human being. In her opinion, though, as she got to know him, he was every bit as smart as Claytor had claimed and as handsome as the rest of the family, with Agnes's eyes made masculine and striking, just as Claytor's were. But he often took on a stern paternal role and rendered himself little more than a condescending killjoy, and even something of a civic bore. Privately Lavinia thought that Dwight was no real friend of Claytor's, although so far she had never said that to Claytor himself.

But now that she was established in her own house, Lavinia was no longer surrounded by her husband's family, and she rarely thought about them one way or another. She thought of Agnes and wished her well as she waited awhile to see if the family of foxes would reappear. Claytor hadn't seemed overly alarmed by his mother's condition the night before; he had been serious, but not scared.

Finally Lavinia moved away from the window and looked in on Julia, who was still so soundly asleep that she hadn't even moved. Lavinia showered and put on a fresh skirt and blouse and phoned Lacey Gillman next door, who agreed to join Lavinia as soon as Lacey got Melanie into her bathing suit.

"We can walk across the golf course to the pool," Lacey said. "No one's playing golf at this time of day. I don't have a car today, either. It was just too hot to drive Walter to work and then have to go back this evening and pick him up. We can treat ourselves. We'll get a sandwich at the clubhouse. A *club* sandwich that someone else cooks the bacon for," Lacey suggested.

By now it was past eleven in the morning, and Lavinia knew the only way to wake Julia was simply to do it. Julia still slept as intently as an infant, not luxuriating in sleep, but burrowing into it determinedly, as though it were a job to get done, and it was never any fun to wake her up. Lavinia wasn't surprised when Julia didn't respond to her voice. But when she bent to push her daughter's hair away from her face, Julia didn't even flinch in annoyance; she lay absolutely still. Lavinia shook her gently against the sweat-dampened pillow, but Julia only opened her eyes to narrow slits in the bright room; she didn't make a sound.

"Julia! Juleee, Juleeee," Lavinia called softly to her daughter. Lavinia sat down on the bed, edging Julia aside with her hip, knowing it would irritate Julia but hoping it might wake her up as well.

Julia's eyes opened only a sliver more and revealed the feverish puffiness of her eyelids when she looked at her mother for a moment, neither of them saying a thing until Julia whispered a plea for water. Lavinia hurried to the kitchen to get a glass and came back and sat down on the side of Julia's bed again to offer it. But Julia grimaced as her mother tried to prop her up.

"Julia, you have to sit up. You can't drink water lying down. Come on! I'll help you sit up," she said, but as she leaned forward again and slid her arm under Julia's shoulders, Julia gave a breathy murmur of reproach, and Lavinia took her arm away.

"Do you want me to hold the glass down to you? Do you want to try to take a sip?" Julia was nonresponsive in agreement, every ounce of her concentration clearly yearning toward even a drop of water. Lavinia tried to tip the liquid into Julia's mouth, but water spilled over the little girl's chin and all over the pillow.

"I'll call Lacey Gillman, Julia. You stay right here. I'll be right back," Lavinia said and she rushed to the phone in the center hall. Lacey was quiet for a long moment when Lavinia explained what was the matter.

"You should call Claytor," Lacey finally said. "I can't come over there if Julia's that sick." Lavinia was quiet at her end of the line, trying to understand exactly what Lacey meant, and Lacey rushed into an explanation.

"If she's that sick . . . I can't take the chance, Lavinia. I just can't. I've got Bobby and Melanie. I can't risk bringing Melanie with me. And I can't risk being contagious . . ."

When she hung up the phone, Lavinia was angry and amazed at Lacey's unapologetic refusal to help, but Lavinia was also shot through with uncertainty, as she always was when she or one of her children was sick. She was deeply ashamed on her daughter's behalf, and — momentarily — even angry at the position Julia had put her in. Simultaneously Lavinia was panicked by her own responsibility for her daughter's comfort when Julia was clearly so sick. More than anything else, though, Lavinia was appalled at the thought of the world without Julia in it. Lavinia was pretty much besotted with her younger daughter, who was so easy and sweet-natured, who was passive where Mary Alcorn had been insistent, who was patient even at six years old, a time when Mary Alcorn had been a whirling dervish of inquisitiveness. But Lavinia could not help falling in with the notion that illness was somehow willful, that it revealed a hidden weakness of character, or perhaps, in a child, a plea for attention.

When Julia had been only three months old, Lavinia's own doctor had glanced at Lavinia with a flicker of disapproval when she had worried to him about numbness afflicting whichever arm she used to hold Julia while feeding her. Several times when Lavinia had sat down in the rocking chair in the nursery, she had come close to losing the ability to maintain her grasp on her daughter. Lavinia was afraid she might drop Julia by accident.

But Dr. Cunningham said there certainly wasn't any physical cause for Lavinia's condition, however it had manifested itself. "Mrs. Scofield, we've come a long way in understanding illness. And I'll tell you, I've come to believe it's true that there *are* no accidents." He suggested that perhaps subconsciously Lavinia hadn't really wanted the baby. "A person's subconscious is not sentimental, Mrs. Scofield," Dr. Cunningham said. "I suppose you could think of this as being a fight for your *self*...for your soul," he had mused, seemingly to himself, and then he aimed his remarks directly to her once again. "But maybe you can trick your subconscious by thinking only of happy things when you feed her. Don't think to yourself that it's the middle of the night. Don't think about being tired. Don't think of the mess and the diapers and doing the laundry.... My wife complained of just those things when I was stationed overseas."

Dr. Cunningham and his wife had three children, one right after the other over a span of seven years before the war, and Dr. Cunningham failed to remember that he truly hadn't missed his home at all when he joined the medical corps, although he had gotten much sympathetic credit for the sacrifice of being parted from his young family. "Think of your daughter's wedding day! Watching her walk down the aisle. Having her own first child..."

Lavinia had come home to Scofields in despair at Dr. Cunningham's diagnosis, although she never revealed his opinion to anyone else, in case whoever she told might agree. She resorted to carrying the baby from her crib to the bedroom she and Claytor occupied in Agnes's house so that Julia was safely supported against a pillow settled on the firm mattress when Lavinia fed her.

The fact was, it hadn't occurred to Lavinia to want — or not to want — another child. She had been excited, she thought, or at least deeply fascinated, when she realized she was pregnant, but the notion of being glad or sorry about it had never once crossed her mind. Having a baby was just what had happened.

Privately, as the incapacitating numbness continued, she wept at her own failure as a mother, and she was plagued by dreams of losing Julia. Literally misplacing her somewhere inside Agnes's large house, looking into the baby carriage on a sunny street and finding it empty. One afternoon when Julia was napping, Lavinia had fallen asleep herself and had awakened in a state of terror and an awful conviction that she was too late. She had run down the stairs and out into the front yard of Scofields, loudly and repeatedly calling Julia's name. "Julia! Julia! Julia, come back!" For almost a minute under the old trees across from Monument Square she remained convinced that Julia was being sent off to space in a rocket. The images in her head dissolved incompletely, like striations of fog, until the monument in the center of the square took shape in her actual sight, along with a woman sitting on a bench who was holding a sandwich and looking Lavinia's way in alarm.

Lavinia believed she had been glad when she found out she was pregnant, but in retrospect she became unsure if she had been deluding herself. In any case, the numbness in her hands and arms gradually abated over the next several months. Ever after, though, she considered illness to be a symptom of some deeply sly and secretly neurotic malady, and, whatever caused it, it was a person's own fault.

Six years later, confronted with her daughter's illness, she still required a few moments to overcome her nearly paralyzing reluctance to make herself and Julia vulnerable to the white-coated phalanx of disapproving authority she imagined would be gathered at the other end of her telephone call. Had it been only Lavinia herself who was sick she would never have phoned a doctor at all.

As it was, she lit a cigarette and paced the little center hall for a moment before finally picking up the phone and, with a note of deep apology, leaving a message for Claytor at both hospitals, saying that he should come right home. That his daughter was sick.

By the time Lavinia had made those phone calls, found a box of plastic straws, and returned to Julia's room with more water, Julia was pressing her arms and legs tightly against her mattress, her fingers splayed and clutching the bedding as though something were trying to dislodge her.

"The ceiling won't stop turning," she said and then suddenly began violently heaving and threw up all over both of them. Lavinia sat holding her daughter and pouring a trickle of water over Julia's face and chin and wiping it clean with a dry bit of Julia's sheet. Nothing would have persuaded her to leave Julia by herself in order to get more water. Lavinia hoarded what she had, and by the time the glass was empty, Julia lay limp and sweaty but shivering, and Lavinia pulled the dry, clean bedspread over them and leaned her head against the wall, and they both appeared to be asleep when Claytor got home nearly an hour and a half later.

Chapter Four

ON THAT SAME Tuesday morning, while Lavinia Scofield waited for Claytor to get home, Agnes Scofield's only daughter, Betts, and her husband, Will Dameron, were interrupted at breakfast by David Hutchins, the farm manager who lived down the hill. Betts and Will lived out Coshocton Road, and they hadn't gone into town for Lily's party Monday night. Betts was nine and a half months pregnant with her third child, and she was supposed to stay in bed, since she had refused to be hospitalized.

David Hutchins had discovered mysterious damage extending randomly over at least three acres of fields planted in clover. Here and there he had come across areas of furiously turned earth, trenchlike gouges, not much more than a foot wide but some as long as fifteen feet, unevenly dug, deeper in one place than another.

Mr. Hutchins wasn't particularly worried about it, but he thought it would interest Will, whose father had managed the property for years until he retired. Will had developed a real fondness for the elegant old farmhouses that dotted the land-scape of Ohio, and he had snapped up his childhood home when it was put on the market by the Claytor family before the war. He had also bought the main house, restored both buildings, and hired a farm manager himself, who was starting a family in the house in which Will had grown up. It was in sight of the main house, but far across a field and closer to the road, and it was where David Hutchins and his wife now lived.

"It looks like it's been *churned*," David told them. "It makes you think of those reports of flying saucers . . . strange lights and so on. The works! Little ladders, little green men . . ." He assumed a wide-eyed expression of mock terror for a moment, raising his hands and wriggling his fingers to indicate the spookiness he was describing, then he relaxed and grinned at Will and Betts. Of course none of them believed in such things for a minute, although Betts was more open-minded about various possibilities than she would ever admit.

"It's just some kind of animal looking for water," David continued on a less animated note. "But I've never seen any-thing that would do that," he said. "A bear *could* do it, I guess, but I've never heard of that. I'll tell you what, though, if we weren't so far north I'd swear it was wild hogs. Just gouged out *troughs* . . . Looks like a herd of elephants've been there."

"I'd like to take a look at that," Will said, glancing toward Betts, who nodded to him to go ahead.

Betts's doctor had wanted to hospitalize her; he insisted her baby was more than a month late but Betts thought not. "Oh, for goodness' sakes! The baby's not late. It's just that Dr. Cunningham's *expectations* are early," she told her mother and her husband and anyone else who suggested otherwise. Betts was undaunted by Dr. Cunningham. At every appointment, when Betts was led away to disrobe and wait for him in an examination room, she slipped out of her clothes and put on the cotton gown as quickly as possible.

When finally Dr. Cunningham entered the room, Betts was never passively waiting, barefoot, with her ankles primly crossed, sitting on the edge of the examination table. She was barely even entirely covered by the too-small cotton robe that was only loosely tied in the back and hit her midthigh. Her immodesty was not the least bit seductive; in fact, her clear indifference to him as a male—as a person at all—always robbed him of authority in her presence.

He would come upon her standing on one side of the room or another, studying the diplomas or the Currier and Ives prints. He didn't see her frequently enough to remember to be wary, and he was always thrown off balance and curiously diminished when she wheeled toward him, moving his way with an upbeat, social aggression, shaking his hand firmly while grasping his other arm with her left hand and bending down toward him with an appearance of exuberant goodwill. Her wide smile never foundered as he peered up at her strong white teeth. Betts hadn't trusted a single doctor since she had been under the care of Dr. Caldwell years ago. She had even become suspicious of Claytor, her own brother, or at least of Claytor's choice of profession. And never in the world—even if she had handed one of her children over to a pack of wolves—would it have crossed Dr. Cunningham's mind to suggest to Betts Dameron that subconsciously she had not really wanted to give birth to her baby.

When Trudy phoned to let Betts know that Agnes was in the hospital, Betts was furious that Claytor—or *someone*—hadn't telephoned the Dameron household the night before.

By the time Will returned, Betts was in a brooding, angry state of mind. Sam Holloway had phoned as well, shortly after Trudy's call, in case no one had alerted Betts and Will.

"I'm hoping that Claytor went home to get some sleep," Sam said. "He thinks your mother might have a mild concussion. She hit her head at school earlier that afternoon apparently. But Claytor also said it might be nothing more than this heat."

Betts thanked Sam for calling, but she wasn't at all certain that Claytor had passed along all he knew. "Dwight and Claytor always treat me as if I'm still four years old," she said to Will. Betts was truly angry when she reported the news to him that Agnes was in the hospital and had been there all night.

She asked Will to drive her into town. "I've been just going along all morning not even knowing Mother was sick. Even Howie knew! They always leave me out of things. They always did, too, the whole time we were growing up. Not Howard so much. But Dwight and Claytor...It was like they were in a secret society and no one else even knew the rules. And they still don't tell me anything. Even when it's important," she said to Will. "I was always the *mascot*. God forbid this baby is a girl, because we'll have to keep having children until she has a sister. No one should grow up as the only daughter in a house full of brothers!"

By the time Will and Betts got to the hospital, though, Betts was in labor, which had come on so fast she didn't have time to worry about anything else.

When Agnes Scofield became entirely alert, in the late afternoon on Tuesday, she was disoriented, especially when she

found Julian Brightman sitting in a chair next to her bed. She
had no idea where she was or why he was there. Julian was as
startled as she when Agnes suddenly opened her eyes, looking
straight in his direction. The only news of her he had had
was that she had likely fainted from the heat, but since he
had been shooting film at the hospital earlier in the day,
he had stopped in to see how Agnes was doing, and to find
out if any diagnosis had been made. It was he, after all, who
had prevented her from having what might have been a serious fall.

Agnes gave up the struggle to orient herself. She was too
light-headed and groggy even to determine if she felt ill or
injured, and she was unable to shake off her fuzzy-headed
confusion. She focused her attention on Julian Brightman's
face, which was apple-cheeked but very slightly slope-chinned,
with dark, shiny brown eyes. Regardless of the subject he was
addressing, his expression was disconcertingly cheerful, as it
was when he leaned toward Agnes attentively.

"What time is it?" she asked him, and he told her it was
exactly 5:07. She heard what he said, but by the time she
grasped it, she had lost the context of the answer, and she
wondered instead where she was as she gathered the impression of an institutional enclosure. Mr. Brightman's voice came
to her jarringly, as though it were a sharp echo.

"Am I at Mercy?" she asked him after she had managed to
organize the question.

Julian Brightman sat back in his chair, appalled, though his
reaction didn't register one way or another on Agnes, who
was still struggling to sort out all the frustratingly vague questions and ideas floating through her head. She didn't even
know if it was early morning or early evening, since either

one would show up between the slats of the Venetian blinds as the same, blank, grayish white.

Mr. Brightman pulled himself together, drawing up straight in his chair and placing his hands firmly on his knees. "No! Of course not! Mrs. Scofield! At my mercy?" He was deeply embarrassed and also scandalized. "Why would you think such a thing? Your whole family... It's my pleasure! Surely a great many people will visit you. Visiting hours have just started. I stopped by to see how you were doing..."

Agnes looked back at him uncomprehendingly for a moment and then was hit by a spate of dizziness and nausea. She closed her eyes against the sight of the blurring ceiling light and floated off into her watery, dreamlike ideas and imaginings, which required nothing in the way of attention on her part.

Julian sat there for a moment before he realized that Agnes Scofield had wanted to know if she was at Mercy General Hospital or at the Lady of the Lake Hospital on the other side of town near the high school. He pressed the call button for the nurse, since he had no idea if Mrs. Scofield's waking up or her lapse back into unconsciousness was to be expected or not.

He was rattled, and having believed that Mrs. Scofield was surprised by an ordinary act of courtesy on his part, Julian remained trapped in that state of compassionate alarm. Julian had admired Agnes Scofield since he had first met her. She was still pretty for her age, although he didn't know exactly what age she was. But she certainly didn't look like a woman with four grown children.

The melancholy sympathy that overtook him as he looked on while she lay with her still-dark hair loose over her pillow and curling around her face, awoke in him a protective instinct on her behalf. He sat at her bedside waiting for the nurse to arrive and relieve him, remaining convinced—even though he realized he had misunderstood her question—that Agnes Scofield was not cherished as she should be by all those people within her orbit.

The next time Agnes opened her eyes Sam Holloway was in the chair where Julian Brightman had been, and Dr. Bass stood at the end of the bed, looking over the clipboard attached to the iron rail.

"How're you feeling, Agnes?" Sam asked, and Milton Bass looked up and came around the other side to stand next to her, taking her pulse with two fingers against her neck.

"Do you know where you are?" Dr. Bass asked her, but not as though he wanted the answer; he was trying to assess her condition.

"Well, not at Mercy," she replied, concentrating hard against drowsiness. "I must be at Lady of the Lake?" But she couldn't hold her place and drifted into an odd semi-sleep.

"That's good," Agnes heard Dr. Bass say, although she couldn't lock her thoughts in place with enough intensity to coordinate any response of her own. She had a good many questions that remained unasked, although she wasn't certain if she had or had not spoken aloud. She could, however, distinguish the voices around her.

"She knows she's in the hospital," Dr. Bass said. "She knows something happened. I think she's probably going to be fine. We're running some tests. But I'm hoping it was the heat plus however she got that bump on her head," Milton Bass told Sam Holloway; he was familiar enough with the Scofields that he was accustomed to thinking of Sam as an extension of their family; it seemed unreasonable to maintain any sort of patient–doctor confidentiality concerning Agnes Scofield.

"How's Betts doing?" Sam asked, rising to leave, gathering the newspaper sections he had stacked on the table, patting his pocket to check for his glasses.

"Well, right now she's mad as hell because no one let her know her mother was in the hospital. Dr. Cunningham's earning his fee, and Claytor's in hot water. No one called the Damerons until this morning. Probably thought there was no point in worrying her. *I* didn't see any point in telling her about Claytor's little girl. If Betts was exposed to her recently it would only drive her crazy. Nothing she could do about it, though. Her labor's going pretty well, but it's going to be a while. Will and Dwight are upstairs in the waiting room. If you'd tell them that Agnes is awake..."

"I'll certainly do that," Sam said. "I don't suppose Claytor can visit either his mother or his sister?"

And Milt shook his head. "No. No, not for a while," he agreed. "At least ten days, I'd think..."

"Well, we may have to think about adding a Scofield wing to this place," Sam said. "I'd say my prayers if I thought it would do any good, but please let Claytor know that if there's anything I can do...," Sam said as he turned the corner on his way to the elevators.

Over the following ten days Julian Brightman held scrupulously to his schedule of visiting Agnes Scofield every afternoon, and as it happened, he rarely found anyone else keeping her company when he arrived, although Sam Holloway often stopped by just when Julian was about to leave. By the end of the week Julian had taken to bringing along a gift or a magazine Agnes might find entertaining. The Eola Arms Hotel, where he was living for the duration of his filming, was next to the Greyhound bus station, which was only a long, dark, narrow space with a ticket counter, a large assortment of magazines and newspapers, glass cases displaying cigars, cigarettes, and other sundries, as well as a dusty collection of souvenirs of Washburn, Ohio, which included a goodly number of intricately beaded or woven Indian-crafted items.

Julian knew enough not to buy a pair of beaded moccasins for Mrs. Scofield, but he did pick out a pretty little woven octagonal box with an elaborate zigzag design around the sides and a brown bear on a bright red background exactingly woven into the top. He had exhausted the supply of magazines for September and October and even the early November issues, glossily illustrated with pictures of beautifully browned turkeys beamed upon by happy families. He always took a copy of the daily paper to the hospital for her. He had noticed, though, that the hairpins she used to put her hair up and hold it in place often lay scattered on the table beside her bed, and he thought the woven Indian box would be the perfect receptacle.

Julian Brightman's intentions were never anything but benevolent in all of his dealings with other people throughout his life, but he had no idea of the turmoil he often left in his wake. Before he began his project of documenting an ordinary American town, he had returned briefly to Poland in hopes of tying up various loose ends of a book he was finishing. He sought the help of the Warsaw press in locating the people whose images he had caught on film when the German planes had strafed the potato fields. He had been elated when he recognized a woman who had been just a young girl at the time. She had been only ten or twelve years old when he had first come upon her, hovering over one of the women who had been killed instantly.

The girl had been speaking insistently, and in Polish, of course. But Julian understood the gist of what she was saying. "Answer me!" she commanded the woman, reasonably enough. "Please talk to me! Why won't you talk to me? What will happen to me if you won't tell me what to do? Where should I go?"

At the time Julian had done his best to help her, and he, too, had wept over her sister, but when he saw that child standing in the offices of the *Trybuna Ludu,* holding an infant who must be her own, he spoke to her with a note of avuncular delight. "Aha," he teased her. "I don't think you have any idea who I am! You probably don't remember me at all. But here you are!" He smiled broadly at her. "Grown up. And your own baby, too. You don't think we have met before!"

She was thin but not fragile-looking, with an expression of fixed courtesy as she looked at him. "I do. Yes, I do remember you. I should," she replied in English. "I first saw you the day the Germans killed my sister. It was the day I first saw anyone die. My older sister—I wanted her to tell me what I should do, but she wouldn't answer me. I had never seen anyone dead. And it was the day that was the first time I met a foreigner. That was you. I didn't know what you were saying. I didn't know if you would also try to kill us."

She spoke to him in English, although there was an interpreter standing by who looked away uneasily, but Julian nodded smilingly at the young woman, in agreement, and patted her shoulder. "Oh, yes, that was me. You do remember. And it was so long ago."

In the same way he never realized that the young Polish woman was made miserable by their reunion, he was oblivious of the fact that Agnes Scofield was nearly crazed by his dutiful visits. When she fought back tears attempting to refuse the gift of the woven Indian box, while also trying to discourage him from bringing her anything more, he assumed she was moved by his thoughtfulness. Other visitors came by to see her, but no flowers or cards were on display, which struck Julian as neglectful. And to be fair, it wasn't Julian Brightman in particular who drove Agnes to despair. She loathed the vulnerability of being trespassed upon by anyone at any moment.

There was a jovial nurse, for example, whose cheerfulness struck Agnes as unwarranted and even frightening. As Agnes's accessibility to visitors became more and more exasperating to her, Deborah Belden's insistently buoyant instructions when she delivered Agnes's medications began to seem alarming. Deborah handed them to Agnes in a small paper cup along with a glass of water and always the same instructions posed as a jolly encouragement. "Down the hatch!" Nurse Belden said, invariably. "Down the hatch and Johnny bar the door!" Her unreasonable delight began to seem to Agnes downright menacing.

"She means well enough, Agnes," Dr. Bass assured her. "Deb's as good a nurse as we've got. But she's tired. She's filling in on the evening shift right now. She's used to working in the maternity ward..."

"I really don't think I can stand being here another night, Milton," Agnes had said when he stopped by on the ninth morning she was hospitalized, and she heard in her voice a humiliating note of supplication. Dr. Bass wanted to keep her over the weekend. He was concerned about her blood pressure, and he had spoken vaguely about running even a few more tests, but Agnes no longer cared if she dropped dead as long as it happened in private and in her own house.

That afternoon Sam Holloway and Debbie Belden, who always checked on her patients when she first came on shift at five P.M., had run into each other in the hallway, both on their way to Agnes's room. They had chatted a bit, walking along the hall together. Debbie's husband was an electrician whom Sam often depended on, and he asked after Art Belden: What was he up to? Would Debbie tell him that Sam would be looking for him pretty soon? The two of them arrived together at Agnes's open doorway in the middle of Julian Brightman's attempt to persuade her to accept his gift of the small woven box.

Whenever Sam visited Agnes, he was used to running into Julian Brightman; Julian seemed to have persuaded himself that there was something afoot from which Agnes needed protecting. He was polite when other visitors happened by, but he was intransigently defensive, firmly planted in the gray metal chair he had early on staked out for himself. Sam wasn't sure if either Agnes herself or Julian Brightman realized that Julian was determined to be her champion. He appeared to believe that Mrs. Scofield was susceptible to mistreatment of some sort or another and had decided to maintain a regular vigil at her bedside as often as he could in order to prevent it. At least that's what Sam had finally concluded.

But the tableau playing out in Agnes's hospital room had been carried too far. Mr. Brightman looked sorrowful and bewildered, and Agnes herself was openly in tears. Deborah Belden and Sam had both stopped still in the doorway, surprised and embarrassed, but after a moment Sam moved forward, approaching Julian with a regretful smile; he meant to signify that he himself was all too familiar with Julian's situation.

"Mrs. Scofield's just suffering from exhaustion," Sam said to Julian, in an effort to explain Agnes's tears. Julian was standing, still clutching the box, extending it in Agnes's direction, but Sam flung his arm over Julian's shoulders and tilted his head toward Julian in an attitude of confidentiality, simultaneously moving him toward the door.

"You see," Sam said in a low timbre aimed only at Julian, "Dr. Bass even made it pretty clear that if Agnes was determined..." Sam paused and seemed to be weighing the propriety of saying more, but then he continued in a rush. "Well, Milt Bass thinks this just isn't the time for a wedding," Sam said conversationally to Julian. "At least not any sort of big ceremony. Any big to-do. It's upset Agnes. Upset everyone. You know how it gets to be with families and weddings..."

Julian crossed the threshold into the corridor and took a long look at Sam. Julian hadn't had the slightest hint that Sam Holloway and Agnes Scofield were in any way involved. Certainly not that they were planning to get married. In fact, he thought of Sam as a sort of bridge between the two generations of Scofields, not firmly fixed in either camp. Taking a closer look at Sam standing in the doorway of the hospital room, Julian couldn't guess what age Sam might be. His hair was dark gray and he had a pleasant angular and rather lopsided face, as if originally he had been perfect but then had been dropped and broken and hastily repaired.

"I'm sorry to hear that," Julian finally replied. "I hope you'll extend my best wishes. And my congratulations, of course," he added, as if reminding himself to do so and then checking it off a list of things he'd completed. "To both of you. Mrs. Scofield is...Oh, she's a very handsome woman. But what I believe is that she's an *admirable* woman. Taking care of all her children when they were young. And even then still teaching school. She was the first person I met in Washburn. I was thinking yesterday that it was probably at that instant I decided I wanted to use Washburn for my film." He paused for a moment to consider what seemed to him the remarkable coincidence of his meeting Agnes Scofield. And then he added quickly, "Oh! Your own hospitality, as well! But that very afternoon when I met her at the grammar school . . . Mrs. Scofield and her family . . . The nice little town . . . You and Mr. Dameron, treating me and Franklin to a fine dinner. We were strangers! But Mrs. Scofield . . . I'm convinced that it is she who is the best example of everything that is ordinary in America!" Julian said, offering his hand to Sam along with a brisk nod, in his oddly European formality.

"Well, that's something. I don't quite know what to say to that!" Sam responded. "I know she'll be surprised to find out that she was your inspiration. I'll pass that along to her," Sam assured him, "along with your best wishes." And Sam withdrew his hand in a manner of finality that sent Julian Brightman on his way with the idea that Sam wanted to talk to Agnes Scofield alone, which, given what Julian understood now, was perfectly reasonable.

Sam stood in the hall, watching while Julian turned the corner toward the elevators, not wanting to intrude on Agnes while Debbie Belden went into the room to check her blood pressure and do whatever else. He and Debbie had come upon the scene together, but she had tactfully hung back in the doorway while Sam Holloway straightened out whatever had upset Mrs. Scofield.

Sam liked Julian Brightman well enough and was fascinated at the unlikeliness of all Julian's various adventures. Of course, there was scarcely a person Sam had ever met who didn't pique his interest one way or another. Sam found Julian's social misperceptions both surprising and a little sad, because Julian always meant well, and Sam was slightly ashamed of himself for purposely misleading the man.

Sam rationalized, though, that he hadn't told Mr. Brightman an outright lie. All he had done, really, was imply a commitment on Agnes's part to some unnamed party. If Milt Bass thought that Agnes was planning a wedding—anyone's wedding—he probably *would* advise against any sort of celebration. Sam convinced himself that he had done nothing more than extricate everyone from a hopeless situation in a way that spared everyone's feelings. He felt certain Agnes had no idea that Julian was besotted with her, and quite possibly Julian hadn't fully realized it himself. But Sam knew full well that Julian Brightman would hound her in his obliviously dogged manner until it drove poor Agnes completely around the bend.

When Debbie Belden left the room, Sam stayed on a little longer, knowing to do nothing more than listen if Agnes wanted to tell him something, or to chat if she was interested in conversation, or simply to sit down and read the paper.

In Marshal County, Ohio, as well as in Knox, Coshocton, and Marion counties, and, in fact, throughout most of the middle and southeastern part of the state, the heat and drought ended in fits and starts, in dribs and drabs—a steamy drizzle late one afternoon, a light but steady rain a few days later—while day by day the temperature dropped incrementally. The maple trees never exhibited the incandescence of fall color; their leaves had browned and fallen and been raked into mulch piles all over Washburn before the start of the school year.

The walnut trees failed even to turn briefly yellow, shedding green drifts of leaves in late September that crisped and browned in the dry grass and that were almost as hard to rake up as the silvery leaves of the weeping willows. The branches of the walnuts held clusters of underdeveloped, yellow-green nuts hanging naked against the sky. Most people were careful not to comment on the peculiar sight, although all the boys in Washburn between, say, twelve years old and, maybe, fifteen simply knocked themselves out with their own observations and witticisms.

Only the pin oaks were beautiful, remaining full-leafed and creamy tan singly or in clusters of two or three along the river. There were two oaks in Monument Square and, of course, rows of them on either side of Oak Street, where they had been planted as saplings forty-odd years earlier. But with the exception of the residents of Oak Street, no one noticed the pin oaks' tenacious light brown foliage. Fall was dispiritedly colorless except for an occasional red flash of weedy sumac.

Thursday, October 15, 1953, the front page of the morning newspaper in Washburn, Ohio, which was the county seat of Marshal County, carried a photo of a canvas hammock that had been picked up by a wind and draped over a chimney in Okolona, Ohio, up in Henry County. All of those flat, northwestern counties along the Indiana and Michigan borders had suffered flash floods, wind and water damage, heavy lightning, and at least three deaths due to storms created when cold air had finally pushed south from Canada. But in Washburn the temperature had dropped to only the low eighties during the day and into the upper fifties at night. It was a relief from the dry heat, but the sky was steadily overcast and the days were dreary.

People running into acquaintances around town — perhaps

at Hayes's Market, or standing in line at the post office—congratulated one another for the good luck of having escaped those storms that had hit the northwestern quadrant of the state so hard. But, in fact, the unrealized expectation of a definite end to one season before the beginning of another was unsettling. In Washburn—and, more than likely, also in Coshocton, Danville, Mount Vernon, and even Columbus—almost everyone was tired of the monotonous sameness of the days. Autumn was passing into early winter with only a flicker of color here and there, and not one singular event to mark the change of season. Weatherwise nothing much at all happened in the town of Washburn in the early fall of 1953.

The day after the appearance of the hammock-draped chimney on the front page of the *Washburn Observer,* when Deborah Belden got off her shift just after midnight, she mentioned to her daughter, who had come to pick her up, that Agnes Scofield had refused the gift of an engagement ring from Mr. Brightman. "Sam Holloway and I walked in at the very minute Mr. Brightman was trying to convince her to accept it. I didn't stay in the room, but Mr. Holloway was trying to sort it all out. He explained that Dr. Bass had insisted that a wedding would just be too much—Oh! Linda! Remind me to tell your father to get in touch with Sam Holloway, would you?" she asked her daughter, who nodded. "He said they were starting a new project pretty soon."

"Okay. I won't forget," Linda said. "But what happened? Had Mr. Brightman already asked her to marry him? Did you see the ring?"

"I didn't," Debbie said. "No. It was in a little woven box. And Mrs. Scofield seemed to be upset that he was offering it to her. No telling what had upset her, though. Almost anything seems to set her off. You know, I was trying not to *listen*. Trying not to pay that much attention. That's all I heard about the wedding. What Sam Holloway said. I just don't know...*I* haven't heard anything else about any wedding. But Mrs. Scofield just isn't entirely back to normal. She won't tell you so...Probably she doesn't even realize she's so shaky on her pins. Someone needs to be *right* there with her when she gets out of bed. But she really wants to get home. Who can blame her? I think Dr. Bass is worried that she might have had a stroke. You'd think Mr. Brightman would have waited for her to be feeling better," she said.

"Well, you're right. You would think so," Linda agreed.

"Mr. Brightman's a nice enough man," Deborah went on, "but I'll tell you, I wouldn't marry him myself. I think he's foreign, but I can't tell where he's from. I just don't think I could ever marry a man I couldn't look at and take seriously. Oh, well. It's just that he always makes me think of Howdy Doody. Not the *teeth*..."—she paused briefly, considering—"but somehow around the eyes."

In an atmosphere as parched as the one in Washburn, the news that Agnes Scofield was *not* going to marry Julian Brightman spread like wildfire, and the fact that she was also not going to marry Sam Holloway flickered and faltered along behind it. Agnes herself, however, as well as Julian Brightman, remained unaware of the connection they were forsaking, the commitment they were not making.

Ordinarily it would have been no more than a two-day topic of conversation and quickly straightened out, but during that particularly dreary autumn of 1953, even Agnes Scofield could not easily be forgiven for having a luxury of choices. It simply was one of those seasons that did nothing to improve—or even support—any person's best qualities. Bernice Dameron, for instance, who knew she probably was Agnes Scofield's closest friend, was secretly—and with considerable shame—downright envious of the two weeks Agnes was hospitalized. Waited on hand and foot, Bernice found herself thinking, as she taught her own fourth-grade class and helped out the overwhelmed substitute teacher hired to cover Agnes's third-graders across the hall.

When Deborah Belden's sister, Sheila Osler, who also taught fourth grade at Jesser Grammar School, said to Bernice casually—as if Sheila were merely referring to something that was common knowledge—that it was really a shame Agnes Scofield had been forced to cancel her wedding, Bernice was nonplussed.

Sheila didn't notice, though, and went on, "I didn't even know they were planning to get married, she's been a widow for such a long time...And Howard's dating Betty Heath pretty seriously...It's a big house for one person." Bernice could do nothing more than smile ruefully and nod at Sheila.

But it required tremendous self-control for Bernice not to give voice to her astonished fury. She went about the business of ushering her class in from recess, but she was paying very little attention. How unkind, she was thinking. How mean-spirited of Agnes not to have said anything. Bernice knew enough not to express surprise to Sheila; she knew enough without even thinking to behave as though she had known all about Agnes's upcoming marriage, because otherwise Bernice would look like the world's biggest fool. Look like an unimportant acquaintance. Agnes's failure to alert her, to confide in her, was unforgivable. Bernice was twice the teacher Agnes Scofield was, and Bernice loved her work, which Agnes never had. In fact, Bernice thought, she had pulled Agnes's chestnuts out of the fire any number of times over the years they taught across the hall from each other.

At home, in the little house across from the school that her brother, Will, had bought for her when he decided to renovate and rent the old farmhouse, Bernice fixed herself a gin and tonic and sat on the glider in the sunroom to read the paper. She concentrated determinedly on the pages of the *Washburn Observer* in an attempt to deflect the overwhelming emotion of betrayal, which still enveloped her. She was being ridiculous! The whole matter was unworthy of the energy it sapped, and certainly it shouldn't disrupt the small habitual pleasures of her day. Bernice was even fairly certain that there was a likely explanation of why Agnes hadn't said anything, but it was too late this evening to infuse logic into her self-indulgent resentment, so she distracted herself with the headlines.

And there was a sort of comfort to be found in the newspaper. She wasn't, after all, in Trieste, where Tito was threatening to send troops. She had not beckoned to the hitchhiker in Columbus, who had just been given a life sentence for murdering the fellow who had been kind enough to pull over and offer him a ride. Bernice knew various and sundry members of the Taft family and had sent a sympathy card following Robert Taft's death in July, but she wasn't particularly interested in Governor Lausche's failure to appoint his successor, which was causing all sorts of speculation and letters to the editor.

Generally Bernice appreciated the serenity of her single life, the flexibility it afforded her to travel, to pursue her passionate interest in music, to do pretty much whatever she wanted to do, as long as she scheduled it around the academic year. But this season she had been distracted and dissatisfied in general, and suddenly, under the barrage of news concerning the Scofields, Bernice felt diminished, somehow, and wrongfully unconsidered.

She browsed through the Classifieds, which she always saved for last, because she could spend her whole supper contemplating and constructing a narrative around the advertisement for, say, *One Haviland teapot, five cups, six saucers.* Who would be in need of an item like that? Why even bother to sell them—and for so little money—since you could still use five of the cups and saucers? She read the paper from front to back in an attempt to avoid coming to terms with the injury it was to her feelings to recognize how little an impression the whole of her life had made upon the impervious surface of the earth.

Variations on this theme occurred with a good deal of frequency among Agnes's friends, and even within her family, although Lily Butler simply dismissed the idea of a refused proposal—of a canceled wedding—as nonsense. Agnes's daughter, Betts, though, was far less sanguine; she didn't entirely trust her mother's forthrightness regarding her private life.

Within a week or so, though, the subject of Agnes's marital plans one way or another was displaced by other events and concerns. Betts Dameron had given birth to a nine-pound-six-ounce boy, Daniel, and the addition to her family was duly noted, but, after all, almost everyone had children and might have more. It was the news of Julia Scofield's sudden illness that finally overshadowed almost every other concern. The news had a gradual effect; it was drawn upward through the generations into the communal consciousness—the way ink travels up a stalk of celery.

In 1953, a case of polio in the midst of a small town was profound. As it was, for that matter, in a large city like Boston. Photographs had appeared in newspapers across the country of families in their cars, lining the streets for blocks around Boston Children's Hospital, sick children bundled in the backseats, while doctors and various other hospital personnel leaned in with flashlights to try to manage a rough sort of triage.

Agnes was hospitalized for two weeks while Milton Bass ran tests on her of one kind or another. No diagnosis was established as far as anyone had heard, but neither was there any dire undercurrent of speculation about Agnes Scofield's future. Julia Scofield, on the other hand, had been hospitalized for only three days, with a high fever, but two weeks later neither she nor her sister, Mary Alcorn, had been back to school. And it was common knowledge that Lavinia Scofield regularly allowed her daughters to swim in the Cardinal Club swimming pool.

No diagnosis had been made in Julia's case, either, but the fact that her sister was also being kept out of school—during the presumed danger period for being contagious or coming down with serious symptoms of the disease—left no doubt in anyone's mind. It was simply a given that Julia had come down with polio and had survived it. That year six people had already died of polio in Marshal County alone, and in the northeastern part of the state the toll had been much greater. In fact, Millersburg, Ohio, had been quarantined.

It was a shame, though, that the communal idea of Julia Scofield, as well as that of her half sister, Mary Alcorn, under-went a subtle change. The very parents whose children most admired Mary Alcorn and Julia Scofield were predisposed to find some count against the two girls. The fact was that the children in Mrs. Fogelman's first-grade classroom had begun bringing home reports of Julia Scofield since the very first day of school, in much the same way her sister, Mary Alcorn's, popularity had broken upon the grammar school scene five years earlier.

"Julia Scofield wants to wear her sandals every day," Sandra Simmons had said the morning of the second day of school, as her mother was fastening the buckle of Sandra's new white Mary Janes.

"Oh, really? Well, do you want to wear your sandals, too?"

"Mrs. Fogelman says we can't because we might cut our feet at recess," Sandra said. Susan Simmons had waited for the answer before she buckled her daughter's other shoe.

That same morning, when Sandra's mother brushed her daughter's wavy long blond hair away from her face and began to tie it back with a green grosgrain ribbon, Sandra ducked her head and slid out from under her mother's reach. "Julia Scofield *hates* ribbons in her hair," she said. By then Mrs. Simmons, who hadn't slept well the night before and was hot and harried, became unreasonably miffed. Who was this Julia Scofield, anyway? But Sandra went off to school ribbonless, and her mother dreaded having to comb all the tangles out of Sandra's hair that evening before Sandra took a bath. In Mrs. Fogelman's first-grade class of 1953, it was Julia who set the tone to which the other little girls aspired, just as her sister had done before her.

By late October, Mrs. Fogelman's two room mothers, Susan Simmons and Rose Johnson, fell into speculating about the first-grade class while they decorated the stage of the Jesser Grammar School auditorium with pumpkins and gourds and cornstalks on the day before the annual Jesser Grammar School Halloween Carnival.

"Sandra and Julia Scofield were planning to come to the carnival together. As salt and pepper. But it's not going to make any sense for Sandra to come alone as *salt*. She's in a state about it—I can't make her understand that without *pepper*... I tried to convince her to wear one of her sister's old costumes, but she's determined to wear the costume Lavinia Scofield made for her."

"How did she make a salt costume?" Rose stopped what she was doing in order to hear the answer. She thought it was a clever idea.

"It's made of cardboard," Susan said, "like a big tube—a cylinder with armholes. A silver-painted lamp shade with holes painted on it is the shaker on top. And then, of course, it says SALT right across the front."

"I don't think that's so bad," Rose said. "You don't really *have* to have pepper. Or maybe she could find another friend to go as the pepper shaker. At least there aren't likely to be any other salt and pepper shakers in the costume parade."

"Well, maybe so. But I wish she'd just wear the princess costume her sister wore three years ago. She'd look so much prettier. And, you know, Julia always looks as if she's just been dropped out of a tornado," Susan remarked. Sandra was driving her mother crazy, complaining every day that Julia still wasn't back at school.

"Oh, Susan! She's cute as a bug!" Rose said. "Like she stepped straight out of *The Little Rascals*. And smart, too. Well.

All those Scofields are smart." She was fond of the whole family, after all.

Susan nodded but raised her eyebrows in an amused but rueful expression. "Well, to tell you the truth," she went on, "I always wonder if anyone ever takes a second look at Julia before they let her out of the house. If anyone ever takes the time to see if her clothes are on right. If she's combed her hair!"

The sash that tied in a bow at the back waist of each one of Julia Scofield's pastel, shirred-bodiced, puff-sleeved Peter Pan dresses — the fashion for every girl in school until the end of second grade — was generally flying behind her in streamers by the ten A.M. half-hour break for "little recess." By then, too, Julia's white socks had collapsed around her ankles above her practical brown-leather Mary Janes, and her pale hair in its Buster Brown cut was almost always out of place because of her tendency to push it away from her face. Sometimes her bangs stuck straight out over her pale eyebrows like a shelf.

The other little girls in Julia's class wore their hair long and curly or sometimes tied up with ribbons into dog ears or a ponytail. But Lavinia Scofield had been appalled by such a style worn by a child. She said to Claytor that she wouldn't allow anyone to sexualize her children at so young an age. "Those dresses are one thing. But the *hair*... Imagine the nuisance for those girls... It's just downright tacky, Claytor!"

In midcentury middle-class America, the climate of the times was saturated with vague, watered-down Freudian theory on every front. The idea was rampant that just about any behavior could be explained as the external manifestation of the subconscious. But simultaneously, the very idea of the *sub-conscious* was suspect to most practical-minded Americans. A person should just pull himself together and get on with things!

And, filtered through the lens of Americans' disapproval of self-indulgence of any kind, the unlucky victim of an illness was implicated as the agent of his or her own malady. Or, at any rate, his or her *mother* was implicated. It was widely known, for instance, that Theodore Roosevelt, otherwise so intently robust, had suffered attacks of asthma as a result of the suffocating affection of his mother, although another school of thought theorized that it was his mother's emotional distance that caused his sudden, desperate gasping for breath—her withheld attention was literally the air he needed to breathe. Or was it *Franklin* Roosevelt's mother? . . . It was FDR who had contracted polio, after all.

Of course, no amount of parental oversight could stave off the sometimes dangerous but run-of-the-mill childhood illnesses passed along through the generations, like measles, or mumps, or chicken pox. But as these new theories were hybridized and adopted into American culture, the notion followed neatly that if you were vigilant and also virtuous enough to avoid any sort of mental chaos, ambivalence, anguish, or repression, your child would do likewise, and his or her good health, in general, would prevail.

As they considered Julia Scofield's sudden illness in light of everything else they knew about her life, it seemed to Susan Simmons and other anxious parents that there had always been something unsettling about the presence of that little girl, which, naturally, no one blamed on the child herself. But there was about her an unkemptness that possibly bespoke a lack of attention to her well-being. It worried the parents of Julia's friends that their children socialized so enthusiastically with a child whose own situation wasn't entirely certain. It made all the parents uneasy.

And, too, there began to be some talk now and then about Claytor Scofield. Too many people had run into him when clearly he had had too much to drink. And word was that he and his wife often fell into terrible, loud arguments, uncivil, with doors slamming and one or the other of them driving off in the car to who knew where. But Lavinia and Claytor's acquaintances were loath to draw any conclusions entirely unfavorable to Claytor. After all, most of the parents of the current batch of grade-school children in Washburn, Ohio, had grown up with Claytor Scofield and Dwight Claytor; those two boys had always been popular and also well liked. The Tarleton Twins, they'd been called, after the two handsome brothers in *Gone with the Wind*.

Dwight, though, had married Trudy Butler, who was as familiar to everyone in town as was Dwight himself. Claytor Scofield, on the other hand, had come home from the war with a small, foreign family in tow. No one knew much of anything about Lavinia Witherspoon Alcorn except that she was from Virginia. She was peculiarly unforthcoming. It was impossible for Claytor's old friends with whom the Scofields socialized not to perceive Lavinia's seeming aloofness as anything other than a slight not only to them but to the very place to which they felt an allegiance.

Lavinia — and by extension her two daughters — remained slightly suspect in the same way that tourists of one kind or another are always considered untrustworthy by the natives of whatever places those outsiders happen to be visiting. And eventually, that hot, dry, colorless autumn of 1953 came to be referred to in Washburn, Ohio, as the time that Lavinia Scofield's little girl did *not* die of polio.

Chapter Five

NOT UNTIL she was home from the hospital was Agnes Scofield gradually able to relax the unthinking, protective vigilance required to maintain an illusion of privacy while nurses, doctors, friends, and goodwilled acquaintances came and went without warning. For the first few days alone in her own house, she was surprised over and over as she discovered the luxury of commonplace, everyday familiarity. For almost a week she was taken aback each morning when she woke up in her own bed.

At first she was nearly moved to tears by the relief of coming into the day tensed and guarded only to recognize once again the unsurprising angles of the furniture in her own bedroom. She found herself overwhelmed—as though some yearning had been quenched—simply by the sight of her vanity table sitting catty-cornered between the north and east windows, the faded chintz-covered chair where she always sat to take off her stockings, the braided rug from her girlhood bedroom that she had failed to mend now for more than thirty years.

In fact, she took in the existence of that unmended rug and realized that somewhere along the way, the trick of avoiding the unraveling edge had become as automatic as knowing that the dining-room door swung away from, not into, the kitchen. One evening before Howard was even born, after a dramatic dustup following a collision when Dwight and Claytor had headed through that doorway from opposite sides at exactly the same moment, Warren had rummaged around in the basement and found an old cut-glass knob, which he screwed into the dining-room side to serve as a temporary door pull until he had a chance to reinstall the whole door and change the hinges. That's where that knob was still, and for the same purpose. For years, now, Agnes had been reminding herself to have the door rehung, but in the meantime she had integrated the nuisance of its backwardness into her everyday life, along with other particulars of the household.

The bottom step of the narrow back staircase, for example, was just half as high as the steep treads leading down to it; the doorway in the extension of the upstairs center hall was only tall enough for someone about five feet seven. Agnes had finally incorporated the hazard of that low door frame the fourth time a child of hers outgrew it, when, at age fourteen, Howard suddenly shot up seemingly overnight to a height of almost six feet. Agnes herself was only a little taller than five feet two, and she passed down the hallway without considering it at all, but Howard had hit his forehead on that door frame with such force that it had knocked him backwards and left a walnut-size bruise that didn't subside for several weeks.

After that, Agnes carefully lettered, cut out, and tacked up a poster-board sign: *Watch Your Head! Low Bridge!* It remained in place even now, helpful to the occasional plumber or electrician, and especially furniture movers.

The unraveling rug could trip someone before he even realized what had happened, just as stepping broadly down that last tread of the rear staircase would cause a person to stumble forward in compensation for taking too long a stride. Clearing the dining-room table after a meal and heading heedlessly toward the kitchen with plates and glasses could still cause a great clatter of broken china and a wide scattering of nubbly bits of glass if anyone came barreling through the door from the other direction. Agnes lingered in bed, ticking off the small conspiracies between herself and the house in which she lived. She hadn't been aware that she had accumulated such a depth of circumstantial intelligence.

For all the time she had lived in the middle house of the three that originally constituted the residential area downtown, Agnes had thought of it as being her mother-in-law's house. In fact, the memory of Lillian Scofield's melancholy dominion had shaped the nature of Agnes's own occupancy. Agnes had lived in the house with the restraint of a caretaker, maintaining the rooms of the house as Lillian Scofield had first arranged them, no doubt with Warren's future ownership in mind. After Warren's death, Agnes's housekeeping amounted to no more, really, than preserving the place for her own children. Ever since she had married Warren Scofield in 1918, and then moved temporarily into his parents' big house in town, she had thought of it only as the place where she happened to live until she and Warren and the children—and then only she and the children—and these past years, only she herself—finally moved somewhere else.

Howard was back and forth from Ohio State, in Columbus,

where he was in graduate school and had finally rented a room, and Agnes no longer considered him to be someone who lived in her house. He was always welcome and never hesitated to stay over, but he was often in town overnight right next door with Dwight and Trudy, or out in Cardinal Hills visiting Claytor, and now and then who knew where he had been when he showed up to have breakfast with his mother before she left for school? Agnes had lived alone, of course, during the war, but she had been inescapably preoccupied with worry about the welfare of her children, which rendered her as caught up in—or pinned down by—their lives as if they had all been right there with her. Whatever else went on in her life during that time seemed to her in retrospect no more than a distraction from the seemingly endless work of waiting for their return.

But in person, any of them—Dwight or Claytor, especially Betts, and even Howard—sitting right there at her kitchen table, for instance, having a cup of coffee and smoking a cigarette, could cause her to grit her teeth in exasperation. The idea that a word of advice or caution from her might still rescue one of them from some sorrow or another was a notion Agnes could not repress, but those children, of course, brushed her suggestions aside. And, too, when they were right there *not* listening to her, the nostalgic version of each child that Agnes had conjured up couldn't possibly be sustained; there they were, no longer cloaked in the near perfection that their absence had conferred upon them.

There were a few slow, lonely mornings when Agnes was finally home from the hospital during which she wondered how one or another of her favorite students was getting along, and moments, too, when she missed the *dailiness* of teaching.

She missed Bernice's company, and she missed her pupils individually, although she didn't miss being responsible for them during all the hours of a school day. The truth was that any roomful of children in the aggregate frightened her. What if they ever caught on to the fact of the power they had en masse?

After Warren's death, Robert Butler had helped Agnes get the job teaching at Jesser Grammar School, even though she didn't have accreditation. Bernice Dameron, who had seemed so worldly when she and Will Dameron were Agnes's childhood neighbors, had very kindly taken Agnes under her wing at Jesser. Agnes had been only thirteen and in her first year at Linus Gilchrest Institute for Girls when Bernice graduated and went off to Oberlin the following year.

Bernice had been a star of that year's senior class at Gilchrest, and had been someone Agnes would have liked to become. The first-year girls had considered Bernice the most elegant of the seniors; she was tall and quite striking, angularly sophisticated, and admirably independent. Once she had been heard unapologetically correcting a statement made by Mr. Morris, who was Head of School. Right in the middle of senior assembly, or so people said.

By the time Agnes and Bernice were thrown together as colleagues, Bernice's glamour and forthrightness had hardened into a lean flintiness, to such a degree, in fact, that her students often passed a year in her classroom without having any idea of her fierce advocacy on their behalf. She was an extraordinary teacher and was generally assigned the children who had the most difficulty learning.

Bernice had patiently and repeatedly advised Agnes simply to assume authority in the classroom. There was nothing tricky about it, Bernice insisted. But Agnes had no idea how to do that; she had instinctively resorted to charm. She was careful not to alert the children to the fact that they were following her instructions, because if they challenged her, she had no faith that they would passively accept her authority just because she was their teacher—or even because she was the oldest, tallest person in the classroom. Some days it was more than usually brought home to Agnes that there were so many of them and only one of her.

Agnes resorted to guile to insure her control. Her students believed that it was they who persuaded her, for instance, to play a game of Travel using spelling words instead of taking a test.

"What? Didn't I tell you about the test? All right, all right. Just this *once* we'll try a game..." They even remained convinced that they had come up with the idea for the contest to see who could be the first in the class to memorize the multiplication table of twelves. But charm requires a lot of energy, and also Agnes was ashamed that her students fell for it so easily. They generally believed that she was the best teacher they had in grammar school; many came back as teenagers to tell her so. But Agnes knew she lacked the talent to honestly *teach*. Of course she persuaded those third-graders to *learn*, but she knew, also, that her commitment was mostly counterfeit, not what she would have chosen to do; she was motivated more by fear and by her urgent need for the salary.

For a little while after she'd come home from Mercy General, and for the first time in her life, Agnes came to terms with the pleasure of leisure and independence. She forced herself to enjoy sitting down with a magazine or a book and reading it with concentration, refusing to act upon the edgy restlessness of thinking she should be doing something else. And the reverse was true as well. The domestic tasks she enjoyed taking on she had always put to the side, doing them in bits and pieces, fifteen minutes here and there, and mostly late in the evening, when she was tired. But these days she left a room undusted, a floor unmopped.

She spent the prime hours of several days cutting and sewing a blouse from a filmy cream-colored silk without imposing upon herself the imperative to *hurry*. Without allowing herself to become convinced that she should simply run it up on her sewing machine in the evenings instead of wasting the most productive part of the day on handwork, making beautiful bound buttonholes, for instance, that no one would ever notice, and that she could have made more quickly but far more crudely on her machine. She took her time to sew French seams in the fragile fabric, although no one but she would ever know how exquisitely that blouse was finished. I'll just take my time, she explained to herself at first, to keep any guilt at bay, and then with a more insistent idea of possession: *my* time.

She put the household bills in a basket on the hall table and was able not to think much about them. McCann's had delivered coal while Agnes was in the hospital; Baynard Grant had tuck-pointed the chimney, finally, and replaced the sieve-like copper cricket. He hadn't yet painted the ceiling in the front room, though, which first needed to be plastered and patched. Agnes expected him to turn up any time in order to drain the pipes in the upstairs bedrooms, the bathroom, and center hall. Over the past few years Agnes had simply stopped heating the second and third floors, which would have caused the pipes to freeze if she hadn't had them drained. She moved out of her big, drafty third-floor bedroom with its bay window, which let in so much light but also let in the cold. For the duration of winter she generally slept in the cozy, windowless little room off the kitchen to cut back on her heating expenses.

Not until Agnes Scofield was over fifty years old and had endured almost five weeks of enforced rest did she find herself entering the first season of carelessness she had experienced in all the years of her life that she could recollect. For the time being, she even pushed aside her looming financial concerns and let the accruing bills remain unopened. There was nothing she could do about them until she could go back to her classroom and once again bring in a salary. Agnes resisted thinking too carefully about her future, though, nor did she have any intention of discussing it with anyone in her family.

Saturday morning, the first weekend in December, Sam Holloway arrived with a perfectly shaped blue spruce in tow, which he set up in the front room, where the tree's vast lower branches spread so widely that Sam had to rearrange some of the furniture to accommodate them. The top of the tree bent against the ten-foot ceiling.

"Gracious, Sam! I've never seen a tree this big in the house," Agnes said, considering the number of lights it would require. "I don't know if I have enough decorations."

"A spruce is going to be pretty wide at the base by the time it gets this tall," Sam said. "But this is one of the trees that had to come down, anyway, so that Will and I can have water and sewers installed all the way up the hill. It seemed a shame to waste it. I brought lots of lights, since I won't be putting up a tree at my house this year. It just stands there unappreciated.

I'm hardly ever there. I'll be glad to string them for you. Unless you'd rather do it. Or maybe Howard wants to do the tree. It always drove me crazy when someone else put up the lights! It's something that you have to pay attention to or it won't look right at all. My mother and sister did an awful job of it after my father died. I'd get home from Vanderbilt and wonder why in God's name . . . Finally they decided that since I complained about it so much, I could just do it myself. All of us were happier."

Agnes heated tomato soup and ran cheese sandwiches under the broiler, flipping them once to brown the other side, and as the two of them sat waiting for the soup to cool, nibbling at their Cheese Dreams, Agnes found herself confiding in Sam about her financial options. "I don't want to teach school again, Sam," she said. "And my children are all set. They don't need my help. I think I'll have about a hundred twenty-five dollars a month. That'll be plenty, I think. But the upkeep on the house . . . I never know when the next thing's going to need to be fixed. All the shutters may have to just come down. They're practically crumbling to dust. Baynard doesn't think they can be repaired. At least not most of them. A few are holding up. Sam, I've been thinking about what would happen if I sold the house. I know it's not worth what it once was, the way the town's grown. But just not having to worry about the upkeep would be a relief."

For a long moment Agnes thought Sam hadn't heard what she said. "Well," he finally replied after thinking it over, "you could do that, of course. I think, though . . . Agnes, if you sell the house . . . Don't you think it would just about break Dwight's heart? You know what I'd like to do? It would really make me happy to buy the house from you. We'd keep it in your name, or if it would make you more comfortable, we could own it jointly. No one would ever even need to know that, and my crew could patch up anything that needs doing. Eventually maybe I could set up an office—"

"Sam! That's ridiculous. You know I'd never do anything like that. We accept too much of your generosity as it is.... But Dwight? Why would *Dwight* care one way or another? It was never *his* house! Not technically, you know? He and I both received a little money when Will bought my parents' house. It wasn't a huge amount because it was split four ways. My brothers and I inherited equally. And ... well ... for goodness' sake! He and Trudy will have the whole of Lily and Robert's house once the Butlers move to Enfield. Why in the world would Dwight care?"

"Ah, Agnes. You know how Dwight is! He's desperate not to have things—not to have his *idea* of things, at least—just pulled right out from under him. And he's always had this idea of Washburn—in fact, it was his idea of the place that got me interested to come see it after the war. If you sold the house where he grew up ... If you sold the last official Scofield house ... Warren Scofield's house. That's the thing, you know," Sam answered.

"Someone would snap up this property for commercial use," he continued. "Say, a doctor's office. Or a little business office. Insurance maybe. The dentist across the square's retiring. In the Drummonds' old house? Dr. O'Neil?" Agnes nodded, and Sam continued, "The Phillipses are buying the building and thinking they'll lease it to their son-in-law. He'd like to put in a branch of Blanchard's Drugstore closer to downtown. A lot of his customers don't have cars. Mike has a delivery boy, of course. But that doesn't bring in any extra business the way it works when people are waiting for their prescriptions to be filled. And I think Mike would rather run the store downtown, anyway. He doesn't like being stuck out in the shopping center all day long."

"Well, I can't do anything about a drugstore going in. Does that bother Dwight? I thought he wanted to stay in Lily's house."

"Agnes..." Sam was subdued for a moment and seemed perplexed, unsure of what he meant to say. "Dwight *does* want to stay in Lily's house. But he wants Lily and Robert to stay there, too. He wants Scofields to be exactly like it's always been. Honest to God, I don't think he's gotten over Claytor and Lavinia moving so far out of town. I think he believes it was an insult—an insult to *him*—when Betts moved to Will's out on Coshocton Road. It bothers him, even, that Howard doesn't seem to be living in any single place you can pin down."

Agnes couldn't think of any reply at the moment, and Sam finally smiled and leaned back in his chair, tilting on its back legs. "Oh, well. Of course you should consider selling the house. It would make a lot of sense. I'm not saying you ought to keep it. After all, Dwight's a grown man..."

"Well," Agnes said, pushing her chair away from the table and clearing the plates, "I haven't thought it through, anyway. I certainly don't have any other place in mind that I want to move to," she said and let the subject drop.

But she hadn't told the truth entirely. Every morning on her walk to school and then again on her way home in the late afternoon, Agnes had passed by the new apartments going up on Gay Street. She had observed the brick building taking shape floor by floor, and the impractical absurdity of living on a fifth or sixth floor intrigued her. You'd look out your windows right onto the tops of the trees. Coming home with her groceries, perhaps, her heels clicking along the marble entry, she might find herself impatiently tapping her foot in the elevator if it stopped on the second and then the third and even the fourth floor, for instance, while she waited to get off on *Six*.

She would be a person who had a lot on her mind. Once inside the modern, efficient, compact space, she would get busy and finish whatever task was at hand. Letters to write, various plans to be made. She liked the idea of herself as briskly efficient, her possessions pared down to an elegant and practical few. She wouldn't give up using the linen napkins, for instance, but she would distribute each child's several scrapbooks, as well as the pair of lamps consisting of bare-breasted bronze-draped ladies bearing lightbulbs in their raised hands. The endless silver trays and bowls and platters packed away with other mysterious silver oddments, as well as the ponderous furniture built specifically to house them.

It was a pleasant scenario to conjure up on her way to school, but certainly she hadn't developed a passionate yearning to move to one of those apartments in what would be the tallest building in town; she had only considered it as she passed by. In fact, she imagined that one of those apartments would be more expensive than the cost of keeping her house in good repair.

Sam spent most of the day arranging strands of multicolored lights among the dense branches of that spruce tree. He climbed up and down the ladder to check his progress, and now and then he would move a string of lights and rearrange them. Across the hall Agnes sorted boxes of old ornaments into categories on the dining-room table, and the two of them took a break periodically to have a cup of coffee, to relax and light a cigarette.

Late in the afternoon Sam finally cleaned his hands with turpentine to remove the dark sap. "I've got the lights up and the top half of the tree done with ornaments, too. I thought Amelia and Mary Alcorn might want to put up the ornaments on the lower branches. Will could bring his boys... And the little girls could come, too. Julia and Martha would have a great time decorating."

"I want to see what you've done," Agnes said, and Sam followed her into the front room, still drying his hands on a kitchen towel.

"You sit down over there," he said, "and I'll plug in the lights." Agnes smiled. She was reminded of the first time she had met Sam, the weekend he had helped Howard produce a remarkable fireworks show. None of the family but Dwight had met Sam when he first showed up in Washburn, but Agnes had heard a good bit about him from Dwight's letters. Dwight and Sam had become close friends during the war. But even Dwight had not realized, that first weekend Sam was in Washburn, that it was simply his nature to embrace almost any undertaking with enthusiasm. Over time the family came to depend upon it; it was one of Sam's most endearing qualities. In fact, Agnes was still disappointed that he hadn't plunged into her idea of selling her house, that it hadn't caught his interest, that he hadn't begun sorting out the best way to go about it. She had imagined that he would be caught up immediately in the subject and would elaborate on all the possibilities before her.

The tree was very pretty, but privately Agnes thought what

she always thought year after year about Christmas trees: They smell wonderful and are thrilling to see the first time they're balanced in their stand, completely out of context. Suddenly there the tree stands, inside a house, where its beauty and symmetry are remarkable, even though every day, going about town, doing errands, you see evergreens all over the place and don't notice them much one way or another. By the time the tree has become familiar, however, tamed with household baubles, strings of popcorn, paper chains and lights—but never enough of them—and is dripping with foil icicles, it fails every single year to meet the expectations its initial appearance inspires.

"I have to say, Sam! It's the prettiest Christmas tree I've ever seen," she said, which was true, and Sam nodded in agreement, but he had reached into the tree to move two blue lights farther apart from each other.

"You know," Sam said, still fiddling with the lights from the second step of the ladder, "I don't think I ever realized how *blue* a blue spruce really is. It almost makes me feel guilty. They're slow growers. Not as guilty as I'd feel if the damned needles weren't so sharp. They're *stiff.* I should have brought my work gloves." He climbed down and backed up to the doorway to judge whether or not he'd improved the arrangement of lights. He nodded to himself, seemingly satisfied.

"I'm exhausted," Agnes said. "I want a glass of sherry, I think. What can I get you, Sam?" She motioned him toward the only two comfortable chairs in the front room, mismatched, orphaned, lumpish wingbacks she had found in the attic after her mother-in-law died. Agnes had slipcovered them in matching chintz, but so long ago that the one nearest the window had faded and lost its pattern, betraying even the pretense of matching the other. But they were far more seductive than the Victorian tight-backed velvet alternatives, and Agnes hadn't taken account of their bedraggled condition.

"Well, what I'd really enjoy would be a cold glass of beer. You wouldn't happen to have any on hand, would you? Or Coca-Cola?"

By the time Agnes returned with Sam's beer and her glass of sherry on a tray, along with a divided dish holding mixed nuts in one half and pimento-stuffed olives in the other, Sam had settled into the faded cushions of his chair as though his lanky, angular frame had simply collapsed of its own volition into a limp *Z* of relaxation. Agnes and Sam no longer bothered with traditional formalities, and Agnes sat down herself, slipping off her pumps and tucking her legs beneath her.

He took a long swallow from the frosted glass and they sat in silence for a little while just admiring the tree. Eventually Sam spoke up. "Well, by now, Agnes," he said, sounding teasingly chipper, "I suppose you've heard the latest news going around town?"

"I don't think so," she said. "At least, not that I know of. But I haven't been paying much attention, and I really haven't wanted company. I've just been glancing at the paper really."

"Well, I'll do my best to catch you up. First of all there's your granddaughter, of course. The word around town is that poor little Julia barely escaped with her life from whatever she caught. Of course, people are positive it was polio—and it may well have been—but a few people are scandalized that Lavinia and Claytor let the girls swim out at Cardinal Hills— Oh! By the way, I ran into Sheldon Simmons at the bank day before yesterday, with his wife, Susan. They asked after you particularly. They wanted me to give you their greetings. And best wishes," Sam said, veering from his account of the gossip in town, and she nodded appreciatively.

"As a matter of fact," he added, "Julia's illness came up. I guess Julia's a good friend of the Simmonses' youngest daughter. Sally? Susan? They all start with an *S* like their parents' do. Anyway, just as we were going our separate ways, Susan stopped me. She wanted to tell me that she'd often seen Lavinia Scofield sitting in a lounge chair by the pool reading a *book* while the girls swam."

"Oh, Lord, Sam!" Agnes passed her hand over her forehead as if she were brushing her thoughts aside. "Well, what did you say?" Agnes asked.

"Agnes! No one would take that woman seriously! I didn't mean to upset you. You know all of this is just about jealousy. Oh, I just told her that Mary Alcorn and Julia were about as likely to drown as two tadpoles, and that Susan shouldn't worry herself about it. I was tempted to tell her that, in fact, Lavinia doesn't even know how to swim. That it was up to Mary Alcorn to keep an eye on her *mother* if Lavinia went in the water."

Agnes was pensive for a long, quiet moment, and then she sounded tired and defeated. "I don't know what it is that makes people always think the worst of Lavinia. But Sam, I *do* wish Claytor and Lavinia wouldn't let the girls swim when all the other pools are closed. It just seems to me like tempting fate. And Julia *did* come down with something that was probably polio. She was never as sick as people thought. I mean, Claytor says that lots of children have had a mild case of polio that they thought was just the flu. But, still, it makes me worry."

"Ah. I wish you wouldn't." He sounded both disappointed

and apologetic. He had thought he and Agnes were in agreement about the foolishness of what seemed to him just petty gossip. "Worrying about that is just a waste of your time. It's no one's fault that Julia got sick. She probably picked up whatever it was at school. All the children who live out that way use the Cardinal Club pool. *Anyone* can get polio." Agnes nodded absently in agreement.

She was anxious in general about Claytor and Lavinia, but she couldn't think of any way to intercede. She wanted Claytor to drink less; she wished Lavinia seemed happier. She was deeply uneasy on their behalf. Agnes was fairly sure her daughter-in-law wasn't very fond of her, and for that matter, Agnes didn't think Lavinia liked anyone else in the family much either, except Howard. Well, but Lavinia and Betts seemed to get along pretty well. Of course, Agnes was worried about Betts, too, and her unbridled outspokenness. Her quick temper.

Sam changed the subject. "Well, I'm sure you've already heard that you're *not* going to marry Julian Brightman after all? The news is all over town. In fact, I thought I better explain," Sam filled in quickly, "that I'm probably responsible for what people think—"

"Wait! What? Wait a minute, Sam! What are you talking about? Why would anyone have an idea like that?"

"—it really is my fault," Sam was saying. "I just didn't realize anyone would be paying much attention. I was trying to discourage Julian Brightman." Sam apologized. "He wouldn't stay away. You were in tears. You remember? In the hospital?"

"Sam! When I was in the hospital, I was convinced that Julian Brightman was put on this earth to plague me," Agnes said. "I know he means well, but I can scarcely abide him. I don't even have a *reason* I can think of. He's a perfectly decent man. It's just...I don't know, just *something*. But why would anybody get the idea I'd be likely to marry him?"

"No, no!" Sam said. "They've got the idea that you're *not* marrying him. That either he misunderstood, or that you turned him down. He was just about to propose to you, and you weren't in any state...I just tried to imply to him that you were otherwise spoken for. I don't think I was *specific*. Of course, people were passing by in the hall...the nurse was standing in the doorway. But that's the story that's got out, Agnes. Well, according to what I've heard — only secondhand, of course. People are probably afraid they'll hurt my feelings. It's not only Julian Brightman you aren't going to marry. You've gone and canceled *our* wedding, too! I don't know where that part got started. I wanted to apologize, though. It's my fault that you're getting a reputation as a heartbreaker. I've tried to set people straight. But it's so much more interesting to them...I don't think anyone suspected Julian Brightman was that *brave!* To ask you!" Sam broke into a short laugh; he couldn't contain his amusement at the thought of Julian Brightman married to Agnes Scofield, but Agnes was appalled.

"That's not one bit funny. That's mean, Sam. That's not like you to make fun of somebody," she said to him sharply. "But, good *Lord!* How in the world...? Julian *Brightman*...That's just ridiculous! In fact, I'll tell you what. I assumed that he was one of those men...I assumed that he wouldn't be interested in *any* woman. Well, you know, in the same way that Lily's friends in Maine — Marjorie Hockett and Dora? They aren't interested...wouldn't ever be interested in men..." She trailed off in embarrassment.

Agnes had grown up with no idea that two men or two

women could be in love. In fact, she could more easily imagine a sexual than an emotional connection. After Warren's death Agnes had never felt in the slightest bit ashamed of enjoying sex without being in love with the man she was with. Not that there had ever been more than one. But Agnes understood lust pretty well; she had no opinion of anyone else's desires one way or another, but it seemed to her much more difficult to maintain sustained affection over time.

She *had* been surprised when Lily had suggested that she not mention Marjorie and Dora to Robert in any way that might imply that they were more than dear friends of each other. "He wouldn't mean to disapprove, Agnes. But he would never in the world really understand a Boston marriage. He loves their company, so why make anyone uncomfortable?"

Agnes brooded silently for a moment, sitting across from Sam, with the image in her head of Robert staying up much later than usual discussing with Marjorie every subject under the sun whenever she visited Washburn. And Marjorie's famous biscuits. Five minutes before she took them out of the oven, he would pick and shuck fresh corn from his garden. Whenever Marjorie visited, Robert's customary reserve evaporated, and he would preside over the table on the back porch urging everyone to help themselves to Marjorie's biscuits and an ear of steaming corn so fresh that it cooked in under two minutes, and plates of Robert's own tomatoes, densely red and firm, and sliced warm just off the vine. Had Warren ever reacted to some other woman in the same way, Agnes would have been jealous, but it made sense to her that Lily was not.

"What makes you think that?" Sam asked in a tone of voice that had lost the buoyancy of amusement. "About Mr. Brightman?"

"Oh . . . I'm not exactly sure, Sam. Oh, Mr. Brightman's so pompous, somehow. Fussy about the lighting being just right. Of course, that's his job. But arranging people's clothes . . . all his mannerisms. Sort of fussbudgety. Like early robins when they all show up, bobbing around the yard in the spring. I can't really explain it. And, of course, I really don't have any idea . . ." She dwindled to a stop.

Well," Sam said, "I shouldn't have made light of him. You're right. I'm sorry I said that. I really am." Sam looked and sounded tired as the light was fading outside; his posture slackened wearily. "But that sort of man, Agnes . . . that sort of man is awfully vulnerable in our society. That would be a terrible rumor to let get around. He might lose his job—he *would* lose his job. His grant from the OIAA would be taken away . . . God! And with McCarthy raving on, it could be ruinous . . ."

"Oh, Sam! Do you really believe that I would ever say *anything* like that to anyone but you?"

Sam held her gaze for a moment and then lowered his head to his hands, rubbing his temples in an odd attitude of melancholy resignation. "I don't know, Agnes. No. No, of course not. Not on purpose. But people don't realize what they give away. Just when they're bored. Just gossip. Beneath the real news that's passed along by gossip . . . there's generally something mean-spirited going on underneath, whatever rumor you might hear. Well. And look at me this afternoon! Making light of all sorts of people . . . people I don't even particularly dislike. But someone hears a bit of information and, without even thinking about it, they file away some little piece of . . . *evidence*. A split second of speculation. As time goes by, it turns into what they think is a memory. Pretty soon it's an actual fact in their mind," he said.

"For goodness' sake, Sam. That seems a little dramatic to me. Besides, *no one* ever tells me any gossip. I never know what's going on. The same way people won't ever tell me a dirty joke. I mean, I don't particularly want to be told dirty jokes, but the fact that no one would dream of telling me... Well, I must seem unsophisticated...or maybe too prudish. The only gossip I've ever heard about *you,* in fact, wasn't really gossip at all. Just after you settled down here. I've meant to mention it for years, though. Betts told me about your fiancée. What happened to her during the blackout in England. That car wreck. I'm so sorry about that. The same way *Lavinia's* first husband died. It seems so stupid somehow, to die in a car wreck in the middle of a war." As soon as the comment was out of her mouth, though, she regretted having spoken at all.

"Oh, Sam! I'm sorry! That didn't come out right. But I meant...Oh, never mind. After all, Warren died in a car wreck himself. But I've meant to tell you for years how sorry I am that happened."

Sam was startled. "Oh, no! Oh, good God, Agnes!" He put his hand solemnly over his heart and his expression grew earnest.

> "The rolling hills and winding lanes
> Of England fair.
> Sweet flowers of the wayside and
> The watery deep,
> Receives those maidens' langorous forms,
> In endless sleep—

"All that business, Agnes...," he said, dropping the stentorious tone of his reciting and giving a short laugh.

"Oh, no. I'll tell you! If the fiancées of all the men... If all those girls died in the war... there wouldn't be a single woman left! Anywhere in England. In France. Don't give it another thought. There were some people I cared a lot about who died in the war. There were two sisters of a friend who died in a wreck, in fact... well, but not a fiancée. A few good friends, though. I don't remember saying anything about it, but maybe Betts misunderstood."

"I probably shouldn't have brought it up at all," she said. "But it seemed to me that you didn't deserve to have that happen. *No one* does, of course."

Sam had finished his beer and was still sitting as he had been, looking almost boneless, and then he appeared to be coming together again—Agnes had seen him do the same thing hundreds of times, and it always amused her.

"What?" Sam asked. "What are you smiling at? You wouldn't think of offering me another one of these, would you?" he added, holding his empty glass her way.

Agnes laughed out loud and rose to take his glass. "You remind me of those old-fashioned wooden toys—little men and women, horses and dogs—always in my Christmas stocking. Hinged with elastic, you know? So that the dog is sprawled flat on the table, but if you pull his tail the elastic pulls tight, and he stands straight up."

Sam smiled back lazily. "It drove my mother crazy. 'Sam,' she'd say, 'I wish you'd sit up straight. You sit there like all your energy has dribbled out through your ears! You'll make a *terrible* impression.'"

In the kitchen Agnes poured another glass of sherry for herself and a beer in a fresh chilled glass for Sam, and when she returned to the front room, Sam seemed fully assembled once more. She handed Sam his beer and they exchanged a slight smile, just a small acknowledgment of enjoying the other's company, of the fact that they knew each other so well. Neither one felt compelled to make conversation, and they sat quietly admiring the tree, which was the only illumination in the room as the streetlights came on outside. Eventually, though, Sam leaned forward toward Agnes.

"I'll tell you what," he said. "I have a proposal to make."

"What's that? What is it?" Agnes asked.

"No. I mean *that's* what it is," Sam answered. "A proposal!"

"Sam...," Agnes said, waving her hand dismissively, "what are you talking about?"

"Good Lord, Agnes! I'm *proposing!*" He was amused but also suddenly a little more restrained. "I'm proposing that we get married!" Agnes didn't say a word; she sat still in her chair. Sam was abashed and quick to elaborate. "It would solve everything," he said. "You could finally give up teaching without even worrying about it... Oh, we could travel, maybe. You wouldn't ever have to be worried about your house—"

"Sam! I'm old enough to be... well... to be your older sister! Besides, I wouldn't ever marry someone just to solve some other problem!"

"Of course, I know that," Sam said, "but it *would* solve your other problems. And it certainly would make me happy. Don't you think we enjoy each other's company?"

"I do, Sam. We're the very best of friends."

"Well, Agnes, you're much more important in my life than any friend! God knows I've got plenty of friends. And I care about them. Well, in different degrees depending on who it is. I don't know how else to explain myself except to say that I'm always happier—I'm just more content altogether—when you're even in the vicinity than when I'm by myself. I didn't even think about the difference in our ages. I don't see what that has to do with anything," Sam argued reasonably. He wasn't trying to convince her of anything; he was simply stating his case. "At least no one can say we're too young to know what we're doing." He paused for a moment and seemed to be considering the possibility one more time. "I really do think it would make each of us happy," he concluded. "Or happi*er.*"

Agnes was surprised by the muddle of her own thoughts. For a long moment she had nothing to say. No questions to ask, no clear objections to make. "I can't think about this all at once, Sam. I can't even make sense of the idea just now."

"I'm sorry. I sprang that on you pretty suddenly. The fact is, I didn't even know I was going to bring it up. I hadn't even realized . . . Well! Let's talk about this another time. I have to get going. I'm introducing the speaker at the Chamber of Commerce dinner tonight. Let's talk tomorrow. Or as soon as we can get a minute by ourselves." He had gotten up as he was speaking and moved around the room collecting his handsaw and hammer and a tape measure he had brought with him. Agnes got up as well, to see him out, and with his hands full, he only bent and kissed her lightly on the cheek before he hurried down the front steps.

Agnes closed the door behind him but stayed as she was, still holding the doorknob, lost in thought. So many young women in town had had crushes on Sam at one time or another, but the only girl Agnes had ever thought Sam might be interested in was Betts, long ago, when Sam had first arrived in town. And Agnes also thought Betts might have cast an eye his way as well. Might have thought about kissing him, thought about the luxury of stretching out full length against his lean frame. But clearly Agnes had been wrong; she had scarcely ever witnessed a more *married* marriage than Betts and Will Dameron's, and of course, Sam was not only one of their closest friends but also Will's business partner.

She pulled herself together and unplugged the lights on the tree. She washed up the plates and glasses and the ashtrays. She stacked the boxes of unbreakable ornaments she'd put aside for the grandchildren to hang, leaving them on a chair in the dining room, and then she wandered through the house to see what else might need straightening, idly making a list in her head of all the things she still needed to get done before Christmas. She steered clear just now of considering anything Sam had said. The whole idea was unsettling, and she didn't want to make any attempt to sort out what the consequences would be of whatever decision she might finally make.

It was almost five o'clock, which was a time of day she had always found irritatingly useless. Eventually she ended up in her makeshift bedroom, where the bed was covered with layers of soft old weathered quilts, and she couldn't resist lying down for a moment. Just an hour's rest, she thought, and then she'd feel better.

But it wasn't until eight in the evening that she woke up, too late for dinner but too early for no more than her usual cup of tea or glass of milk before bed. And having lost an entire segment of the Saturday of that first weekend of

December threw everything off. She knew it would the moment she'd awakened and realized it was dark outside, that no light came in through the kitchen window. She had a strategic arrangement with sleep, and her carefully established pattern of sleep and waking was out of order for almost a week, during which she was inordinately unsettled and restless.

Chapter Six

FOR YEARS and years Agnes had been suspicious of any long-anticipated celebration; inevitably the event failed to meet expectations, and too often some sort of unforeseen disaster occurred. But in the last month of 1953, she allowed herself to look forward to Christmas. After all, she was no longer solely responsible for the success of the occasion, and as a bystander she was looking forward to all the excitement. She went with Lily to the annual bridge club Christmas party, where gifts were drawn from a pile, and although she came home with one more box of dusting powder, she and Lily won at Duplicate.

Agnes accepted Lily and Robert Butler's invitation to join them at the Garden Club Christmas dinner and dance on December 23, but the three of them didn't intend to stay for the dance. Occasionally Agnes had attended the event with the Butlers. The past few years, though, she had skipped the whole thing with a good deal of relief, but this year she thought she should make an appearance.

Three long tables had been set up along the perimeter of the ballroom at the Eola Arms Hotel, each accommodating thirty-six people. Smaller tables, intended for as many as eight, were arranged diagonally across what would be the dance floor as soon as the tables were cleared after dinner, folded, and whisked away. Robert was at the head of the table dominated by various Scofields and their spouses, along with a group of friends connected to the family through one generation or another, and Dwight was at the foot of that same table, where the younger members of that group had gathered.

Agnes wasn't entirely sorry that Sam was out of town; she had not discussed any of her current situation with anyone in her family; all of her children had very full plates of their own to deal with, and Agnes was in no mood to debate or justify whatever decision she came to. She and Sam had continued to discuss all sorts of possibilities, but Agnes decided not to bring up the issue at all until the whole family gathered at her house for their traditional Christmas Eve dinner. Howard couldn't be in town, and Sam would be at the radio station. But otherwise she imagined that everyone would be in good spirits and in a fairly receptive state of mind. In fact, her attendance at the Garden Club dinner was primarily motivated by her desire not to ruffle any family feathers before they congregated at her house the following evening.

The morning of that same Garden Club Christmas dance, December 23, out in the Cardinal Hills subdivision, Lavinia and Claytor Scofield had gotten up a little before five A.M. Lavinia wasn't entirely sure she had slept at all the night before, because she knew she would barely have time in just one day to finish making and assembling the beribboned tins of pecan puffs that she put together each year at Christmas as gifts for their neighbors. She lay in bed feeling headachy and uneasy, staring at the ceiling, and finally she slipped out of bed and went to the kitchen, still in her Lanz flannel nightgown printed with columns of candles in old-fashioned holders. She went straight to work.

Claytor came into the room to find out what she was doing, and without saying much at all, he sluiced water over his face at the kitchen sink and got to work himself, lining the tins with tissue paper, deliberately fashioning the luxurious satin bows while he was still in his pajamas.

"My God, Claytor," Lavinia said, "this has really gotten out of hand."

He was sitting at the kitchen table making out gift cards while waiting for Lavinia to pull more cookies out of the oven. He and Lavinia also gave cookies within the family in town as well as mailing them to Lavinia's mother and former mother-in-law, almost always too late for the gifts to arrive by Christmas. They sent them as New Year's gifts instead, but the list had gotten so long that it required almost three whole days of baking to fulfill all their obligations, now that they were in the seventh year of their marriage.

Claytor turned to look at her. Lavinia always insisted that the cookies needed one more—a third—roll in powdered sugar after they had cooled and just before they were packed. That time-consuming extra step had become a sore point between them after a year or so. About the time Julia was born, Claytor and Lavinia's marriage had grown familiar enough that the first disagreement over the extra layer of sugar had begun snappishly, but it was over with apologies offered within a half hour. By now, more than five years later, that same argument was a traditional, weary tirade hauled out every year by one or the other of them, and that morning when Mary Alcorn and Julia woke up about an hour after their parents, they got dressed and cleared out of the way during this final day of the family's traditional Christmas cookie making.

In the first go-round, the small domed cookies just out of the oven were so hot that the sugar hardened into a grayish glaze, and each cookie was rolled once more while still warm. But they looked and tasted so much better, Lavinia claimed, if she rolled them in sugar a third time, just before carefully placing them in their small red tins.

"Lavinia," Claytor generally said, "we don't have time! The third layer of sugar will all fall off by the time the tins are opened, anyway! Why do you care? You don't even like half the people we give these to."

And Lavinia generally replied in an angry mutter, saying something along the lines of "As long as I'm making these damned cookies, I'm going to make them the right way! This is something people know that *I* do! No one eating these cookies will think it's *your* fault if they're not good. *You* don't have to do anything but put the packages together!"

"Goddamn it!" Claytor would—and did—explode. "I don't know another husband who would put up with this... I'm skipping rounds at the hospital! I haven't had a decent night's sleep. A decent meal..." And on it went, enlarging far beyond the issue of a third coating of sugar for those cookies all the way to the questionable fondness of each for the other's family, escalating predictably into a great fury ranging over incidents of Lavinia and Claytor's courtship, early marriage,

Lavinia's oblivious spending habits, and Claytor's drinking too much or not. The Christmas before last, as Julia's parents appeared to inflate with a terrifying fury, she hid in the built-in linen closet, and Mary Alcorn trailed after her parents, insisting that they stop it.

"Shut *up,* Mama! Don't say that! Daddy! Stop it! Both of you, just shut up!"

When Claytor and Lavinia finally noticed her, they both turned angrily in her direction. "Don't you speak like that to your mother! None of this is any of your business!" Claytor said to her.

"For God's sake, Mary Alcorn! Can't you mind your own business for once in your life?" her mother said. "Can't you leave us alone for a single minute?"

The year before this Christmas, as the very same argument heated and expanded and inevitably spiraled into a vortex of genuine rage throughout the household, Julia, who had been only five years old, simply started screaming, stopping only to gasp for breath. Lavinia couldn't get her to be quiet and finally bundled the girls into the car and drove away, getting lost somewhere along the winding roads of central Ohio, wandering aimlessly for hours.

This year, though, the gift list had grown so long that Lavinia needed to bake sixty-two dozen cookies. By one o'clock in the afternoon she still had seven dozen to mix and roll and bake, and she was exhausted. "Hand me half of the tins you have left, Claytor! No one else's getting extra sugar this year. I'm *never* doing this again!" Her face and sleeves and most of the front of her flannel gown were powdered white, and a glossy, whitish streak of sugar had hardened in her hair as she had pushed it back behind her ear time and time again.

Her hands were caked with sugar, and she leaned over the sink to turn on the faucet with her elbow.

That the two of them had gotten caught up once again in this increasingly miserable enterprise struck Claytor all at once as...just silly. He laughed out loud in spite of himself. Lavinia turned toward him with a murderous expression, but then she caught her breath, put her hands on her hips, canted backwards a little, and gazed around the kitchen. She, too, began to be taken over by a kind of shocked amusement. Claytor and Lavinia Scofield were thrown into an intimate, absolute sympathy with each other for a moment in the hot, vanilla-scented kitchen.

The air was hazed with powdered sugar, and the efficiently planned counter space was overwhelmed with bowls of every size, empty cellophane bags that had held pecans, and empty boxes of confectioner's sugar that littered the counters and spilled onto the floor, and a leaning sack of flour—simply ripped open, not carefully unfolded—dribbled its contents over the edge of the sink. The meat grinder, which Lavinia used to grind the nuts, was clogged with oily pecan meal and still fastened upright, and over everything lay flecks of ground pecans and a light frosting of powdery white sugar. Measuring cups had been used, misplaced, and replaced with others brought out of the cupboard. Spoons were put down haphazardly and therefore rendered unusable, so another spoon was snatched from a drawer.

In the living room the Christmas tree—carefully glue-coated and glittered during a surge of creative enthusiasm with which Lavinia had infected Claytor as well—lay bristling on the floor, still not dry after three days. In the house, in fact, there was chaos throughout every room—the bathroom sink speckled with toothpaste, toothbrushes scattered, damp towels in a sour heap on the floor, no laundry done, no beds made, no supper except frozen chicken pot pies and carrot sticks for three nights in a row.

There they were, Lavinia and Claytor, the adults in charge of this holiday, which came spinning at them like a hurricane centered around the eye of their domestic tribulations. Here it was: Here was the life they led together, and it wasn't even miserable on a grand scale. They didn't hate each other; they weren't even locked into a hard-shelled dislike of the other, not always, at any rate. They found themselves trapped in a dark but slapstick comedy that was no more than ridiculous. Unspeakably absurd, given the two people they might have become.

For a moment in the fuzzy-sweet air of the small kitchen, memory and circumstance came together at once and simultaneously. Each suddenly recalled that at some point in the past he or she had had nothing but the other one in mind, a shared obsession, having yearned after the other when they were apart for very long. And here they were, together by decree, amused far beyond the situation of the moment, both laughing about something else altogether, something complicated and inexplicable to anyone but the other, and maybe even then impossible to articulate.

They bent forward, grasping their sides to stave off escalating, unreasonable hilarity, which dwindled almost to a halt and then started once again. They gasped for breath, quieting for a moment in a slow, sputtering halt, and then each was struck with a spate of helpless laughter once more, until finally they were spent, taking long, shuddering breaths of air.

Lavinia swiped her arm across her forehead to brush her

bangs aside, leaving behind a sticky streak of even more sugar. "I've got to get a bath," she said. "If I don't, my hair won't be dry by the time we have to leave for the party."

Claytor, too, finally got dressed. He found the girls outside bundled up in their winter clothes and subdued, sitting on the trampoline reading comic books. He got them into their good dresses, their matching navy blue coats, and their nice shoes, and the three of them went on their way to deliver cookies to their neighbors while Lavinia ran water into the bath and searched for the ironing board, because she still had to iron her dress.

It was only a little after three in the afternoon when Claytor and the girls set out, but the day was already edging toward nightfall. By the time they reached the house at the end of Fairway Lane, Mary Alcorn and Julia had exhausted themselves along the way, playing for a while with their friends at each stop, and Claytor himself was worn out with the long afternoon of spreading good cheer. He barely knew the Bankstons, who lived at the end of the lane, except to exchange greetings with Dave and his wife — Eloise? Lois? Louise? — and their two tall teenaged sons, whose names eluded him at the moment.

Julia dragged along, a little whiny, and Mary Alcorn asked if she and Julia could start walking back home. Claytor told them to go on and head back up the lane, and he would catch up with them. "But you two stay together," he said. "Mary Alcorn, don't leave Julia by herself. Okay? It's just not a good idea."

Dave Bankston answered the door in a state of some agitation, or so it seemed to Claytor when Dave grasped the offering of the red tin abruptly and then stepped forward onto his

front porch, forcing Claytor to back down a step and interrupting him in the middle of wishing Dave's family a merry
Christmas. Dave was a man who ought to have given off a
cheerful air. He was about Claytor's height, slightly plump,
with dark, round, shiny eyes and a thin mustache, but the
impression he gave off was one of intemperate self-assurance,
as well as an undercurrent of impatience.

Just before Thanksgiving, Lavinia had been asked by the
local organizers of the March of Dimes to collect contribu-
tions on Fairway Lane. She hadn't wanted to refuse because
the request was one of the few overtures made to her by any
civic group since she had arrived in Washburn. She knew
Claytor would be pleased—or, if not Claytor in particular,
then all the rest of the Scofield family. But she set out armed
with pamphlets and envelopes in a state of dread. If she could
have gotten away with it, she would have donated for all of
her neighbors without their knowledge, but each contributor
had to fill out and sign a donation card. Her neighbors on
Fairway Lane had been chatty and generous, however, and she
was less intimidated by the time she reached the last three
houses.

She had scarcely explained her request, though, before
Dave Bankston held up his palm, signaling her to be quiet.
"No, no. That's something we don't approve of. We never give
to door-to-door solicitors. Or buy Girl Scout Cookies. Citrus
boxes for the marching band. We don't do that sort of thing."
And he had stepped away from the entrance and closed the
door while Lavinia stood there with a pencil poised over the
March of Dimes sign-up roster.

Claytor was still so irritated on Lavinia's behalf that he

hadn't wanted to extend any Christmas cheer in the Bank-stons' direction.

"Don't you see, though," Lavinia said, "that's exactly why we have to. I don't want Dave Bankston to think he got away with being so rude! I don't want him to think I even gave it a second thought."

And Claytor noticed that Dave wasn't at all reluctant to accept a gift from someone going door-to-door. "I've been wanting to talk to you especially, Dr. Scofield," he said. "If you have a minute or two—"

"Well, the girls are walking home. I really should catch up with them—"

"I'll walk along with you, then, for a minute," Dave Bankston said, tucking the tin of Lavinia's fragile pecan puffs under his arm and tightly grasping Claytor's elbow in order to steer him down the steps and along the front walk. Claytor disengaged himself when they reached the paved lane by extracting his arm from Dave's grip and lighting a cigarette, cupping his hand around the flame from his lighter.

Claytor had grown fairly used to having people recite symptoms to him out of the blue and ask for a diagnosis on the spot. Now and then he could point a person in the right direction, but more often he could only offer the suggestion that either he or she make an appointment with a doctor or—more happily—simply wait a week and see if the symptoms persisted.

Doctors complained to one another about this syndrome on the part of total strangers and even close friends, but it didn't bother Claytor at all. He himself had come down with just about every minor symptom of all the diseases he had studied in medical school, and he knew how obsessed people could become, how ashamed of themselves they were, but also how mortally terrified.

He and Dave walked along a little way before Dave spoke up. "Do you always smoke?" Dave asked him, and Claytor turned to try to read Dave's expression, but Dave showed nothing more than curiosity.

"I'm afraid so. It's a bad habit," Claytor said. "Is that what's bothering you? Have you been having coughing spells now and then? Say, first thing when you wake up? When you've just gotten out of bed?"

But Dave ignored the question and delved straight into an explanation of what he wanted to consult Claytor about. "Claytor—if I may?" and Claytor nodded. "You stay caught up on civil defense guidelines, I imagine? In your line of work," Dave began, but he immediately sensed Claytor's impatience. "Well, I know you want to catch up with your daughters, so I won't try to fill you in on every detail. This summer, though, after they tested that bomb—"

"What? Who do you mean? Who tested a bomb?" Claytor said. He was caught entirely off guard. "What are you talking about, Dave?"

"Sorry! Sorry!" Dave said. "I'm getting ahead of myself. The Russians. The bomb test in August. It just seemed to me and Louise that finally it was time to get prepared. You remember that photo in *Life* magazine of the newlyweds who spent their honeymoon in their new bomb shelter? I realize that was just for publicity . . . but it did give me an idea. That's what made me think of building a shelter that could be used for just everyday things, too. Maybe if one of the boys wants his own room. Or Louise might use it as a sewing room.

"Anyway, we're putting in a shelter. It won't be finished

until spring, but the walls are poured and reinforced. We just have the storage to secure and the bunks to get installed. We had the builder enlarge the original plan. It'll be fairly comfortable for as many as six people. It'll be stocked for that many. Three months' worth, at least.

"But just now," Dave went on, "I was wondering if cigarettes might put a strain on the ventilation. . . . Anyway, Louise and I agree that you certainly wouldn't be turned away if you sought cover—"

"Hang on a minute, Dave. I'm not following you. I'm not sure what you're getting at," Claytor interposed, although he felt gloomily certain that he *did* know what Dave was getting at.

"We're putting in a fallout shelter," Dave repeated, with a hint of exasperation at Claytor's puzzlement. "It's not a bad space. Fairly comfortable. We'll stock it with games. Scrabble, maybe. Monopoly. Decks of cards. Poker chips. And books and tools we might need.

"But what I'm saying is that we would certainly welcome you if you wanted to take cover. We've thought about all of it pretty carefully. Louise and I and even the boys."

"You mean if the Russians start dropping bombs on us here in Washburn?" Claytor asked.

"Well . . . anywhere within seventy-five miles. That's right," Dave agreed. "Granted, we're probably only about tenth on their target list. . . . But with the engine manufacturing that goes on in Washburn, they've got us in their crosshairs. You can bet on that."

"Umm-hmm. Well, but Dave," Claytor put forth mildly, "I just don't know exactly what I'd do . . . what about my family?"

Dave put his hands in his pockets and ambled on alongside

Claytor for a few steps. "I expect they'll be evacuated. But civil defense is going to need doctors. I'm afraid we just can't accommodate more than six people." He wasn't sheepish exactly, but low-voiced and cautiously patient. "I'm trying to protect my *own* family... I just can't start making exceptions. And, to tell you the truth, I think even six people is pressing our luck."

"Well, then...," Claytor said, "your offer's certainly generous, but what about the rest of *your* family... uncles and aunts?... cousins? Doesn't any one of them live in town?"

"You're a doctor!" Dave pleaded reasonably. "You could be a real help. And you're close enough that you could probably get here in time. My sister lives in Granville..."

Claytor didn't say anything for a few steps more, and then he paused and turned to Dave, who came to a stop as well. "Dave, I just don't know... I'll have to think about it a little while. I can see you've put a lot of planning into all this. It's thoughtful of you to consider me, though. And I hope you and your family have a good holiday!" He turned away, assuming that Dave would go in the opposite direction. Dave stepped forward with him once again, however, matching Claytor's stride.

Claytor paused once more. "Well, Dave, I'm pretty certain this won't work out. What would I do about my dog, for instance?"

"Your *dog?* Dr. Scofield! Have you thought about this at all? Do you understand what it's going to be like? I'll tell you the truth! It's going to be terrible. I don't think we can even imagine it! It's going to be the worst thing that's ever happened."

Claytor murmured an acknowledgment, feeling sorry that he hadn't taken Dave Bankston more seriously. People could only do the best they could do, Claytor was thinking, as they walked a few steps farther, and then Dave stopped to turn back toward his own house.

"Thanks for the gift," he said on a relieved and lighter note. "I know we'll all enjoy it." He raised the red tin in illustration. "Tell everyone at your house Merry Christmas from the Bankstons!" Dave added, and then he paused for a moment and turned all the way around to face Claytor once more.

"I didn't know you had a dog," Dave said, abruptly shifting gears as well as his tone of voice, which was mildly annoyed and suddenly brusque. "I've been bitten twice by the Morrisons' dachshund. I warned them that they ought not to let their dog out. I don't want to end up making a fuss. Going to court. But I ought to be able to walk down the street! And their dog chases cars. He's going to get himself killed. But I've never seen a dog at your place."

"No," Claytor agreed. "No, we don't have a dog. But I've got my eye on one." And even though a moment earlier he had felt guilty not to have taken Dave's anguish more to heart, Claytor found himself annoyed at being caught red-handedly dogless. "A Great Dane," he embellished. "They're known for having calm temperaments. Gentle giants of dogs...I'll tell you the truth, Dave. I don't think I'd be able to leave an animal like that behind. The thing is that you can't explain it to them. Your dog will trust you more than most people ever would.... Well. It's just about impossible to disappoint that kind of devotion. But you have a merry Christmas, now!" he said. "And a happy New Year."

He saw Mary Alcorn and Julia ahead of him, leaning over the railing of the little bridge that crossed Bell's Creek, which ran diagonally across the golf course. He hoped that if an atomic war broke out, they would never know about it, that they would be the first to perish, while they were contentedly and soundly asleep. Just atomized. Gone. Without a single minute of playing Scrabble in a bunker while clouds of radiation swept across the oceans and continents of the world as the winds shifted, season by season, over the tiny planet.

Lavinia and Claytor arrived at the Garden Club dance later than they had intended, after dinner had been served, although places had been saved for them next to Will and Betts. Agnes didn't realize they had arrived at all until the general murmur of the room quietened like a receding wave. She had been making idle conversation with Julian Brightman's assistant, Franklin Cramer, which was easy to do, since she knew nothing about him and could rely on a great many legitimate questions to ask. But her attention was caught by the cessation of conversation, as was that of their whole table, and she glanced around to see what was happening.

There was Lavinia, in a startling, entirely backless, black satin, halter-neck dress, wending her way among the tables followed by Claytor in his dinner jacket.

Agnes's breath caught for an instant when Lavinia came into full view. She looked remarkably beautiful; she wore no jewelry at all, and the sight of her was as disconcerting as coming upon that freshly cut Christmas tree standing in the living room before it had been decorated, immediately diminishing all the other objects around it to nothing more than ordinary, unnecessary, and common decorations. Lavinia's dark brown hair fell in its usual pageboy, not elaborately pinned up, as the women in town considered appropriate for a dressy occasion. It swung freely against her shoulders, and she was unencumbered by the frilly corsages worn by every other woman in the room except Betts, who had always refused to pin flowers on whatever dress she had chosen to wear. But Betts could get away with it, since she had come up through the ranks, as it were, never pretty or even cute until, in her late teens, all at once she was stunning.

Agnes was overtaken by a sense of dread and even pity on behalf of her daughter-in-law. Lavinia had unwittingly committed a transgression among the young married couples in Washburn, where a wife striving for anything more than prettiness was considered overtly predatory. Even, perhaps, considered somehow subversive in the fragilely rigid postwar traditions that were establishing themselves in the sudden new and relative democracy of American society. It was something Agnes wouldn't have known to warn Lavinia about, even if she had believed a warning would be advisable, because it wasn't until this very minute, as she caught a quick glimpse of the expressions of other women who turned Lavinia's way, that the new boundaries of communal decorum became clear to her.

Only Betts had earned a special dispensation, and it was Betts, in fact, who rose from her seat at the table to wave Lavinia and Claytor her way. She, too, looked extraordinary, and Agnes realized for the first time that evening that Betts was wearing the long-sleeved, high-necked white silk cocktail dress that Agnes had made for her daughter's trousseau. Betts, too, was without further decoration except for a pair of diamond earrings. She had pulled her blond hair back severely, and the comparison of her daughter and her daughter-in-law to Snow White and Rose Red flashed briefly through Agnes's mind. How had those stories ended? Agnes couldn't remember.

But Lavinia, with her slightly absent expression, seemed to

have no idea that she stood out like the slash of an exclamation point among the seasonal scoop-necked plaid taffetas, or the red-velvet-jacketed sheaths with jaunty, tailored bows at the waist. The vague uneasiness swirling through Agnes's thoughts suddenly coalesced around the phrase "like a lamb to the slaughter." Although unfortunately, Agnes thought, Lavinia lacked the sweetly mitigating expression of stupidity that characterizes a sheep of any age. Agnes tensed in anticipation of the rest of the evening stretching out ahead of them.

Rose and Dave Johnson, as well as Susan and Sheldon Simmons, shared the long Scofield table, sitting at the younger end with Dwight and Trudy, Buddy and Jeanie Hunnicutt, and Howard Scofield and his fiancée, Betty Heath. Will and Betts Dameron bridged the gap between the two generations on one side of the table, and Lavinia and Claytor sat down across from them, where Lavinia was sandwiched between her husband and Buddy Hunnicutt, whom she didn't know very well at all.

When a waiter approached, Claytor waved away dinner and ordered drinks for himself and Lavinia, explaining that their babysitter had canceled at the last minute and that they had eaten a bite while they tried to track down someone else. "We finally left the girls at Lily's, Dwight. With your sitter. I promised her I'd more than double her money. She's Celia Chrisman, isn't she? Charlie's oldest daughter?" and Dwight nodded in Claytor's direction, because he wasn't sure he could be heard over the sound of cutlery and conversation that had paused only momentarily.

The conversation Lavinia and Claytor had temporarily interrupted picked up again, and in the background the band began to tune their instruments. Buddy Hunnicutt had been holding forth on the *Washburn Observer*'s morning editorial, which had decried Walter Lippmann's attack on the U.S. attorney general. Jeanie Hunnicutt was leaning away from her husband, discussing some school business with Trudy, who was also a member of the school board.

Somehow Buddy's train of thought had wound around to the execution—just this past June—of the Rosenbergs. "...glad that's all over with. I wasn't sure about Truman, but I knew Eisenhower wouldn't go soft..."

Buddy's wife simply raised her voice a little and determinedly continued to speak over her husband's. "...and we need someone who knows enough to help us hire a librarian...," Jeanie said.

But her husband rambled on. "Truman knew White was a sympathizer, but now they'll know that spies caught in this country will be executed. Lippmann's as red as Stevenson! But now Ike's finally come around. *No* question about it! No exceptions. Don't use a mother with children unless you want those children to be orphans—"

Buddy was talking across Lavinia, addressing Will and Claytor. She had leaned away from the table and was sipping her drink and had just lit a cigarette, but she exhaled an elegant, slender stream of smoke and bent forward, resting her elbows on the table, face-to-face with Buddy Hunnicutt.

"You *can't* believe what you're saying!" She spoke in a subdued voice that was nevertheless filled with outrage and conveyed contempt. "You can't mean that!"

Buddy tipped back in his chair, rocking a little, lifting the front legs off the floor, and smiled at Lavinia, and then inclusively around the table. "Well, there are some things that have to be done. They've *got* to be done." He had been admiring her since she entered the room, but he was startled at her objection. Startled by her matter-of-fact outrage. Her whole manner seemed arrogant to him, with her teasing Southern accent and unabashed air of disrespect. "These things have to be done. And that's what I mean. *You* might have a soft spot for that woman and those little boys —"

"I don't think this is a subject any of us much wants to pursue, Buddy." Dwight spoke up from his place at the end of the table. He was avuncular, slipping on a mantle of responsibility as though he were an elder statesman.

But Lavinia's voice rose. "There's not one single intelligent person in the *world* who could condone what we did to the Rosenbergs!" Lavinia was adamant, now, in Dwight's direction. She wanted his affirmation on the subject.

"Oh, well, Lavinia," Dwight said to her, "it's a complicated business . . . It's not so cut-and-dried. But let's get down to some serious business, let's enjoy ourselves. I'm about dead from Christmas frenzy in our house, and it's mighty nice to see everyone — especially you ladies — all dressed up and glamorous when there's not a child in sight." He smiled at Lavinia and then inclusively around the table in general.

"For God's sake, Dwight," Lavinia snapped, her voice enlarging with frustration. "I can't think of a *simpler* subject in the world than the Rosenbergs! It's about as simple as . . . well, anything you can think of! Stopping the Germans! Kindness to animals! Kindness to *children!* You're just flat *wrong!* The . . . *awfulness* of what we did to the Rosenbergs is as simple as having a pot to pee in." Lavinia's father had used that expression whenever he fell into his Southern version of hail-fellow-well-met, and it had become a handy bit of familial shorthand, not shared, however, by the family Lavinia had married into.

Dwight shook his head, smiling amiably, and held his hands up to signal surrender. "Now, don't get overexcited about all this. I'm not saying I think it was justified, I'm only trying to explain that it's a slippery issue..."

Lavinia realized that the rest of the crowd were trying to pretend she'd never said anything so brashly crude, and Dwight eased them all through the awkwardness by convincingly assuming authority with a dash of ironic charm, as though he was reluctant to be the voice of reason but what else could he do? Someone changed the subject, and they began discussing Christmas and how little they had understood the exhaustion of it until they had children of their own.

Lavinia had nothing to add; in her own house the Christmas tree still lay sprawled across the living-room rug, because she had painted it with Elmer's Glue-All, thoroughly covering every branch, every needle, and then she had sifted handfuls of silver glitter over every inch of it. It looked gorgeous, although the glitter hadn't thoroughly dried, and the tree was still too heavy to remain upright in its three-legged stand. But she was so angry, anyway, that she just sat among the other guests in an emotional simmer.

The girls were asleep by the time Claytor and Lavinia arrived to pick them up, and Trudy insisted they sleep over. "Just bring their clothes when you come tomorrow, since we'll all be at your mother's for Christmas Eve, anyway," Trudy said to Claytor.

That December night of the Garden Club's Christmas dinner and dance, when Claytor and Lavinia were all by themselves in the car on the way home, Claytor suddenly said out of the blue, "Good God, Lavinia! Sometimes I think we don't even live in the same world! You're so naive you don't even know when you're upsetting people. *Insulting* them! You don't even know when you're being insulted yourself!" He was tense and exasperated.

She looked out the window, shocked, in fact, to be so insulted by her own husband. "I know how you feel about the Rosenbergs!" she said. "I didn't hear *you* say anything, Claytor. I know how—"

"I don't even try to talk to Dwight anymore!" Claytor interrupted. "God knows I wouldn't try to persuade Buddy of anything at all... But I don't know why you can't just let things go along. I don't even enjoy *seeing* Trudy and Dwight anymore when I know you're liable to start some sort of argument." And then he leaned forward and switched on the radio.

"Oh, goddamn it, Clay!" Lavinia leaned forward and turned the radio off. "Wait just a minute! You mean to tell me I should let Buddy Hunnicutt go on and on in his horrible... whiny—*unctuous*—voice! Like some insect droning around your head—and just...just not even object? *Why*, for God's sake?"

"Buddy's a horse's ass. He's *always* been a horse's ass—my God! Even in the second grade. But what's the point in arguing with him? What do you care *what* Buddy says?"

"Then why should I have to worry about hurting Buddy's feelings? I *hated* what he was saying. I know how you feel about the Rosenbergs! I know Howard feels the same way, too! Even Dwight. I've heard him say so. All of you just *sat* there. You know what? I hate Buddy! Period! I don't care— in fact, I *hope*—I never see him again. Oh, Lord! What's the matter with the rest of you? You think it would be better just to keep sitting there being polite to Hitler? What about when we're at a party with Buddy the next time and—"

"Polite to Hitler?" Claytor interrupted.

"Oh! You know what I mean! You wouldn't want to be at a swanky dinner party somewhere. Ambassadors and presidents and prime ministers and so forth. And in the middle of the first course, say, you wouldn't *dream* of embarrassing Hitler by mentioning anything as indelicate as the concentration camps. Don't bring up the Jews! Don't say the word *homosexual!* Don't plead for the Catholics or the Gypsies! So you just talk about the weather in the Rhineland. Or the quality of... oh, God, I don't know... the wonderful German beer! Or maybe the bratwurst... Good grief! I grew up in Virginia thinking that Northerners must be so much smarter than the Southern men I knew. I thought you hadn't gotten yourselves all messed up with the stupid, stupid, *stupid* idea of your pride. Or *honor,* and race, too. But there's not much difference at all. I *am* naive! I thought the girls would be smarter than Southern girls, too. And they *did* seem smarter when I was at Wellesley... Until I realized that they just had different ambitions."

Claytor switched the radio on again. He was angry in general and also in particular—at his wife, and also at Dwight. And, too, Claytor was angry at Ethel and Julius Rosenberg, who had allowed themselves to get caught, and who might or might not have been guilty of a conspiracy to commit espionage. Who might or might not have been passing information about the atom bomb to the Soviets. As if it mattered. As if that genie wasn't already long ago out of the bottle.

As soon as the car came to a stop in the driveway, Lavinia jumped out, slamming the passenger-side door behind her, and went straight into the house without a word, but Claytor sat where he was, in a state of mild drunkenness and sorrow. Sadness had crept up on him after he and Lavinia had fallen silent, and by the time he pulled the car into the drive, it overcame him just the way nausea sweeps away any other sensation.

He was certain he had tipped the attendant at the Eola Arms Hotel who had retrieved the car from the parking garage. He was sure he had held the door for Lavinia, had driven around Monument Square and then through town, and up the long incline to Belmont Drive, which was the turnoff to the Cardinal Hills development. He had passed Orchard Road and Singletary Street and rounded the curve to Fairway Lane. By the time the car door shut behind Lavinia, though, he couldn't recall having done so. He couldn't recall even one particular incident of getting from town to his own driveway. He had no idea whether the three traffic lights he had navigated had been red or green, whether or not he had been forced to yield at Monument Square. And, although recounting the drive home didn't serve any particular purpose, he found it unnerving that his thoughts were both heavy and blank.

He sat behind the wheel as though he were still steering the car, looking out the windshield at the enormous gum tree that towered over the garage, dropping its spiked seeds everywhere, looming above the one-story house during every windy lightning storm. It occurred to him that if he turned on the motor, aimed the wheel a little to the left, and floored the accelerator of his big Buick Special, he would smash directly into that tree, probably leaving very little impression at all against its massive trunk.

Being polite to Hitler. He leaned back and relaxed his grip on the wheel. In the long run, Claytor knew there was no one else in the world but Lavinia who could have summed up the evening with as succinct a description. It punctured the balloon of Claytor's self-righteous indignation at her for her indifference to having possibly upset Dwight or Trudy, or anyone else at the long table. Her indifference to the possibility of having humiliated Buddy Hunnicutt.

Claytor's anger dissipated into weary, amorphous fatigue as he sat parked in his own driveway. He had no way to name whatever he was grieving, but his chest constricted and he was short of breath as he fought not to teeter in either direction off the narrow wire on which he balanced between a great, tumbling despair and a defeated acceptance of the way his life was turning out. What in God's name was he doing sitting in the freezing car? What was he doing on a December night almost numb with cold in his own driveway in Washburn, Ohio? He wondered if he could sustain the effort of continuing to live in his own chosen community day by day. If he himself might eventually throw up his hands and give up the effort. If he might one day let Buddy Hunnicutt know that he was and always had been a jackass.

But of course, being polite to Hitler was the way the world worked. It was, he thought, what held society together, how people got through every single day. Everyone he knew — even Lavinia most of the time — held fast to propriety in the face of chaos, desperate etiquette in the face of despair and terror. The difficulty, though, was in realizing those rare occasions when it was, in fact, *Hitler* to whom you were extending such instinctive courtesy, and therefore it was time, at last, to abandon any niceties at all. But the impulse to maintain an unruffled surface in one's own brief life was inescapable. It was all to do, Claytor thought, with the unquenchable human desire simply to be happy.

Chapter Seven

LAVINIA HAD SLAMMED the car door as hard as she could and left Claytor sitting in the dark, her mind still taken up with outrage as she made her way along the nearly invisible stepping-stones and into her own house. The sight of the glimmering, arduously glue-painted, glittered Christmas tree lying on a white sheet diagonally across the living-room floor startled her for a moment. She had intended to get home early enough this evening to pull down the attic stairs and retrieve the girls' Christmas gifts and wrap them. She couldn't remember where she had put the Christmas paper she had ordered from the Metropolitan Museum of Art's gift shop, along with matching satin ribbons, which Claytor knew how to turn into lush, shiny, chrysanthemum-like bows. Around Christmastime he always took their several pairs of scissors into the hospital to have them sharpened, and, generally, he took along Lavinia's cooking knives as well. The scissors had to be razor-sharp in order to cut notches in the thickly wound ovals of ribbon that he then turned into the glistening, many-looped bows.

She took off her coat and gloves, put them and her evening bag down on the couch, and bent to grasp the trunk of the tree to see if she could lift it now that the glue was drier. It wouldn't budge, and her attempt only produced a silver patter of falling glitter. She approached from the narrower top of the tree, lifting it enough to gain a purchase and then walking it upright, leaning into it and righting it hand over hand. And there she was finally, holding the heavily glitter-weighted tree straight up, with her arms submerged in its branches where she grasped it about midway up its trunk. But she was in the house all by herself, and she didn't dare let go.

She held fast to the righted tree, waiting for Claytor to come inside until she heard the engine turn over and realized he had pulled out of the driveway. She stood in the middle of the living room a little longer, but she had no idea where Claytor had gone or when he would be back. Finally she leaned farther into the branches and tightly embraced the tree, turning her face to the side so that glitter and evergreen needles didn't get in her eyes. She swayed from side to side in a peculiar, clumsy dance, slowly walking the tree close enough to the wall that she could prop it upright. It remained standing as she cautiously released it, and she fetched three dining-room chairs and arranged them, ladder-back inward, in a semicircular fence against the lower branches. She hoped the tree would remain upright until she and Claytor could fasten it in its stand and wire it to the ceiling.

She was still angry, but she was also feeling desperate with only one more day to assemble the magical Christmas morning she had envisioned for months. She ignored the kitchen and stood in the hallway, looking up at the pull-down door of the attic, which unfolded into a steep, narrow ladderlike staircase. She thought about the elegant brown genuine-horsehide rocking horse she had ordered for Julia from FAO Schwarz, and the sturdily made wooden child-size soda fountain with real dispensers for water and milk and ice cream. They were stored in the locked back room of the garage, but she couldn't move them by herself.

Her favorite gift for Julia and Mary Alcorn was a beautifully carved and hollowed tree trunk about a foot and a half wide and probably three feet tall. It was hinged on one side and opened to reveal a family of Steiff mice: two graying but jolly grandparents, two cheerful parents, and a little girl and a little boy mouse dressed in tiny-scale plaid-tartan taffeta and red velvet for Christmas morning. A baby mouse sat in a playpen. Each of the mouse children had a Christmas gift of his or her own, the wrapping paper discarded in a tiny crumple at their feet. The girl held a Raggedy Ann doll; the little boy had a spinning top with a pump handle that really worked, and the baby had a tiny teddy bear as well as a Calder-like mobile that turned lazily overhead in the slightest puff of air. Lavinia was charmed by the mobile's implicit tip of the hat to the contemporary. In the corner next to the mouse-house fireplace, the mouse family had decorated a white-tipped Christmas tree with tiny glass ornaments, paper chains, and gingerbread men.

Lavinia had spent hours at a time in the attic, examining the intricate details of that mouse house, the green-gray moss at the base of the trunk, three mushrooms, scarcely visible among the tree roots, a snail climbing upward, a ladybug nearly concealed beneath a leaf. Each time she studied it she discovered another detail that filled her with admiration. The last time she had gazed into the three-story space, she had noticed on the bureau of the parents' bedroom a silver-framed portrait of the bride and groom in full wedding regalia. She had been so pleased at the discovery that it left her feeling grateful, just in general. She thought she might be able to bring the mouse-house tree trunk down from the attic by herself.

And then Lavinia remembered all the books still in boxes in the attic. The E. Nesbit she had ordered from England, Albert Payson Terhune, the Lawrenceville Stories, *Penrod and Sam*. And C. S. Lewis — she had forced herself not to read the ones she'd never seen so that on Christmas morning they would still be pristine and crisp. And other books, too; she couldn't remember them all, but now that she considered them, it occurred to her that each volume still needed to be wrapped.

Lavinia returned to the living room, where the tree stood braced inside the chairs with its heavy, glittered limbs starting to droop, the silver glitter here and there coming loose from the underside of the branches in dime-size clumps, like hail. She had intended to decorate the shining tree with nothing but lights and silver ornaments, but as she studied it she realized that if she didn't get it into water, it might drop its many arms to its sides before morning.

It dawned on her gradually, too, that there was no way to string lights on the tree without dislodging nearly every trace of glitter, and as her vision of Christmas morning evaporated in the glare of practicality, she was plunged into despair at her failure once again to construct any single moment as grand as any one of the various tableaux she had put together over the years in her imagination. She sat down, and then she finally curled up on the unforgiving stiff-cushioned but beautifully simple Danish teak sofa, pulled her wool coat over herself up to her neck, folded her arm under her head for support, and simply went to sleep.

Under the bright overhead light, Lavinia's dark hair and her exposed profile glimmered with specks of metallic glitter; shiny silver dust was caught even in her eyelashes. She was sound asleep when Claytor got home from Giamanco's Bar and Grill out on Route 20. He didn't even notice Lavinia asleep on the sofa, and he went straight to bed, unaware that his wife wasn't next to him on her usual side of the mattress. The righted Christmas tree gradually snowed itself back to mostly green again, its liberated branches springing upward one by one in apparent celebration.

About four o'clock the following afternoon, the extended Scofield family assembled raggedly at Agnes's house for their traditional Christmas Eve dinner, which, within the family, was referred to as Agnes's "catch-as-catch-can." Agnes imposed no order on the supper. The meal was an informally laid-out collection of all of her children's favorite childhood treats, and now her grandchildren's favorites were incorporated as well. It was a childhood dream of a cold supper, and everyone helped him or herself whenever—and to whatever—he or she wanted. After supper, or even with a plate in hand, the company settled in the living room in order to listen to Sam Holloway's ninety-minute Christmas radio broadcast, which began at six-thirty in the evening.

Each year, however, Agnes was surprised to discover once again that the menu was more of a production than putting together a formal dinner. At one time or another during the day of Christmas Eve, Agnes would think to herself that this was hardly how she would define "catch-as-catch-can," an expression her husband, Warren Scofield, had coined to indicate some fun was afoot and that they shouldn't waste time on an organized supper. Originally he had meant that everyone should fend for him or herself, although at the time, the children had been too young to manage it, and Agnes had thrown something simple together.

When her children were young, Agnes had felt a surge of anticipation whenever Warren arrived home in a heightened state of delight and engagement with the family. He had been wonderful at spontaneous enjoyment. "It's catch-as-catch-can tonight, kiddos! And be quick, too, because they've already got that engine on the sled and are hooking up the tractor to haul it down to the river."

Agnes would put together a stack of cheese sandwiches and some apples, say, or a bunch of bananas, and bring them along for the children to eat while they watched the engine eventually move down the river on a barge, headed for installation somewhere else. Or they'd all troop to a street fair that had sprung up in another part of town, where Warren handed out dollar bills to the children as though he were dealing cards so that they could choose from among the hot pretzels, fried dough, corny dogs, cotton candy, and snow cones.

One October he had gotten wind of a haunted-house tour put on by the Carpenters Union for the children of the workmen at Scofields & Company. Betts—who at age three was too young, Agnes had protested—had become hysterical with terror when she caught sight of her father and herself in the long, eerily lighted hallway fitted out entirely with funhouse mirrors. Warren had swung her up to sit on his shoulders, and she and her father were reflected from every surface, recognizable but distorted—short and mashed, tall and thin, genie-like, appearing to have expanded grotesquely as they emerged from a narrow bottle. Betts simply began an odd, horrified, breathless keening. She could not look away from the image of the two of them looming menacingly in her direction.

Warren had finally persuaded John Danville, whose house it was, to let Betts take a tour of the inner workings of the guillotine and the horrified, grimacing rubber head the blade had supposedly severed from its cloaked body. John revealed to Betts the peeled-grape eyeballs of the plastic skeleton Betts had mistakenly embraced in the dark, the steaming cauldron of dry ice in which floated a disembodied hand that turned out to be a water-filled, frozen green-rubber workman's glove. In fact, though, when Agnes thought of that particular experience, she still regretted it, and she had apologized to Betts several times over the years, but Betts claimed she didn't remember it at all.

"Oh, Mama! For goodness' sake. I know you think I was traumatized. But all I really remember was how much fun it always was when Daddy came up with one of his plans. I don't remember much more than being thrilled. You know that fluttery feeling you get as a child. It was almost better than Christmas, because it was a surprise."

Agnes was never mollified by Betts's assurance and, in fact, was downright annoyed by Betts's overly generous memory of that ordeal. Generally Agnes was able to keep secret from herself the unreasonable and tiny bit of envy she had repressed as she witnessed Warren's straightforward, uncomplicated adoration of and delight in the children, whereas her own affection was equally passionate but entwined as well with stubborn strands of "what if's" and "if only's." Warren had been careless of his children that long-ago evening. On his way home that afternoon, he had stopped in at Darcy's Tavern on River Street with some of the workmen, and, in fact, that was where he had first heard of the haunted house. But he had had too many glasses of beer as he bought rounds for the group from Scofields & Company. Of course, the children didn't know that, and Agnes hadn't thought it worth protesting enough to trigger his irritation, so she was equally to blame.

Sometimes, though, when Agnes had watched the children when they were with Warren, she had wished more than anything that she could find a way to abandon her caution, to experience the same joyous, ungoverned enthusiasm that was Warren's genuine response to Dwight and Claytor, Betts and Howard. On her own, though, Agnes had only learned how to pretend spontaneity with the hope of one day falling into it naturally.

By now she realized that she would only ever manage to enjoy *orchestrated* spontaneity, in the manner of her annual Christmas Eve dinner. Nothing had to be done at the last minute, and no rules were imposed on the children as to when they could help themselves to whatever they wanted. No rules for the adults, either. That was pretty much the extent of Agnes's attempt at being carefree, and even that she managed only once a year. That Christmas Eve's casual supper was planned within an inch of its life so that Agnes could relax and enjoy the meal herself.

She had made fruit punch, and the children helped themselves. The liquor tray in the pantry was stocked, the ice bucket filled, and the adults were left to mix drinks for themselves. Everyone made a supper of fried chicken and a variety of favorite cookies and assorted sandwiches cut in the shapes of clubs, hearts, diamonds, and spades with cookie cutters Agnes had received years ago at the bridge club's Christmas exchange. She made German potato salad, as well as ambrosia—one bowl with, and one bowl without marshmallows and coconut. She put out platters of sliced turkey and ham, pumpernickel and rye bread, with assorted condiments, bowls of sugared almonds and other small dishes of roasted and salted pecans, celery festively fringed at the ends, carrot sticks and pimiento-stuffed olives, and rolled Swedish wafers filled with her famous green cheese. By now no one remembered how or when this Christmas Eve supper had become a tradition, but the ritual was generally a godsend for the adults trying to occupy their overly excited children until it was time for them to go to bed on Christmas Eve.

On the Christmas Eve morning of 1953, however, there was mutiny in the air of every household from the moment the youngest of the extended Scofield family awoke. At Betts and Will Dameron's house, the new baby stirred the entire household at a little after five in the morning and continued to cry in inconsolable gusts of anguish all the moments of the day during which he wasn't sleeping. It was the first time since he and Betts had come home from the hospital that Daniel Scofield Dameron had asserted his presence. His older brothers hadn't taken much account of him one way or another until that morning, and then they had been appalled the whole long day of Christmas Eve. By the time Douglas and Davy arrived at their grandmother's, they were cross and clingy around Betts, reluctant to let their mother out of their sight, and Betts and Will had a strained air of jolliness under duress.

As for Trudy and Dwight Claytor's house just across the

way, little Julia Scofield had awakened at the crack of dawn, bewildered and distressed to find she wasn't where she expected to find herself, although she knew enough not to be so rude as to say so. Not one of the four cousins — best friends under normal circumstances — was happy with the unexpected situation their parents had casually abandoned them to. Trudy and Dwight, and Lavinia and Claytor, who had all been children once themselves, of course, had lost track entirely of the fact that any child in the world — at least in those parts of the world where children have the luxury of an opinion about their circumstances — requires a bit of preparation in order to settle into familiarity with adults who aren't their parents, or to be comfortable in any house that's not their home, or even to be graciously welcoming to guests they had not expected.

At breakfast the four girls sat soberly around the kitchen table while Trudy grimly applied various combinations of spreads to slices of toast. She had already discarded two pieces of toast she had made for Julia after Julia, when pressed to eat while the toast was hot, replied that she couldn't eat it because there was no *J* written in honey across its face.

"For goodness' sake, Julia! You'll like it better with the honey spread over the whole piece, anyway. You're too big to be so silly!" Trudy said. But before she had even finished speaking, Martha declared that she wanted toast with an *M* on it.

Mary Alcorn, looking on, didn't want her sister to suffer Aunt Trudy's disapproval — she and Julia adored Trudy, who wasn't so tall or booming as Aunt Betts could be — so Mary Alcorn tried to intervene. She offered to make the toast for Julia and Martha herself, but by then Trudy was even further annoyed and longing to sit down with what she thought of every morning as just one cup of coffee.

"No, no! My Lord, Mary Alcorn! I hardly think we need any more cooks in this kitchen!"Trudy said, meaning to imply gratitude while refusing the offer, but sounding so snappish that Mary Alcorn sat down in surprise and ducked her head because her eyes stung with rising tears at what she perceived as a rebuke. Julia got down from her chair and went around the table to lean against her sister in some idea of solidarity, or perhaps of giving or receiving comfort. But as she slid onto the wedge of chair available to her when Mary Alcorn scooted over, Julia lost her purchase and threw her arms out for balance, and Mary Alcorn's glass of orange juice went flying.

For one instant the kitchen fell entirely silent, until Julia backed away from the table, covering her face with both hands. "I didn't *mean* to!" she said. "I didn't *mean* to!" she wept.

Trudy pulled herself up short and put aside her perfectly natural dismay at the chaos in the kitchen. "Oh, Julia! Well, sweetie, of *course* you didn't mean to! It's just orange juice, sweetheart. We can always go milk more oranges out in the barn! There's plenty more where that came from." She cajoled them into better moods, and finally Julia relaxed and even laughed when Aunt Trudy suggested that after they milked the oranges, they should pick some more bacon from the bacon trees and see if the hens had laid more scrambled eggs. But it was an all-day battle on Trudy's part to keep spirits up and tempers down, her own included.

Finally, as the family began arriving at Agnes's house, and the Dameron boys came together with their older, seemingly superior, female cousins, it was as if some sort of combustion took place. Douglas, who was almost four, and who had spent the day in an effort to separate his mother from the suddenly imperious new baby, went wild with the release of all the energy he would have expended otherwise. And his brother Davy, who was a speedy toddler, did his best to keep up. The little boys went up the front stairs and then scuttled through the hallway and down the back stairs with their cousins Julia and Martha in pursuit. Douglas had brought his cap gun with him, and long strands of smoking, blackened, red cap-paper emerged from the chamber of his pistols as he fired at his cousins through the banisters, which brought even their older cousins swarming after them. When Davy took a tumble down the short back step, tears and bedlam ensued, and finally Agnes stepped in.

"All right, now! That's enough running around, Douglas! Davy, come over here and let me see your knee!" She infused her tone with the schoolteacher expectation of no more non-sense, and as usual she was surprised when everyone did exactly what she said. Davy snuggled into her lap and sucked his thumb while she sat down at the kitchen table.

"Well," she said as she peered earnestly at Davy's knee, "that's pretty serious. Does it hurt?" And Davy nodded but didn't speak. "All right, we're going to need to do something about that. And Amelia? Mary Alcorn? You take Douglas around and help him fill his plate with whatever he wants, and one of you fill a plate for Davy. The boys can eat here at the table while I fix up this knee. Then you girls can take your dinner plates and sit around the Christmas tree if you'd like to."

When the group dispersed a little raggedly to do as she asked, Agnes explained to Davy that she would need him to direct her as she fixed up his knee. "Tell me exactly where it hurts," she said gravely, and Davy nodded mutely once more, dazzled into silence by being taken so seriously. She took an ice cube from her glass of punch and made a wide circle around Davy's kneecap. "What about here?" she asked him, leaning over to see his face. He shook his head, and she gradually lessened the diameter of the circle she rubbed over his leg.

"There!" he said. "It hurts there!"

"Aha," Agnes said, "now we're getting somewhere. Most people don't know this, but if a person concentrates very hard, they can evaporate away most sore knees. There might be a bruise, though."

"Okay." And as Agnes continued to rub cold circles over his knee and instructed him to close his eyes and tell her when he was rid of every last bit of pain, he sat perfectly still for a little over a minute, and then his eyes popped wide open and he grinned.

"Okay!" he said, and he hopped down and climbed onto another chair just as Mary Alcorn put a plate full of all sorts of bite-size portions of his favorite foods in front of him.

"All right, Davy," Agnes said. "I'll go get a plate and come back and have my supper with you and Douglas if you'll save a place for me."

"Okay," he said, and Agnes returned with a piece of chicken and some German potato salad. Douglas and Davy both ate plenty of dinner while Agnes told them all about Sam Holloway's Christmas program that they would listen to in a little while.

"He even gets radio messages from the Air Force so he can

keep us posted about where Santa is anywhere in the world," she explained, and they listened intently, their mouths full.

Shortly after dinner, though, Dwight drew his mother and Claytor to the side — Lavinia had sent her regrets and was at home wrapping presents. She and Claytor had barely managed to wrench the household back into something approaching a state of what they considered to be normal domesticity.

Dwight declared that the children weren't going to make it through Sam's program this year. "We'd better get them home," he said. And Claytor, who had spent the day wrestling with the heavy, still-glittering Christmas tree, agreed right away. Lily took Agnes aside as well. "Robert's not feeling well, Agnes, and to tell you the truth, I'm exhausted. Your supper was just wonderful, but I think we'll listen to Sam's program at home."

"Oh, of course, Lily," Agnes responded while Lily retrieved her and Robert's coats. "I'll see you tomorrow." She turned back toward her son.

"There's so much food, Dwight. Do you just want to give it a try? I've got blankets and pillows to spread out for the children. Around the tree. Sam'll be on in only about...let's see...less than half an hour." Agnes didn't want to see the occasion fall apart, although it was clear that the children were dog-tired. "Do you want to just see if the children are ready to settle down? The thing is, I hope you can stay. I have an announcement I want to make when everyone's a little calmer and I can hear myself think," she said, although only Dwight and Claytor were near enough to hear her.

Agnes's children had speculated among themselves about whether or not their mother would — or should — go back to teaching after her illness, and they had discussed with one another various ways to ease any financial problems she might run into if she retired. Dwight was certain that it was that decision one way or another that she wanted to announce to the family. She probably wanted to discuss the pros and cons. "I'll tell you what, Mother. Why don't you save that announcement until New Year's. Howard'll be here then. And the children *won't,* so we —"

"Well, but Dwight," Agnes interrupted him, "I'm not sure that *I'll* still be here..."

Claytor was stooping to get Julia's foot into one of her overshoes, and he looked up at his mother in alarm and slight exasperation.

"Mother! Of *course* you'll *be* here! What's been going on? Have you had any more dizzy spells? Rapid heartbeat? You know, you have to let Milt Bass —" Julia's foot settled into her rubber boot at last with a sudden squelch, and Claytor stood up, finally able to speak directly to his mother. "Have you talked to Milt —?"

"No! Oh, no. It's nothing like that! I'm fine," she said, although now that Claytor had categorized the possibilities, his mother realized that she'd experienced all of them in the past few weeks at some time or another. "I have something to tell you. It's just... Well, it's a surprise. But I wanted to tell everyone at the same time. I have champagne in the icebox. Apple cider for the children. I wanted to tell the children, too. They'll want to know. At least Mary Alcorn and Amelia will want to know."

"Mama," Claytor said, catching hold of Julia, who was pretending she was too tired to stand up and was making a show of sliding to the floor, "this bunch is in no shape to be interested in anything but Santa Claus right now."

Agnes glanced around the broad entryway, where Will was trying to pry Douglas's hands off the banister, which Douglas seemed to think was a game they were playing, and Betts was holding the baby while extending Davy's jacket toward him and shaking it slightly, as though she were trying to attract a bull, although Davy pretended not to see her.

"You're right, Claytor. Everyone's too tired. You go ahead and get the children settled in the car. That'll give me a minute to pack up some food for all of you to take home. Get everyone into their coats and hats and mittens, and then I'll have snacks packed up to send home with you," Agnes said as she headed in the direction of the dining room.

By the time she had lined up three grocery boxes on the dining room table, one to send home to each household, Julia and Mary Alcorn were already waiting out in Claytor's car with the motor running to warm it up. Betts had wrapped her children in such cocoons of winter clothes that the restraint itself seemed to have calmed them down. The same theory that must explain straitjackets, Agnes thought.

Her three oldest children, as well as Trudy and Will Dameron, were grouped in the hallway also ready to go, wearing their coats and gloves and scarves, and even the sound of their voices was muffled and padded.

Agnes directed the husbands to collect the dinner she had packed up, and when they all milled about at the doorway once again telling one another good-bye, leaning forward to offer a kiss on the cheek, she spoke up to get their attention while she had them all in one place. "You know, there's no need to make some sort of big announcement," she said to them. "It was just an idea. Just silly. Especially on Christmas Eve, when everyone's busy. But I did want all the family to be the first to know. I'll probably go to the midnight service at St. John's tonight, since Bernice is playing the organ. I'll certainly tell *her*. I don't want any of you to hear my news from someone else, and I just wanted to let you know..."

The faintest twinge of impatience crossed both Dwight's and Claytor's faces; they were eager to get their children home and in bed. "Well," she continued, "I thought all of you should know that Sam and I are getting married. Not any big sort of to-do. But the thing is, we might be going away before New Year's, since Sam has to be in Boston..."

Agnes wasn't speaking with any particular urgency; in fact, she had raised her voice only a little to be heard above the various endearments and insistences of leave-taking going on in the front hall.

Claytor and Dwight and Betts looked at her blank-faced in surprise. Trudy had been bustling about, getting Amelia and Martha ready to go, and she hadn't heard what Agnes said, but she snagged Dwight's arm to urge him to hurry. "Honey, they'll start taking off their coats if we don't get going," she said, tugging slightly at his elbow. Will had already gone outside before Agnes had announced anything, luring Douglas and Davy along with him by asking them to carry their presents out to the car. Daniel had fallen asleep on Betts's shoulder.

No one replied for a moment, and then Claytor smiled at her and leaned forward to give her a kiss. "Well! Congratulations!" he said, although he didn't know what to think, and simultaneously Betts exclaimed, "But you can't do that! You're old enough to be... I don't know. But you're too much older..."

Agnes smiled and responded to Claytor while Betts was still protesting. "Well, thank you, Clay. But I don't think you're supposed to congratulate the bride." Dwight, under Trudy's urging, moved his daughters toward the door, but stopped once more and turned back to Agnes. "Oh, well. That's ridiculous, Mother. That doesn't make any sense at all. You and Sam," he said in a pleasantly conversational but authoritative tone of voice. "You wouldn't even be a Scofield anymore." But he was being tugged away by Amelia and Martha, and the hall was suddenly empty before anything else could be said, which, Agnes thought, might be just as well for the time being.

Agnes stood still and watched through the glass as the cars pulled away from the house, one by one, and then she cleared and put away all the food while Sam's voice emanated from the radio. Finally she brought a slice of the Dr. Bird Cake into the living room and had her dessert by the Christmas tree while listening to Sam's broadcast. He always wrapped up the show with the story of "The Little Match Girl," and then "The Happy Prince."

He edited freely so that all the beautifully ominous visions the freezing match girl saw turned out to be her real life after all, and she went home to a wonderful Christmas feast with her grandmother, who had been looking for her everywhere.

And the gloom of the happy prince evaporated as the originally doomed swallow found clever ways to solve all the problems perceived by the bejeweled statue without dismantling the statue itself. Sam turned the strange little tale into a Robin Hood fable, bringing it to a glorious end in which the greedy merchants, the unfeeling scientists, and the literal-minded schoolteachers learned the folly of their ways, and the village made a remarkable fiscal recovery. The swallow lived out the rest of his days—which were many—on the sun-warmed golden shoulder of the genuinely happy prince.

Agnes was always amused when she heard Sam telling old fairy tales to whichever child happened to be in need of calming entertainment of one kind or another. The first time she overheard the tale of Rumpelstiltskin as he reinvented it for Amelia and Mary Alcorn, she and Lily were in the kitchen and had sent the two girls out to the porch to ask Howard or Sam to tell them a story. The tale Sam told floated in through the window:

"Father, I have met a very lonely little man who tells me that if I can guess what his name is, then he will teach me how to spin gold from a cart of straw. But he is very proud of his name, and I have heard him many times singing it out loud as he works. Once I spin straw into gold, the king will be very glad to have me marry his only son, who loves me beyond all earthly treasure. The kingdom can build a farmer's cooperative, and then the king can choose among the finest offerings in the land, and no one in the village will go hungry over the long cold winter."

Later in the afternoon Lily had said to Sam that she had always been thrilled by the evil and greediness of fairy tales. That children relished imagining such horrors.

"Well," Sam said, "I never saw the point of that. After I heard the story of the 'Three Billy Goats Gruff,' it took me about five minutes every day—coming and going—to convince myself to cross the footbridge on the way to school. My God, it made me miserable every damned day until I was almost ten years old. What's the point of that? I already knew to be careful crossing that bridge. There were snakes in Louisiana. I didn't need to be worrying about a *troll!* Mary Alcorn and Amelia have their whole lives to hear the gloomy versions of Hans Christian Andersen and the Brothers Grimm, but it won't be from me."

It occurred to Agnes that it was one of Sam's greatest accomplishments, his talent for—his insistence upon—spinning any dross he came across in his life into pure gold.

Chapter Eight

IN THE SUMMER of 1957, the schools in Tangipahoa Parish in Louisiana, just north of New Orleans, opened as usual in mid-July in order to accommodate the needs of an economy that relied almost exclusively on a successful spring strawberry harvest, at which time the schools obligingly closed for the year. By late August, however, an ominous epidemic of a new strain of Asian flu broke out in the area, and ten of the twelve colored schools closed for several weeks. All but two of the seven white public schools in the parish, and the two parochial schools, remained open, although there were a few days each week when absenteeism reached fifty percent.

The outbreak spread northward, exploding in September, when schools in the rest of the nation began to hold classes. In Mississippi, Georgia, Florida, and Alabama, the situation caused many school boards to close their schools for a period of two or three weeks in a preemptive effort to halt the contagion. In Huntsville, Alabama, however, even though the schools had closed September 30, first-grader Margrit von Braun, the younger daughter of the rocket scientist Wernher von Braun, came down with a high fever on the first Wednesday in October. It would be remarkably good luck, her mother thought, if her older daughter, Iris, didn't catch it as well, and privately Marie von Braun thought that most troublesome of all would be if Wernher himself came down with the flu. For several months he had been growing increasingly restless and depressed, frustrated with the pace of his work under the auspices of the Army Ballistic Missile Agency at the Redstone Arsenal in Huntsville.

Wernher had enthusiastically accepted every recent invitation to travel, which his wife, Marie, had long ago realized was one of the few distractions that allowed him to weather his frequent spates of overwhelming anxiety. Being lionized, giving talks and speeches and explanations, kept him engaged and busy. His hurried departures were an occurrence Marie had come to terms with by now. In fact, she was sometimes relieved to have him out of the house during those sullen spells of pessimism and despair that swept him up and rolled him under like a wave.

The first week in October, however, Major General John Bruce Medaris, the officer in charge of operations at Redstone, had required Wernher von Braun to remain in Huntsville. Through the days of that week Wernher had suffered through hours of glad-handing; he had gone out of his way to exert every ounce of his considerable charm upon visiting dignitaries from Washington. By Friday, October 4, he was rapidly descending into an exhausted spell of humiliation and self-loathing, which wasn't helped by his younger daughter's complaints and whining when she was awakened at nine o'clock in the morning to pose with the rest of the family for a photograph to be published in *Life* magazine.

Wernher had no patience for all those people who couldn't see the larger picture of space exploration that he had envisioned since he was as young as three or four years old—a notion entrenched so early on that it became the elemental structure around which his sensibilities were shaped; his belief in the importance and greater good of the endeavor was, in essence, his religion. His zealotry allowed him to rationalize all that he knew about the horrors he himself, among many others, had ignored in pursuit of the imperative goal of insuring a resource for the tiny planet Earth. Even, perhaps, an escape.

He suffered through long spells, however, when his faith abandoned him. If he was not absorbed in the work itself, or when the notion of progress leached away into a gray futility, he was assailed by the issue always before him of the many masters he had served—was serving now—in order to enable his pursuit of the one single idea of conquering space that propelled his life forward.

The chore of currying favor over and over, abasing himself to whoever was in charge of the purse strings, was an increasingly repellent task, and the grating irritation of his daughter's whining, combined with his larger discontent, ignited a slow-burning disgust that took its place alongside the parched indignation he had kept to himself all week. He threw his arms apart, fingers splayed, in a gesture of dismissiveness. "You stay in bed, then, Margrit," he said, annoyed and fatigued. "When people see the rest of us in that magazine picture, they will not know that you even exist."

She ached all over, but she got out of bed and let her

mother comb her hair and find a pretty robe for her to wear, because her father was the hero of her life and she couldn't stand to have him be disappointed in her. After the photo session, her father carried her back to bed and tucked her in himself, apologizing for his earlier brusque and unkind behavior, although Margrit was embarrassed by the apology and didn't reply. It hadn't occurred to her yet that her parents didn't know exactly what she was thinking, and the misery of spending an entire day under a cloud of her father's disapproval was unbearable. The photographer, Wally Sanders, and Wernher left the house together in order to get photographs of Wernher with the Washington dignitaries Neil McElroy, secretary of defense, and Army secretary Wilbur Brucker.

Wernher didn't trust either man to support his space program; military men, he'd found, lacked the foresight to want anything more than ever more powerful weapons. And to that end, Wernher had bundled his space exploration research into weaponry development, but he would rather have pursued a more direct course. Privately he considered these visitors too stupid to understand their own folly, and Eisenhower too much of a penny-pincher to proceed with a full-fledged effort to conquer space.

Neither Neil McElroy nor Wilbur Brucker suspected Wernher's disdain, however, which he asserted only by continuing to avoid calling either man by his first name, pretending he hadn't understood their offer of that friendly informality when General Medaris first introduced them. But if either man noticed the slight at all, he no doubt put it down to Wernher's German formality.

About two o'clock in the afternoon Wernher escorted the guests back to General Medaris's office and made an excuse of work he needed to do before he collected Marie and met them again for cocktails and dinner at the Officers' Club. He sought the silence and refuge of his office. He wasn't feeling well, and he leaned his head back on his chair and closed his eyes against a blossoming headache. He was startled awake by his phone ringing, and when he saw that the time was nearly four-thirty, he assumed it was his wife, wondering what time they were going to dinner.

"Yes," he said as he picked up the receiver, but he heard the buzzing hiss of a long-distance call, and he waited patiently.

"Dr. von Braun," he finally heard over the staticky delay.

"Yes. Yes, I am here," he said overloudly, which was a habit he couldn't break whenever he was speaking long-distance.

"This is—McDerm—ew York. I'm with the—ish paper—I hoped you would tell me—think."

"We have a very bad connection. Did you say you want to know what I think?"

The line suddenly cleared. "I was hoping you'd give us a statement," his caller said.

Wernher hadn't been able to hear the initial question, but he was used to being asked to comment on various issues by reporters, who sometimes telephoned from other countries and other time zones in the middle of the night.

"Yes. But tell me the question again, please," he asked patiently. "I couldn't hear what you said."

"The satellite! The Russians have launched a satellite. I wondered what you and your people had to say."

Wernher sat a moment with the receiver to his ear and then simply hung up the phone. He made his way to the Officers' Club and sought out Neil McElroy, who was chatting with General Medaris.

"If you go back to Washington tomorrow, Mr. Secretary," he interrupted in a voice that was clearly straining not to burst out of his chest, "and find that all hell has broken loose, remember this!" He was a menacing intrusion on that warm October afternoon with his knotted, flushed expression and his bunched, muscular posture, as if he could hardly contain himself within his own skin. "We *knew* the Russians were going to do it! We have the hardware on the shelf! For God's sake! Turn us loose and let us do something! We can get a satellite up in sixty days!"

His words were running over themselves, dividing and reuniting in German and English in his urgency and frustration, and finally General Medaris interrupted. "No, Wernher. No, no. Maybe in ninety days." But Wernher didn't seem to have heard him and simply left the room through the glass doors open to the outside, just as he had come in.

After the completion of his film, Julian Brightman had long hoped to be able to return to Washburn, Ohio, and the Office of Inter-American Affairs—under the aegis of the State Department—had arranged for a screening of *This Is America* as an appropriate courtesy to the town in which it was filmed. Although the planning had begun the first of the year, the earliest the committee's secretary could coordinate Julian Brightman's schedule with the availability of Memorial Theater in Washburn was the evening of Monday, October 7, 1957. Editing had taken a long time and had been painstaking, and then had come the arduous and time-consuming chore of obtaining satisfactory translations as well as exercising careful diplomacy in order to avoid the appearance of condescension when distributing the film to forty-six foreign countries.

There was almost a full house at Memorial Theater by seven o'clock in the evening a little more than four years after Julian had completed the film of contemporary life in post-war America. Unfortunately, the documentary had never been intended for American consumption, and the only copy Julian had available to him had a Portuguese sound track.

Mr. Brightman positioned himself at one side of the stage in order to provide a running commentary in English that followed the Portuguese translation as closely as possible. The film was about an hour and a half long, and Trudy Claytor's attention was wandering after watching *The Town,* with Mrs. Fletcher Devlin in the leading role, and then *The County Agent,* starring Mike Wolf, who was, in fact, the Marshal County agent. But in the middle of *The Doctor,* she sat up straight and leaned forward when she recognized herself running toward the camera with her hair wrapped on perm rods and a towel around her shoulders while she embraced her daughter Martha, and then glanced straight into the lens with a strained smile.

The warm female voiceover swelled with maternal assurance:

Sua mae esta aliviada. Ela foi interrompida enquanto enrolava o seu cabelo, como muitas mulheres americanas modernas fazem na sua propria casa.

Julian Brightman read the loose translation with a good deal less expressiveness: "'The doctor explains that the little girl has only been stung by a bee. She will be fine. Her mother is relieved. She was interrupted while curling her hair, as many modern American women do in their own homes. The emergency is over. All is well and it is time for the doctor to go to his office, where he will attend to those patients who are well enough to visit him.'"

Julian didn't speak Portuguese, and he had no idea that the Portuguese reader had assumed that this section of the film was to point out the curious fact that American women arranged and cared for their own hair. When she was working on the translation, Silvia Guimaraes had glanced over that section of script twice to see if she could discover what advantage there was to that much modernity.

As it happened, Julian Brightman's film had far more impact when it was shown in Portugal and Brazil than it did where it had been filmed, in Washburn, Ohio, where it failed even to stir much interest or debate or criticism during the coffee hour that followed that evening's screening. Most of the audience had dwindled away after the show, and only a handful lingered in the foyer to congratulate Mr. Brightman, to ask after his welfare and what he was working on now, to find out how the film had been received wherever it had been shown.

By that Monday evening of October 7, 1957—over the space of just one weekend—the film illuminating the lives of postwar Americans going about their business in their prosperous, flourishing country was rendered no more than a naive bit of nostalgia.

In just three days, America's idea of its place in the world had shifted; the country was thrust from the postwar era straight into the space age. And though it was alarming to various military and elected officials—as well as to Dave Bankston and his family on Fairway Lane—that the Soviets had been first to succeed in launching a satellite, it was also thrilling to most Americans that the feat had been accomplished at all.

Nearly everyone in Washburn had spent the weekend

before the Monday showing of Mr. Brightman's film—the evenings of October 5 and 6—in their yards, or they had gone in groups to have a picnic at the fairgrounds or on the rolling treeless acres of a farmer's field, peering up to see the small light of Sputnik cross low in the sky.

On that same Monday morning in Little Rock, Arkansas, Linda Hardin and Elizabeth Sims, coeditors of the Little Rock Central High newspaper, *The Tiger,* were chatting as they walked to school together, until they had to fall into single file in order to pass through the lines of the 101st Airborne Division. The Screaming Eagles had been dispatched by President Eisenhower to insure the safety of the first colored students to attend Little Rock Central High. In the October issue of *The Tiger,* which had been distributed the previous Thursday, October 3, Linda and Elizabeth had editorialized:

If the current friction at Little Rock Central High cannot be amended, then one day we will look back on this year with regret. The integration of our schools is now the rule of law, and we will be sorry that it was not implemented peacefully, without incident, without publicity. We encourage each student, as well as the parents of that student, to maintain a sensible, peaceful neutrality.

We urge our student body and the community of Little Rock Central High School to accept the situation without demonstration or complaint, no matter what personal views are maintained. Perhaps there is still an opportunity to make these, your years at Little Rock Central High School, the brightest ornament in the crown of your personal and academic education.

It would have been difficult to find many people in Little Rock who welcomed the crowd of screaming protesters—many of whom had been bused from a fair distance and were being housed in several local churches—who thronged the main entrance to the school morning after morning, hurling insults at the colored students and working themselves into a frenzied mass. But in 1957 that seemingly mild editorial enraged and scandalized the white citizens of Little Rock who would never have considered taking part in such an ugly mob scene but who, nevertheless, bitterly resented and opposed the integration of their schools. Linda and Elizabeth had both spent the weekend fielding and then avoiding furious, often obscene, telephone calls, and each stayed inside her respective house as a precaution against whatever might be the intention of the boys—boys they didn't know, whose cars they didn't recognize—circling the streets, slowing to a crawl and revving their engines as they passed either girl's house. Elizabeth's father loaded his hunting rifle, although he locked it in the coat closet near the front door.

Elizabeth and Linda had been too preoccupied to watch for Sputnik, and they passed self-consciously through the two rows of paratroopers and then fell into step with Brad Smith as they emerged from that tunnel of large armed men and made their way up the wide and graceful granite stairs to the entrance of the school. The three of them had gone to school together from first grade on, and they were good friends. Brad was also president of the student council and a star athlete on the football team as well as in track and field. When he ran into Linda and Elizabeth that Monday morning, he said with relief, "This'll pretty much be the end of this. With Sputnik launched, no one's going to be paying that much attention to us anymore."

Minnijean Brown, on the other hand, was just as angry as

she had been since she had entered Little Rock Central High in September as one of only nine colored students to integrate the school. Of all of them, it was she who had the most difficulty repressing her outrage when she discovered that she was expected to respond with indifference to the constant harassment of any of the white students.

Not for one moment did it seem to her, or to her family, that the launch of a satellite by the Soviet Union had even the remotest connection to any of them. And in fact, by February she left Little Rock and finished high school in New York. She had been concerned about her safety at the school even with the world's eye fixed on the events at Central High; she certainly didn't want to stay there when no one outside Little Rock was paying any attention.

Not a single white student at Central High School, however, was at all sorry to see the Soviet launch of Sputnik push the news from Little Rock right off the front pages of papers all over the world, as well as out of the headlines of the national six o'clock TV news broadcasts in the evenings.

All over the world people gazed at the distant horizon. The black American musician Richard Penniman, professionally known as Little Richard, who was billed as—and considered himself—"the Architect of Rock and Roll," was touring Australia performing at an outside venue when he saw the satellite move across the skyline. Behind him the band was winding up the traditional closing number, "Tutti Frutti." Little Richard suddenly shot his arms straight up into the sky, lowered his chin to his chest, bent his knees slightly toward each other in a wide-stanced crouch, waited for the beat, and then leapt into the air in what seemed to be an ecstatic frenzy.

"Awoo-oo-ooo,
Woo-oo-ooo."

A falsetto shriek in midair and then, leaning toward the audience when he landed at the edge of the stage, a final baritone challenge:

"A-wop-bom-aloo-mop-a-lop-bam-boom!"

He left the stage while the band was still playing and dropped out of the music business altogether. The Sputnik sighting, along with other recent and ominous events in his personal life, threw him into a state of dread he hadn't felt since he had been a child.

He had been helpless and mystified by being actively despised by his father ever since he could remember. Richard's early, unwitting effeminacy as he became a toddler and then a little boy enraged his father, Bud Penniman, who was a minister, a bootlegger, and a brutal drunk. He kicked Richard out of the house before he was quite twelve years old. From that point on, Richard was pretty much left to shift for himself, and he had always known that there was no one on earth to whom he was the most important person in the world.

By the time he spied the blue-white light of Sputnik crossing the Australian sky, he was twenty-five years old and exhausted. He was grieving, as he had been his entire life, although, since grief was a constant, he was unable to isolate and recognize it. On top of that, he was involved in a nasty royalty dispute with his record company as well as working to win over—night after night—white audiences who were ready to be hostile to a black performer.

During that Australian tour, when the Russian satellite was flung into orbit like a tiny moon, the event catalyzed for him his own singular isolation. God was signifying his damnation of the music Richard made and the debauchery he had indulged in. That small round bluish marble of light moving low across the sky seemed to Richard Penniman to be a harbinger of the impending end of the world. He cut his tour short, flew home to be baptized, and entered a seminary that was located, oddly enough, in Huntsville, Alabama, not far from the Redstone Arsenal.

The ramifications of the successful launch of a Soviet satellite were swift. As early as the Monday morning of October 7, 1957, plans were being made all across the United States to upgrade America's strengths in math and the sciences. By late October in Washburn, Ohio, Mary Alcorn and her cousin Amelia Claytor, both of whom had just started eighth grade at Henry Knox Junior High, discovered that they would be moved from their regular math class to what was being called the "new math" class. It turned out to be unfortunate for Mary Alcorn, who sat right behind David Becker, on whom she had a crush, and who had lent her his copy of *The Catcher in the Rye,* which he swore he would read again at least once every year.

"What do you think it *means* that he lent me his own copy?" she asked Amelia over the phone as soon as she got home from school that day.

Eventually Mary Alcorn was moved back to the regular class. She was uninterested in knowing, and confused by being taught, for example, why a fraction was inverted before it was multiplied, or the history of pi. Nevertheless, she did invite

David Becker to escort her across the football field when she and Amelia Claytor were elected to be the two princesses representing the eighth grade at the Henry Knox Junior High School homecoming football game.

In 1957, across the whole spectrum of American life, a new culture of lean modernization was taking hold. The popularity of shiny blond-maple Early American—style furniture, for example, was gone in a flash, as were the ball-fringed café curtains over the windows above kitchen sinks across the country. And the color turquoise—used sparingly until then only by automakers—was everywhere: bathroom and kitchen tiles, kidney-shaped, molded plastic ashtrays, new carpeting, interior paint, even lamp shades.

Simultaneously, the most popular china pattern of all time in the United States, Franciscan's sweetly pastoral Desert Rose, was given a temporary run for its money by the company's own new china pattern called Starburst, which was characterized by elongated, cream-colored, rimless plates and platters with varisized representations of bronze-, turquoise-, and olive-colored explosions scattered across their surface. Starburst's new inward-curving coffee cups and cereal bowls were decorated with the same surprising asterisks.

Lavinia Scofield was one of the first women in Washburn, Ohio, to replace her chipped and scanty set of everyday china with the clean new pattern, but brides-to-be were registering Starburst as their everyday china preference in bridal registries of department stores all over the country.

The postwar period in America came abruptly to an end, and the citizens, in their everyday lives, were less inclined to rehash those darkly ambivalent war years. They were ready to move on straight ahead into the possibilities of the future. There was a new, progressive adventurousness filtering through the atmosphere, although it was too soon for anyone to realize that the impulse was collective and not just particular. In fact, not until the second decade of the twenty-first century would Sputnik's connection to the demise of Desert Rose dinnerware, as well as Early American–style furniture — and even the disappearance, by and large, of ball fringe — be noted and remarked upon in a novel written late in the career of one of those three-named women writers who initially cropped up in the 1980s.

Agnes and Sam were in Maine when the Soviet satellite launch occurred. For several nights in a row they sat out on the rocks, or when the evening was too chilly, they retreated to Sam's house, with its remarkable view, to watch for Sputnik. Sam set up the radio so they could pick up the beeping signal emitted by the satellite, and although Agnes heard it, she never did see Sputnik, just as she never saw falling stars or found four-leaf clovers. Wherever grass grew Sam could generally find a four-leaf clover in less than two minutes flat. He pointed out the satellite to her three separate times, but the sky was bright with stars, and it eluded her. It was one of the many ways in which one of them complemented the other: Agnes never expected to spot the satellite, and Sam never expected not to.

It was Sam and Agnes's fourth summer and fall in Maine since their marriage. The week following Christmas of 1953 and then through the early days of January 1954, the collective Scofield family had continued to haggle with Agnes — but never with Sam — over the wisdom or even the seemliness of her forthcoming second marriage. Agnes had been anxious to pacify each one of them separately, since no two of them had the same complaint. Even Lily and Robert Butler had expressed concern.

Lily had waited until she and Agnes were on their way to play bridge, and even then she had been uncharacteristically awkward in getting to the point. "Have you thought very carefully about marrying Sam?"

"What? *Lily!*" Lily was driving, and Agnes crossed her arms and stared out the passenger-side window, surprised at the sudden turmoil of anger that swept over her, causing the hairs at the nape of her neck to prickle. "Of *course* not! Why brood about it? I've hardly given it a thought! After all, we can always get a divorce!"

Agnes was really angry, which Lily rarely witnessed, and which startled her. "I'm not trying to be intrusive!" Lily said. "Not trying to irritate you. Naturally you've thought about it. What I mean to say is, have you thought about it being Sam you're marrying . . . Sam in particular?"

"Lily—"

"I'm *not* trying to annoy you! You know how much I like Sam. It's just I think that marrying him . . . Have you ever thought that Sam might be homosexual? Or . . . Well, I don't know . . . *something?* How could anyone as charming as he is not be attached to someone?"

"Honestly, Lily! Do you think I just fly through my life not considering anything at all? I'm really absolutely delighted with everything about the idea of being married to Sam, and I've had about as much of this as I can take! I've had no end of *moralizing* and lectures from my own children! Wouldn't you think they'd wish me well? Why would any of them care a whit? And I'll have this conversation with *you*, Lily, just one time! And that's damned well more than I'll do for anyone else."

Lily was not only taken aback, but she was reminded of the first time she had actually taken Agnes Claytor Scofield into account, just after she and Warren were married. Agnes had been leaning over the rail of the mail boat as it delivered her and Warren to Port Clyde, Maine, on the last leg of their honeymoon. Lily had been standing on the dock, looking up, while Agnes was smiling and making an effort to restrain her hair, which the wind had picked up. Agnes was so pretty, but even more than that, she possessed a powerful sensuality. Lily had been jealous and wary simultaneously. For all of her life until that moment, she had considered both Robert Butler as well as her first cousin, Warren Scofield, men who would always *belong* to her, in the way of first loyalties, of admiration. All of a sudden, though, Lily had understood how ripe with consequence Agnes was within the Scofield orbit. This young girl. Just out of Linus Gilchrest...But then, over the years, Lily had forgotten how essentially formidable Agnes was, and they had fallen into friendship.

"And I don't ever want to talk about it again," Agnes said with crisp, unfriendly insistence. "It's not anyone's business at all. But I know that you sometimes think I'm an unsophisticated nitwit—"

"Oh! I don't think—"

"Lily! Let me finish! I want you to know that Sam's... Sam and I... There's plenty of attraction between us. But the fact is that I don't really care much one way or another, anyway. I do love Sam. You know, Lily, we're so *careful* not to... Well, I can't quite put my finger on it." And she lapsed back into the familiarity she and Lily had established over the past thirty years.

"We're *kind*... really nice to each other. I'd never realized that somehow all that passionate *yearning*... it brings out some kind of grudge between men and women. Almost like you're in some kind of... contest. A sort of *battle!* It's so wonderful. So exciting! All that *lusting* after everything. Even for the phone to ring... So exciting to be lusted *after*... Oh, I'm not explaining what I mean. But it's all about a kind of tension. About balancing on a tightrope," she said, relaxing her defensive posture and leaning back against the seat.

"But Sam and I are kind to each other! We're almost like each other's favorite cousin. You know, that one relative you can instantly pick up with exactly where you left off. Even if *years* have gone by. Of course there's more than that between us, too. I'll tell you the truth, I can't even imagine going through all that sort of grand drama I went through falling in love with Warren. I'm just too *tired* to go through all that again. Just too tired! Too exhausted by the drama of watching my own grown children... But when Sam's around I can put things in perspective. And, you know, Lily? Well, it seems to me that it's my turn."

"Well, I'm really glad for you, then. I know it isn't any of my business. But I just thought..." Lily pulled the conversation into a less intimate seemliness. "That's wonderful. Sam is probably the nicest person I've ever known. Well, of course, Robert, too. I just wasn't certain... But I *am* relieved to know you've thought it all out." And it was a subject they never revisited.

Apart from Lily, not a single person had any concern about or complaint against Sam; it was Agnes whose wisdom they questioned. And, really, Agnes thought, Lily's worry had been grounded more in a not-unreasonable assumption of Agnes's naïveté; Lily and Sam got along like a house afire, and she wouldn't have cared if Sam was a Martian come to earth. Lily's concern had been on Agnes's behalf, and Agnes knew it.

Christmas Eve of 1953, when Agnes had announced to her children—just out of the blue, they would later recall—that she was planning to marry Sam Holloway, they had all been so busy with the holiday upon them that no one had given it much thought beyond the moment. Dwight had reminded his mother that she wouldn't be a Scofield anymore and then hadn't mentioned it again over the holiday. Howard wasn't there, and Claytor had absently leaned forward and given his mother a kiss on the cheek and congratulated her, and Betts had gone off on a tangent about what she considered the huge difference in Sam's and Agnes's ages—although Betts had lost track of how old either her mother or Sam actually was.

Not until New Year's Eve had the subject come up again. Howard Scofield had returned from spending Christmas with his fiancée's family in Cleveland, and he was back in Washburn, staying with Betts and Will. He would rather have stayed in the relative peace and quiet of his mother's house, but she no longer heated any of the bedrooms or had running water above the first floor in the winter, and the temperatures were only in the teens. He came into town to spend New Year's Eve day at Scofields, though, and when he and his mother sat down for lunch, he finally told her that Betts was in a state over the whole idea of Sam and Agnes getting married.

"Betts is still upset?" Agnes asked unworriedly. "I went out to watch the boys open their presents Christmas morning. She didn't say a thing about it then."

"Well, Mama...you know it'll cause an uproar in town. Good Lord! All those women who've been considering Sam. All those single women." He had almost said *younger* women but had caught himself in time. "And, after all, Betts and Sam were quite a couple before she fell for Will. I was still in the service. I didn't know about all that, but it's like she feels you betrayed her. She says no one should be the single daughter among four children. She's even mad at *me!*"

"Oh, for goodness' sake! Betts is... Well, it's true enough that I don't like her these days as much as I love her..." Agnes had fallen into an exasperated musing, but Howard was horrified.

"My God, Mother! What a thing to say—"

"Oh, never mind all that, Howard!" She snapped out of pondering the situation and was unsentimentally brisk. "Betts and Sam were never anything more than good friends. They'll still be good friends. Will and Sam are business partners, after all," Agnes said, but not with any defensiveness; she was matter-of-fact and clearly unworried. Indifferent, Howard thought.

"Mother! How could you know that? That's surely not the way Betts remembers it. She's fit to be tied, and I think she doesn't realize that she's really hurting Will's feelings going on and on about it. And, Lord, with the baby and Doug and Davy...No one's having a good time in the Dameron household, I'll tell you that."

Agnes gazed up at Howard as he leaned over the kitchen table where she was sitting, and she was touched by his worried expression and his anxiety on behalf of all of them. Agnes didn't love any one of her children more than she loved the others, but Howard was the youngest, and probably because of that he was the least self-absorbed; he was by far the most likable.

"Well," she said, "don't worry about Betts being mad at you! I promise you, Howard, I'll never tell Betts you told me any of this."

Agnes had already been through this debate with Betts, anyway, years before. Sam and Betts *had* spent a lot of time together when he first arrived and settled down in Washburn. It was Agnes herself who had assumed it was Sam Holloway that Betts would marry. In fact, Agnes had been horrified initially by Betts's intention to marry Will Dameron. Long before Will and Betts had even noticed each other, Will had been Agnes's occasional lover during the several years her children were away during the war.

Agnes had never said a word about that to her daughter. Betts had lived in Washington, DC, for the duration of the war, and Agnes suspected she was very much in love with some man also posted in Washington. But certainly Agnes didn't think her own brief and casual companionship with Will Dameron during the war had anything to do with *any* of her children. After all, Agnes and Will had each been widowed; they were more or less the same age, the same generation, and they had grown up next door to each other. If there was an issue of age discrepancy to be made, surely it was the one between Agnes's daughter and Will. He was twenty-five years older than Betts.

But, in fact, Agnes hadn't cared one way or another about that. Her concern was based on her opinion that Will was simply not as interesting—not nearly as quick, as bright—as Betts was. Agnes worried that Betts didn't really know how ordinary a man Will was, although he was perfectly nice. Agnes didn't dislike him. But it worried Agnes that Betts might be tying herself to someone who would eventually seem tediously predictable and dull. She had tried to explain that to Betts, but Betts refused to understand what her mother was getting at, and, luckily, Agnes had turned out to be wrong. Will and Betts had the happiest marriage of any of Agnes's children.

More than anyone else in Washburn, however, it was Dwight Claytor, Agnes's youngest brother, who had been raised as her and Warren Scofield's first son, who fell into a broodingly silent state of resentment regarding Agnes's re-marriage on behalf of Warren Scofield. It was absurd! Dwight knew it was unreasonable. Even so, his anger was compounded by delayed and terrible grief. It had been Warren Scofield whose approval and acceptance and affection Dwight had most longed for all his life — and which Warren had provided. But it seemed to Dwight that Warren's existence on the earth would be nullified — would be made irrelevant — by the remarriage of the woman Dwight thought of as his mother, and whom he also thought of as Warren Scofield's wife.

Dwight had been eleven years old when Warren Scofield, driving the icy roads winding over the mountains of Pennsyl-vania, had apparently lost control of the car and slammed into a staunch maple tree, which was the only thing preventing the car from sailing out over the steep valley below. Warren and his uncle Leo Scofield had been thrown a good six feet on either side of the car, against the brittle brown grass, among the fallen, withered leaves and the spiky stalks of reeds, and killed instantly by the impact. But at age eleven Dwight was unable to register the entire significance of Warren's absence. He knew, of course, but didn't absorb the fact that it was permanent.

But the Christmas Eve when he was thirty-five years old and Agnes announced her intention to remarry, Dwight was all at once overwhelmed by the final resonation of the loss he had incurred. He was nearly paralyzed with a sorrow beyond his control, and anger, too. He could scarcely speak amiably to Agnes. In fact, he would begin a conversation and feel the muscles of his jaw freeze shut; his lips would become numb, so that occasionally he literally couldn't speak to her at all. She didn't seem to notice, and Dwight didn't talk about it to anyone—how could he? Trudy was indifferent to Agnes and Sam's marriage one way or another, and she and Dwight were having enough trouble without adding what he knew intellectually was a selfish and ridiculous concern.

One Sunday evening shortly after New Year's, Sam stopped by to have dinner with Agnes and whoever else might be around. She gave over the kitchen to him. They were the only two in the house, and she sat down at the kitchen table with a cup of coffee. "You know, Sam," she said, "I don't want any sort of wedding at all. Let's just go down to the courthouse tomorrow and get married. Then we can invite the family to dinner—everyone. The grandchildren, Bernice Dameron. I know your sister was planning to come up from New Orleans, but we can visit her there. Or she could come another time. Oh, and the DeHavens, too, of course. Let's just get this whole business over with."

"That sounds to me as if you think it'll be about as much fun as taking castor oil," Sam said.

"No, no. It's not about you and me . . . There's nothing that would make any sort of ceremony much fun, Sam. Weddings are overrated. Just tedious and exhausting. And it's not that anyone disapproves of me marrying you. It's just that they don't really approve of me marrying *anyone*. It makes sense, I guess. It's easier for them if nothing changes. They just haven't figured that out yet.

"But I don't want to deal with it anymore. I'm tired of being polite just because they don't realize they're insulting me. I'm tired of worrying about how they feel. Once it's done they'll just stop thinking about it. To tell you the truth, Sam... they just seem to me so... *greedy!* Like those pictures of gaping baby robins in a nest. Well, that's why I guess we have to invite everyone for some sort of a reception afterwards. There's no point in causing any more ill will..."

On January 24, 1954, Sam and Agnes got married unceremoniously at the clerk's office next to the courthouse, with Lily and Robert Butler as witnesses. That evening all of the extended Scofield family and a handful of friends were invited to celebrate the marriage at a wedding supper Agnes had arranged at the Monument Restaurant. The entrée was chicken croquettes, and she had wisely had cupcakes made for dessert instead of any kind of ceremonial wedding cake. By the end of supper most of the parents had departed with frosted cupcakes and tired, cranky children in tow.

Sam was off on a trip to Massachusetts two days later, and Agnes flew into rounding up carpenters, painters, electricians, and various other workmen to address the flaking plaster ceilings, the water-rotted bases of wooden cabinets and porch steps, the electric sockets that sometimes sparked when she plugged in the toaster or a lamp, the leaking slate roof that seemed to be ominously deteriorating over her head. And, on the first day of relatively mild weather, she got in touch with Baynard Grant to have him turn on the water in the pipes upstairs, and that night she moved back into her light-filled bedroom on the third floor. She fell asleep remembering the struggle to coax her young children to let go of their defenses and give themselves over to sleep. They were safe, she had promised them. They were warm. Each one of them was as snug as a bug in a rug.

Chapter Nine

A FEW MONTHS after their marriage, Sam traveled once more to Boston, where he got together with his friend John Bemis, who had developed an efficient, modern post-and-beam house that integrated prefabricated elements sold by Deck House. Agnes had gone with him, and they were spending a week at the Park Plaza Hotel. Sam wanted her opinion of the Deck House models. He thought the houses had enormous appeal and potential, and he was fascinated by the several homes they toured, each one inconspicuous within its setting.

The entryways were determinedly modest, but just beyond the threshold the structures seemed to unfold like a succession of gleaming wood-and-glass boxes, which were interrupted here and there with elements of gray stone: sometimes a floor-to-ceiling fireplace but sometimes no more than a fieldstone planter serving as a partition. Some of the rooms were unnervingly cantilevered above a stepped-back lower story, and their walls of immense glass panes extended directly into the receding surfaces of a rugged rock face, or into the interior of a lightly wooded forest.

"I didn't think these houses would seem so elegant," Sam said to Agnes, who agreed. "I thought the emphasis would be utilitarian. No *gimmicks*. None of those small rooms crammed full of overstuffed furniture. Or those inlaid tea tables that fall over at the drop of a hat. The spaces seem crisp. Cleaner... There seems to be more of it than there actually is." Sam was satisfied that this was the sort of house he wanted to build on the coast of Maine as a retreat for Agnes and himself.

"It does, Sam. But there's not a stick of furniture in any of them. I can't imagine how we could make a house like this comfortable to live in." She agreed with Sam that the clean lines of the houses were elegant, but she equated that with the purity of austerity. Agnes's own house could be said to be full of stuffed furniture—if not *over*stuffed—and certainly her house had its share of fragile, fold-down, inlaid piecrust tables, most of which had been repaired several times over by now. But she was curious to know what it would be like to live inside a house designed to nullify the idea of enclosure, as though the structure were little more than a scrim between the private and public presentations of domestic life.

They traveled from Boston on to Maine, making a late-evening arrival at the Scofield farmhouse in the town of Martinsville. The following morning, on the way to the grocery store in nearby Tenants Harbor to buy coffee, milk, eggs, light-bulbs, and various other staples, they passed a small gray-shingled house where two men were in the process of removing the front door under the not-altogether-friendly eye of a large, dark, shaggy German shepherd and a scruffy gray terrier. The windows had already been extracted intact, it seemed, and were stacked along the winter-browned but grassy slope across the road. A fire truck was parked farther along, and Agnes asked Sam to pull over.

"My Lord, Sam. The fire truck . . . I think they're planning to raze that litte house. I don't want them to burn that place down." It was a modest but handsome small house, typical of those built well over a hundred years earlier, long before the founding of Dragon Cement in the late 1920s. But by the time Agnes and Sam came upon the house that spring, the pre-dominant view across the cove on which the house sat were the six towering, stout white chimneys of that industry, each one emblazoned with a red dragon exhaling a flame bearing the slogan BUILDING YOUR ROADS AND BRIDGES.

Dragon Cement was the largest employer between Rock-land and Camden, the second-largest being the Maine State Prison in Thomaston, and locally it was proudly touted as the only cement plant in the whole of Maine. Dark, substantial columns of smoke rose from all six chimneys straight into the sky, uninflected by any minor, regional breeze, rising steadily until the ashy smoke was caught by the prevailing winds from the west.

By evening, Agnes had bought the house for one dollar, and had paid another one hundred and thirty-five dollars for the front door as well as the two side-entry doors and all eighteen windows. "This would never be the kind of house you'd buy for yourself, Sam, but I've always loved them. They have all sorts of tucked-away rooms. I'm hoping I can have it moved. You know where the woods edge the bottom of the meadow at Lily's farmhouse? That stand of tamaracks near the shore? Maybe I could buy that from Lily. I don't think either the farmhouse or this house could be seen from the other, so it wouldn't spoil anyone's view."

Lily refused to allow Agnes to purchase any property, but she agreed at once to Agnes's plan. "It'll be my wedding present," she said. "For all I know, you may already own that land through Warren's estate. I'm not certain about the title," Lily said, "except I know the farmhouse is in my father's name. My uncle George, and probably Warren's father, too, owned some of that acreage. There's over a hundred acres. I don't know exactly what it entails except I know it includes the ocean frontage from the Martinsville line all the way until you come to the little swimming beach in Port Clyde. No one cared about that frontage then. It's too shallow for any good-size boat to drop anchor, and it's too rocky to swim. I can't see any reason not to go ahead as long as you don't have any problems with local permits, or whatever. We can work out anything else that needs working out when Robert and I come up in July."

Agnes and Sam had phoned Lily from the grocery store in Tenants Harbor, since the phone at the farmhouse hadn't been connected yet for the summer. Sam also made a few local calls to get a start arranging the removal of the house from its current site. He already had connections with builders and all sorts of people in Tenants Harbor, Thomaston, and Martinsville, Maine. Port Clyde, as well. In fact, over the years he had been coming to Maine, he had gotten to know just about everyone on the St. George Peninsula.

The only phone at Curtis's Store was right behind the counter, and Joyce Curtis simply leaned out of the way against the cash register, making no bones about listening to the negotiations. Her eyebrows shot up in an expression of skepticism, and when Sam finally hung up and was reimbursing her for the long-distance calls, she tucked in the corners of her mouth and gently shook her head in the way Sam had noticed that people often do when they know something that you probably would be better off knowing yourself.

"What, Joyce?" Sam asked.

She was sorting the bills and coins into the cash drawer, but she paused to study him a moment before she said anything. She was never certain about the reactions of people from away, but she liked Sam Holloway. "Well," she said, "if you're moving that Woodcock house to somewhere on Scofields' property, you'd better first make sure about your well. It won't be any piece of cake to tie into the well of the main house. And anyway, it used to go dry almost every summer when the Huppers were still farming."

The spring of 1954 in Maine was unseasonably warm, day after day, and mud season was early. No one had even considered the difficulty of moving the house in the uncertain quicksand of the soupy earth. The fire department had planned to burn the house down as a practice exercise in fire containment, since a commercial building was slated to begin going up on the site in the next few days. But Sam had found a fellow who suggested a way to relocate the house using his team of draught horses to navigate the muddy spring soil, pulling the house on a sled behind them.

Four days later, Agnes positioned herself at the head of the newly cleared narrow road that led through the stand of tamaracks so she could signal the driver that this was the spot where the horses should make their final turn to deliver the house to its new site. Mr. Meekin joined her as he shouted directions to the driver, and the two dogs dodged in and out among the horses' hooves, nipping and barking. "What are the dogs *doing?*" she asked Mr. Meekin. "They could get killed!"

"Oh, the horses know them. The big dog, Abel, he's a herding dog. He knows what he's doing. Jimmy Woodcock kept a flock of sheep over in Friendship. He bought a piece of land over there before he was married. He could leave those sheep with Abel and Bella for a day or so at a time. A good bit longer than that if he could get someone to feed them. Jimmy always said that those dogs were cheap at the price and that they never complained. I don't know what happened to Bella. The terrier — that's Shirley — she just does whatever Abel does."

"I thought the Woodcocks had moved out of the area," Agnes said.

"They're down south of Portland. In York. They might as well have moved to Massachusetts."

"But who takes care of their dogs? Who feeds them?" Agnes asked, and Mr. Meekin turned a considering gaze on her while a cloud of nearly transparent gnats filled the air around and between them. The insects were as insubstantial as dust motes in a shaft of sunlight, but they stung, though not so fiercely that you knew it until you were indoors and discovered, for example, that your hands were covered with a red rash of pinprick-size welts. Only then did the bites start itching like crazy, although the itching stopped in about a half an hour. The bugs got caught in Agnes's hair, and every evening she had to painstakingly comb out the tiny gray gnats as she searched her hair for their transparent wings.

"Well, that's up to you, I guess," Mr. Meekin said finally.

Agnes turned to size up Abel and Shirley. She liked dogs,

but she didn't trust them to be careful of the investment of her emotions. Every dog to whom she'd offered shelter eventually chose to leave her household and move elsewhere, and she expected that these two would soon wander off, but she gave them each a sandwich from the basketful she'd made for the crew moving the house.

It turned out as the summer wore on that Abel wasn't a particularly clever or cagey dog in the way that Agnes's previous dog Pup had been. Pup had seemed to read her mind. He had known, for instance, to slip quietly off the velvet sofa as soon as he heard Agnes moving around elsewhere in the house, unable to do anything about the telltale tufts of undercoat he left behind. Abel was clearly affronted, however, at the insult to his dignity time after time when Agnes repeatedly shooed him off the couch that she had carefully slipcovered.

On the other hand, Abel's loyalty was absolute; his world revolved around Agnes and her welfare. Pup had liked Agnes fine, but he moved on to whatever children were in the vicinity, gradually becoming Amelia and Martha Claytor's dog. Absurdly, and in spite of herself, Agnes had felt jilted.

Abel clearly believed that he was solely responsible for protecting Agnes. He became still and watchful when another woman approached, but he was openly hostile when a man arrived, grumbling low in his throat, his hackles raised in a wide ruff across his shoulders. He was indifferent to children as well as to Shirley, who had a terrier's block-headed perseverance in trying to engage Abel in play.

It took the entire summer of 1954 for Abel to recognize that Sam was an accepted member of Agnes's household, but Sam was mostly amused and would sit down on a stump outside the house and let Abel decide to approach him. When Lily and Robert arrived, Abel wouldn't let Robert cross the threshold of the cottage. Outside on his own, though, Abel was indifferent to just about everything. He didn't want to herd, or fetch, or even chase squirrels. When Agnes was elsewhere, Abel appeared to be off duty, sitting statuelike, in the same posture as a crouched marble lion at the entrance of an important civic building, or at the end of a curving drive that presumably led to a house of some consequence. He lay with his elbows together and his legs extended straight in front of him in the grass leading down to the rocks where the tide came in. His head remained up even when he seemed to be asleep, his nose held just slightly aloft to catch whatever scent the sea breeze brought his way.

Agnes was flattered by his devotion even though she knew that it might be no more than a genetic imperative on his part to take care of his flock. But even so, it was only she whom he had chosen to protect, and she couldn't help taking that as a compliment. It was also a responsibility, and it never even crossed her mind that Shirley — as loyal to Abel as Abel was to Agnes — could be subtracted from the equation.

She filled the entire summer of 1954, and late into the fall, with the work and business of rendering the skeletal cottage into livable space. Sam had gone ahead, too, and begun construction of his contemporary Acorn Deck house on a bluff overlooking the steep, rocky drop to the ocean, just over the Martinsville line in Tenants Harbor. Sam had bought land that abutted the property Leo Scofield had purchased from his friend Andrew Hupper after the First World War.

Sam and Agnes wore a trail between their two enterprises, visiting each other for consultations during the day, or to eat lunch together. They slept in the farmhouse at the top of the meadow, since not until the following summer did either of their houses have running water. They had sought out a professional opinion, which turned out to be even more dire than Joyce Curtis had predicted.

As a result of starting with a clean slate, all through the small rooms of what Agnes began to refer to as the Cottage — as opposed to the Farmhouse — there were spaces that became familiar to Agnes apart from any previous association. She had decided to install a window seat in the upper hallway, for instance, really no more than two broad planks she had painted and fitted out with a slipcovered cushion, but she had acted on a whim; she hadn't consulted a soul. The Woodcocks' attic had been full of discarded linens and odds and ends of furniture, and Agnes had cut salvageable panels from the torn, moth-eaten quilts and fashioned them into pillows to use all over the house. She had unearthed a beautiful beige-and-brown gauzy wool blanket that was perfect in a chill.

When she discovered that blanket, carefully folded away in tissue paper on a shelf in a downstairs closet, she had thought about getting in touch with the Woodcocks, ferreting out their address in York, Maine. Clearly they had left that handmade blanket behind by accident. But Agnes had developed an oddly adversarial and defensive attitude toward their very existence. They occupied her house by being absent, and she could only see their cavalier abandonment — not only of their dogs, but of their house as well — as an overall universal betrayal of what she hoped had been their better selves.

She often found herself defending her renovations to what she imagined was the Woodcocks' unfrivolous and critical eye, and she never convinced herself that she had gained their approval. She folded the blanket that she had initially brought into the kitchen with the idea of packaging and mailing it to them, and draped it over the sofa across from the fireplace, where it was exactly the right weight to pull over herself during the evenings. Bit by bit her house turned out to be exactly what she wanted.

Early one morning in late September of 1958, toward the end of the fifth season Sam and Agnes had spent in Maine, she was idling over a third cup of coffee and the *Portland Press Herald* longer than usual. Abel was lying under the table. Agnes had shaken off her slippers and planted her feet in the thick fur of his belly. He loved to have his stomach rubbed, and Agnes didn't realize that he managed to manipulate her into this same ritual every morning. Sam was in Boston, and she planned to spend her day getting the houses in Maine packed up for the winter, hers as well as Sam's, and also tying up any loose ends that needed doing at Lily and Robert's big farmhouse at the top of the meadow.

Robert and Lily had come and gone; Howard and his wife, Betty, had visited for two weeks, along with Trudy and Betts and all the grandchildren in tow, including Mary Alcorn and her sister, Julia. Claytor and Dwight had been unable to get away, and Lavinia had stayed at home as well. During their visit all four of Agnes's granddaughters, along with Trudy, were housed at the cottage, and Betts and her three boys had stayed up at the farmhouse with Howard and Betty and Lily and Robert. By August everyone but Sam and Agnes had departed, and when the various visiting nieces and nephews left, the sense of urgency that prevails in a house full of children had gone with them.

Agnes was lazily enjoying being all on her own, browsing

over an advertisement in the Portland paper for a line of new fall hats, marked down ten percent at the Besse-Clark department store. She had never liked wearing a hat; it was a terrible battle to have with her springy hair. And she always felt sorry for Mamie Eisenhower whenever she was photographed in a hat perched over her jauntily sad, ringlet-like bangs. As Agnes looked over the illustrations of wool pillboxes, a crushed satin pancake hat with a feather quill, and a handsome, brimmed, modified felt fedora, she realized that it was unlikely she would ever buy another hat for herself as long as she lived.

The idea took her by surprise on various levels—the casual acknowledgment of her own mortality, as well as her sudden conviction that only she would ever again be the source of her autonomy. If someone within that small orbit of people she cared about and lived among—even Sam, even one of her children—wished she *would* wear a hat to some occasion or another... Well! If wishes were horses, beggars would ride. Warren had used that phrase all the time, and it popped into her head out of the blue.

Agnes's mind veered to other little slivers of memories of Warren and the children. She remembered his saying ruefully about the boys, whenever they got into a spat of some kind, that they were *just like dogs in the manger.* She had always nodded and agreed, but she realized just now that she had no idea exactly what that meant or where it had originated. Eventually she decided that Warren had employed the familiar phrase about the beggars and horses whenever he was refusing some desire of one of his children... Well! It had the pitch and cadence of hard-earned wisdom—the heft of a conclusion. But the fact that beggars might ride if the world were a fair and generous place; if anyone could get what he wanted merely by *wishing* for it... It was a statement that never appeased anyone at all. It was really no more than a way to say *no*—justifiably or not—without being responsible for the ensuing disappointment.

As her mind drifted from one thing to another, the thought suddenly occurred to Agnes that she had attained a goal she had never sought nor even considered. Not about hats, in particular, of course. And it would be going too far to think of it as sloughing off greed or desire altogether. It was a recognition of the end of vicarious yearning. It was about reclaiming and slaking her own desires after the long years of their being defined by the people to and for whom she felt responsible. She was neither glad nor sorry to discover that a curious detachment had insinuated itself into her expectations of what remained possible during the rest of her life.

But what happened to a woman whose desire all through her childhood as well as the ambition of her adult life was no more than to be thought well of? She had always wanted everyone to like her even if they couldn't or didn't *love* her; she had wanted to be necessary to the people she loved. But at last, as she sipped her sweetened, creamy cup of coffee and looked out the window at the sparkling ocean, she realized she had become indifferent to anyone else's opinion of her. Well, not indifferent, but disengaged in the effort to sway them to view her favorably, because finally she had figured out it was impossible.

People either liked or loved you or they didn't, according to their own needs. Not a single night of the months in Maine had she lain awake agonizing over the possibility that she might accidentally have slighted someone, or that she might have exhibited favoritism to some member of the family as opposed to another. She knew perfectly well that she was capable of—and had indulged in—a certain spitefulness now and then, and generally she had apologized. If she happened to slight someone by accident or through ignorance, or just through a failure to rein in her tendency toward bossiness... Well, she no longer tormented herself about it. Her newly hardened indifference was unexpected; it was a state of being that she hadn't even known existed.

She sat for a while longer, then she took the last swallow of tepid coffee, put out her cigarette, and turned her attention to what still needed to be done to batten down the houses so they would safely withstand the winter. Abel followed right along, heeling on her left side, his nose aligned with her left hand, although Agnes didn't realize his behavior was habitual; she only knew that she could always expect him to be at her side. Just as she knew that Shirley would have gotten herself creakily to her legs and followed along behind them.

Their first year in Maine, Sam and Agnes had left the two dogs behind under the care of Mr. Meekin, but when they returned the following May, they found Shirley her usual self, but Abel was skin and bones, his coat spiky and lusterless, his eyes appearing sunken in his bony skull. Within a few weeks of being reunited with Agnes, however, he filled out again, regaining his health and his self-confidence, and Agnes never again left him in Maine over the winter. She and Sam traveled back and forth to Maine strictly by car in order to transport Abel and Shirley, even though it made for a long and dodgy trip having to find overnight lodging en route that would accept pets. But still, after a cool and leisurely summer, Agnes was always glad to be returning to Washburn, Ohio, even though she knew she had a few weeks of negotiation ahead of her persuading Abel that he must allow the rest of her family to come and go as they pleased.

Now that the upkeep of Agnes's house was not a constant drain on her emotional and financial well-being, she always looked forward to getting home again. Sam would have arranged for a crew to come in while they were away, to patch whatever needed patching. He also alerted Mrs. Ballister, his former housekeeper, to take charge of arranging for fresh sheets to be put on all the beds, the windows to be washed, the house to be thoroughly cleaned, and all the rooms aired out. It was a pleasure to come home from Maine, although increasingly Sam and Agnes's reception by the rest of the family became more and more complicated.

When Agnes Scofield had married Sam Holloway, right after Christmas of 1953, the Scofield family had staggered a bit, shaken by Agnes's abdication, although none of them named it quite that way. It was a moment, however, when there was a permanent shift in the hierarchy of their elaborately connected group. But one way or another, over the years, the whole extended family of Scofields had gotten used to the fact that Agnes and Sam were married, although Agnes was never considered a Holloway; instead, Sam was considered a Scofield. Everyone in the family had enough complications in their lives that they rarely even thought about it anymore. In fact, it hadn't crossed anyone's mind in several years to approve or disapprove of Agnes's marriage.

But not one of her children could forgive her for blithely indulging every bad habit of that dog that had attached himself to Agnes in Maine. They didn't like Abel, and they disapproved of and were annoyed at Agnes for being devoted to him. They were even jealous, perhaps, although that was never a notion any one of them but Lavinia considered likely. Who in the world, after all, would be jealous of his or her mother's *dog?*

On the other hand, not a single adult but Sam—and, oddly enough, Lavinia—could approach Agnes straight on without Abel moving to stand crosswise in front of her and issuing a low, murmuring grumble of discouragement, and Agnes never even scolded him for it.

"Oh, don't pay any attention to him. He's just forgotten who you are," she would say. "He doesn't *bite* people. He never has." She would often make a sweeping gesture with her arm to disperse any criticism of him. And at that, he would lie down alertly at her feet, not relaxing his attention but understanding that she was agreeable to being with whoever had come her way. And Abel never, ever challenged a child, so, really, what could her family say? What logical criticism could they make? If their mother cared more about the company of the dog... Well, there wasn't anything to be done about it.

In spite of themselves, though, her family held Abel's hostility toward *themselves* against Agnes, and Agnes, in turn, held their fear and disdain of her dog against each one of them. In late July of 1958, when Trudy and the girls had arrived at the cottage, Abel had greeted the girls with restrained enthusiasm, just barely wagging his tail and cocking his ears at an amiable angle. But when he spotted Trudy he crossed the threshold and braced himself to bar her entrance. Trudy wasn't used to dogs; she had never been all that fond of Pup when he had adopted her children. But Abel terrified her; she thought the dog might attack her. She climbed up out of his range onto the picnic table in the yard. "Aunt Agnes! Agnes! Please hurry! Can you call him off? Agnes! Please call him off?"

But when Agnes reached the door she was annoyed. "For goodness' sake!" Agnes said. "Do you really think Abel couldn't get to you on that table in two seconds flat if he wanted to? Don't be silly, Trudy. He just doesn't recognize you. Come inside and stop behaving like a four-year-old. Abel won't bother you!"

Trudy was sincerely hurt by Agnes's dismissiveness. Surely her aunt, whom Trudy had admired and counted on all her life, realized that Trudy would have preferred *not* to be so frightened of that hulking German shepherd. But Abel had paid attention to Agnes's voice, and he lay down in a tentative crouch near the doorway in order to let Trudy pass back and forth while he still kept a watchful eye on her.

Two weeks later, when she and the girls were packing up to go home, Trudy was no longer discreet about her opinion of Agnes's dog. Trudy rarely even noticed Shirley, who hardly attracted anyone's attention. She was old and tired and generally did nothing more than stay out of the way, lying in some corner on the floor like a heap of dirty laundry. Over the days in Maine, though, Trudy became downright angry at Abel. "He is the *stupidest* damned dog I've ever known," Agnes overheard her say to Howard. "Every time I leave for more than ten minutes, he won't let me back in the house until your mother's there. And *she* gets cross at *me!* 'For goodness' sake, Trudy! Just tell him who you are! You can't expect him to know *everyone!*' But that dog doesn't give a damn *who* I am! He *knows* who I am! He just doesn't like me, and I think he's dangerous."

Trudy was only half right about that; Abel would never have harmed Trudy. He understood that she was no threat, but he had a very low opinion of her. Of course, his instinct in the matter was no more than an apt interpretation of how Agnes herself was beginning to feel about Trudy.

By the time Sputnik orbited the earth in the late fifties, Fairway Lane, where Lavinia and Claytor Scofield had settled, was no longer considered a new part of the town of Washburn, Ohio. In no time flat the neighborhood had taken on a quality of having always been established, while other developments popped up, organized around new shopping centers, branch banks, and brilliantly lit, sparklingly new pharmacies. It was seldom necessary to make a trip all the way into town, where it was hard to find a parking place in any case.

Lily and Robert had moved to the village of Enfield, where Harcourt Lees College was located, about eight miles distant from Washburn. They moved to a house they had mostly designed themselves, and the streamlined features delighted them, but privately their family and friends thought the look of it could only be described as a Victorian Ranch.

And, too, by the time the sixties arrived, houses were no longer being built with returning GIs in mind. The wealthier families in the community began to leave behind the elegant but old-fashioned houses south of Monument Square that they had inherited or with which they had encumbered themselves during the early years of the twentieth century. Most of those families drifted north to the swanky new area of town named Beau Cage, where not one of the houses resembled another and each was built in a particular style.

On Sunday afternoons young families of more modest means often drove through Beau Cage on an outing, the children in the backseat, to take in the Japanese house with its little footbridge and pagoda, or to see what was often called the Sherlock Holmes house, partly because the Rathbones, who lived there, were cousins of Basil Rathbone, who played the part in the movies, but also because it was a tall, dark, half-timbered affair that might reasonably sit at the edge of Grimpen Mire.

The Hawaiian-themed house had a fish pond that was filled and stocked in the summer and extended from an outside lanai right into the living room, so the fish moved freely back and forth in what was intended to be a living mosaic. But so, also, did the mosquitoes come and go, and once during a cocktail party, a harmless but three-foot-long blacksnake came in as well, quietly winding its way out of the water and through the room amid gasps and startled exclamations, disappearing down the hallway and then the basement steps, and was never seen again.

There were more modest homes in Beau Cage as well, but each one was fitted out with every possible new convenience, and no matter what the price of the property, each kitchen was attractively designed for use by the lady of the house, not for her cook. There were no more privately employed cooks in Washburn, and housewives fended for themselves, for better or for worse.

In time, the large old oil-burning or coal-heated houses were left behind, with their gloomy black linoleum or stone-floored kitchens, their stained soapstone workspaces worn to a slope beside the sink, their clanking radiators and uncertain temperatures rising and falling throughout their meandering rooms. Local businessmen bought them up cheaply and turned them into two- or even three-family dwellings with hastily flung-up staircases spiking down the exterior walls. Regulations had been put in place during the war years, when housing was so hard to find, to ensure that a multifamily household had a separate exit for each unit in case of fire, although almost everyone used the fire escapes as a main entrance just to avoid the bother of running into neighbors by the mailboxes in the communal front entryway.

It would be another thirty years before those run-down but beautifully built houses began to be snapped up by young couples who made an adventure of furnishing the turn-of-the-century houses eclectically, using original, scavenged items in clever opposition to their original purpose. A Brazilian coffee grinder from an old plantation, for instance, as a drinks cabinet, iron egg baskets picked up for a dollar and recycled as trash cans, or an old wooden sled used as a coffee table in front of a small Victorian sofa reupholstered from its original velvet with sturdy navy-and-white-striped mattress ticking, say, and white piping delineating the seams.

Until the late fifties Agnes had managed not to pay much attention to the changes in town that distressed much of her family, especially Dwight, and many of her friends. It was pointless to spend time bemoaning the inevitable modernization that happened over time, although she, too, occasionally couldn't help but feel a pang of regret.

In the early sixties little sentiment was expended over doing away with the elaborate, old-fashioned brick architecture that lined the main streets of most small towns in Ohio. Very few people in Washburn, for instance, thought much one way or another about the razing of Rudin's department store, with its ridiculous pneumatic tubes to make change, the slowest elevator in the world, and no escalator at all. Most towns in Ohio backed up against a river, and, as in Washburn, the downtown couldn't expand, so one building had to come down in order to put up another. In place of Rudin's, a modern new women's clothing store went up that made architectural use of black, slightly undulating, aluminum panels for the first and second stories, and silver-gray panels for the third. One morning Agnes was doing errands across the street from the new Goldrings Building and realized that it reminded her of one of the boxlike two-toned cars that were so popular these days.

Only Dwight Claytor and his family were year-round residents of any one of the three houses in the Scofield compound, which was generally referred to by townspeople these days as the Claytor Place, and occasionally—by a few local wits like Buddy Hunnicutt—as Peyton Place. Sam and Agnes were at the Scofields compound over the winter, of course, but now and then Agnes seriously considered suggesting to Sam that they sell the house and move permanently to Martinsville, Maine. There was plenty of family to stay with whenever they wanted to visit Washburn, Ohio.

Chapter Ten

I T WAS DWIGHT Claytor who had first introduced Michael DiSalle to Sam, when DiSalle was mayor of Toledo. Dwight was intricately involved in Democratic politics in the state, even weighing the possibility of a future political career for himself. By the time DiSalle had finally managed to win the governorship, he was calling in every favor he was owed and pulling every string he could grasp in an effort to pass the Ohio Civil Rights Act. Dwight and Sam and Will Dameron became increasingly involved in the effort as well. All three of them carried some weight in the central part of the state, but the issue wasn't going to enhance their authority, and privately all three thought that if they were successful, it would cost DiSalle any chance of reelection.

But when Sam and Agnes returned from Maine to celebrate Thanksgiving and Christmas of 1958 with the rest of the family, they stayed on in Washburn for the longest stretch of their marriage so far. They settled into Agnes's comfortable old house in the center of the Scofield compound and remained established there until May of 1960.

"There's no better way for a person to become a racist than to grow up in the middle of a society that generally has no idea of the bigotry they all live with. Later on you can't believe you were part of it. You perpetuated it. You finally just can't believe the things you've absorbed growing up. Just imagine! In nineteen forty-four, I was in a B-seventeen flying over Czechoslovakia," Sam said. "The flak guns suddenly opened up, and we were hit...oh, at least eighty times. We made it home because those P-fifty-ones just showed up out of nowhere. They covered us like glue. It turned out they were the Red Tails. The Tuskegee Airmen. And I couldn't get over it—I'll never get over it, I guess. The base where we were stationed was segregated!

"So there we were! In a godforsaken muddy swamp of a place and I looked around. Every one of us was sure that the next flight would be the one when we'd get blown to bits. But God forbid you eat in the same mess hall as any of those black pilots!"

The Ohio Civil Rights Bill passed in 1959, and Agnes and Sam stayed on until the spring after the 1960 elections. They each made short separate trips to Martinsville, Maine, when something needed to be taken care of, but once more, during those many months, the notion of *home* conjured up in Agnes's mind the idea of her house in Washburn.

In fact, Sam was in Cleveland for a three-day political-strategy meeting, and Agnes had just returned from a hurried trip to Maine to discuss with her contractor some construction she planned—a screened porch and a garage—the first

time Lavinia and her daughters arrived at Agnes's house unexpectedly, and well after midnight. It was a weeknight and late
enough that there was virtually no other traffic in town. Abel
sprang to his feet at his self-imposed post on the first landing
of the staircase, where he could keep an eye on everything,
and he broke into a frenzied, high-pitched barking as soon as
he heard tires on the gravel of the front drive.

Agnes hadn't heard anything and was unpleasantly jolted
out of a deep sleep. "Hush, Abel!" Agnes called to him. She had
awakened so abruptly that she prickled with a surge of alarm,
and it annoyed her. "It's nothing! It's raccoons! Abel! Quiet!"

But Abel's bark dropped into a serious, deeper register of
warning, and Agnes heard a car door slam underneath her window at the front of the house. She didn't remember if she had
locked the door, and Abel would appear to be dangerous to anyone who came in just by habit, although Agnes had told them
over and over that he wouldn't hurt a flea. "For heaven's sake!"
she had repeated over and over, "can't you see he's all *bark?*"

But even if it was only Howard who had driven in from
Columbus late, or been visiting Betts and Will and then
decided to stay overnight—no matter who it was—Agnes
didn't want Abel to frighten anyone. She had decided that this
long spell in Washburn would be the perfect opportunity to
make peace between her dog and her family. She slipped her
robe on over her nightgown, and the scruffy little terrier,
Shirley, looked up from where she was lying on the cool
hearth of the bedroom fireplace and gave one brief bark to
illustrate her usefulness and then tucked her head and went
back to sleep. She was a very old dog now, and almost completely deaf.

Agnes grasped Abel's collar as she descended the staircase

with him at her side, preparing to grab his collar in a firm grip at the doorway, but he stopped barking and swept his tail back and forth before they were all the way downstairs. He moved away from the door and sat of his own accord, watching while Agnes opened it to discover Lavinia, who was fully dressed in a linen skirt, a tailored white cotton blouse, and a string of pearls. She was grasping her handbag so tightly that her knuckles were white. Julia stood behind her, a little to the side, as though she and her mother might be visiting Agnes separately but had arrived at the same time.

If Agnes had been more alert, she would have realized as soon as Abel relaxed that it was either Sam or Lavinia at the door. The first year Sam and Agnes had returned to Washburn with the dogs in tow, Lavinia hadn't given Abel's presence much thought; she had simply stooped to receive him when he bolted her way, barking and grumbling. Lavinia had extended her hand toward him, palm down, and then had risen again, not even seeming to notice Abel, although she was idly scratching the top of his head. Lavinia's unflinching lack of interest in him— her obvious ease around Abel—had cemented his affection for her forever after.

When Agnes unlatched the screen door Abel nudged forward to greet Lavinia and then Julia, who was ashen-faced and scarcely moved when Abel jostled her, expecting his usual affectionate hug.

Julia remained standing behind her mother, and she didn't greet Abel at all. Agnes and Lavinia stood facing each other for quite a few moments without speaking, as Agnes tried to take in her daughter-in-law's presence on her doorstep. "Lavinia," she said finally, unable to come up with any context that explained her presence.

"I didn't know where else to go," Lavinia said, and Agnes pushed the screen door open wider to invite them inside. Julia was carrying her small train case, and she stepped inside without glancing at her grandmother.

"What's happened?" Agnes asked. "Is everything all right? Are *you* all right?"

Lavinia moved a few feet farther into the entryway and scratched Abel's ears absently. "We just got away too late," she answered. "I thought we'd drive down to Charlottesville. Visit my family for a while. Mary Alcorn and I will switch off driving... *I* won't be driving the whole way. One of us can read the map while the other one drives. But by the time we got packed... We were on our way, but it got so late. And Mary Alcorn said she'd rather go to Natchez and visit *her* family, anyway. She and my mother... Well, even *me* and my mother..."

Of course Agnes realized that even Lavinia wouldn't set out for a long car trip in the middle of the night, and Agnes stood watching her daughter-in-law with growing dread as Lavinia went on about seeing the Alcorns again in Natchez. They were her first husband's parents, she said, and Mary Alcorn's grandparents, and, as Lavinia began to convince herself of the likelihood of the trip she had invented on the spot, her words flew faster. "She only met them at Phillip's funeral. But she was just three months old. And then when she was five she saw them again. She doesn't remember them at all. I don't remember why we haven't stayed in touch. We did for a while—"

"But where *is* Mary Alcorn?" Agnes interrupted.

Lavinia stopped speaking midsentence and simply closed her mouth in an expression of bewilderment, and Julia reluctantly spoke up.

"Mary Alcorn's taking the first turn driving. She's waiting for us in the car."

Her grandmother studied her a moment and then shuddered involuntarily, more of a shiver, a much smaller rendition of the way a dog shakes off water. "It's too late to go any farther tonight, Julia," Agnes said. "Run out and get her...No, never mind. I'll go get her and help her carry in whatever you need. You and your mother go on upstairs, or if you want something to eat...There's ham in the icebox. Help yourselves to anything you want. Lemonade or iced tea. Make yourselves comfortable in the second-floor bedroom. The beds are all made and there're towels...Well, you two go on up. I'll put Mary Alcorn in the little bedroom at the other end of the hall."

Agnes slipped out the door and closed it behind her before Abel could lurch through and storm the car. She paused for a moment on the porch until she could see clearly without the light from the house, and then she circled behind the idling car and approached the driver's window. Mary Alcorn had crossed her arms over the steering wheel and leaned her head against the brace of her forearms, but when Agnes knocked at the closed window, her granddaughter turned to look at her and rolled it down. She didn't say anything, and her eyes were swollen in the aftermath of tears.

"It's too late to travel any farther tonight, sweetie," Agnes said to her matter-of-factly. "Pull the car around back and I'll help you bring in anything you think you'll need for the night." Mary Alcorn nodded and put the car into gear. It was nearly fifteen minutes, though, before she appeared at the kitchen door, carrying her own small train case. Agnes had put together a quick tray of peanut butter sandwiches and a plate of apples cut into wedges.

"Are you all right?" Agnes asked Mary Alcorn. "Is there anything I can do? I was just going to take this tray up and leave it on the bureau in the hall. I didn't know if any of you had eaten." Agnes was explaining all of this slowly in order to give Mary Alcorn a chance to say something if she wanted to, but Mary Alcorn had put her suitcase down and was pulling her long hair up into a ponytail, doubling a rubber band around it to hold it off her face. Her expression was uncertain, but then she regained her composure.

"Thank you," she said. "Thank you so much for letting us stay over. We'll be able to get an early start in the morning. And Mama wanted to stop by T.G. and Y. and get a portable ironing board, anyway."

"That sounds like a good idea, then," Agnes assured her, signifying that she would not ask for information that Mary Alcorn or Julia or Lavinia didn't volunteer on her own. She followed Mary Alcorn to the second floor and deposited the tray on the bureau and then went up the second flight of stairs to her own room, and Abel followed right behind her.

That early April morning not one person slept soundly, nor even any creature except the old terrier, Shirley. Abel lay down at his post on the landing with a grave sigh and remained alert to the uneasiness within the household.

Julia Scofield was caught in a state of precocious sorrow. By age twelve she had already experienced spates of sobbing grief over breaking up with a boyfriend, over losing the election for vice president of the seventh-grade student council, over the death of her cat, Frieda, whom Julia had loved her whole life. Even as she had been heartbroken over her cat and various other disappointments, however, she had known she was safe enough in her social standing, cherished enough within her own orbit, that the degree of misery she allowed herself was not dangerous. She knew she would feel better in a day, in a week, or even a year. She had even known that her genuine grief over Frieda's death was, in fact, permanent, but she would love other cats, too, over her lifetime.

But lying in bed in her grandmother's house, she was filled with pity for her mother, her father, herself, and even Mary Alcorn, and she was aware of the possibility of a free fall. She had always believed there was a safety net to catch her family if they all toppled off the high wire they navigated during all the hours they were awake. Julia no longer believed it would hold all four of them. Now that details of her family's personal collective life were escaping the protective cloak within which she believed she kept them concealed, would it really be true that she would never see her father again under any comfortable circumstances? That for the rest of her life she would exchange information with him only in awkward moments during family events where her mother was not? Or when he and she went horseback riding together out at Aunt Betts's? Julia didn't know how she would be able to manage being bereft of ordinary pleasure. She tried to imagine feeling carefree ever again, but since it would depend on her ignorance, it would be impossible. It would require more than simply forgetting. How could she *un*-know the situation of her own life?

She didn't give way to the unregulated sobbing of childhood, because her mother was in the other bed, and Julia was unwilling to have anyone know that she was terrified and grieving. Each time she resigned herself to the future that loomed ahead of her, she almost fell asleep, but then she wasn't able to restrain herself from climbing aboard the same train of thought all over again, trying to reach some other destination.

The result of stifling her full-throated grief was that tears trickled onto her pillow off and on all night. She wished she could forget what everyone else needed her to do and simply behave like Mary Alcorn did. She, too, would like to leap out of bed and smash her pillow against the floor, cursing her mother and father as loudly as she cared to; she would like to bang her hand against the wall while detailing her fury.

But having witnessed Mary Alcorn slowly losing any authority she might have had, having seen the injured expressions on her parents' faces when Mary Alcorn hurled her furious accusations at them, weeping, and gasping for breath so she could say even more, Julia had become determined not to draw attention or even to give voice to her own rage and sorrow. The price she paid for the iron-willed restraint of her despair, however, was never to be rid of it.

Lavinia lay between the crisp, cool sheets that were always on the beds in Agnes's house with dozens of thoughts trapped inside her head, spinning through her mind, paralyzing her with their whirling fervency. Bits of music—a verse by the Adams Sisters over and over—

> You'll find me dancing,
> Though I'll be blue,
> My heart will greet you,
> 'Cause I've been true—

Beneath all of those flying bits of irrelevant detritus she tried to form a narrative. She *had* made a start at redoing all the rooms of their house—well, even better than that. She and Julia had managed to scrape away every last bit of wallpaper during the past week while Claytor had taken two weeks at a cabin at the lake on doctor's orders to get some rest, to get his blood pressure under control. Or so Claytor had said.

Lavinia had become increasingly preoccupied with the idea that Claytor must be involved with another woman, and her frantic redecorating was interrupted now and then by an ominous, brooding bass note reverberating beneath the high-pitched orchestral horns blasting through her exhausted mind. At those moments she would have a glimpse of the abyss beneath her gathering rage. For a moment—only a few seconds—she felt that chasm's gravitational pull, but then she went skidding off once more into a wild flurry of ideas and conclusions and myriad other thoughts.

She had no idea that Milton Bass had taken Claytor aside and firmly made the suggestion that Claytor pull himself together, that he get a handle posthaste on his drinking, because word was getting around. And he also declared that Claytor needed to get all the rest of his life sorted out as well. The debts he owed, and so forth.

Claytor had presented his getting away for two weeks to Lavinia as his own idea, claiming fatigue. He knew he was too vulnerable to tell Lavinia the truth, to reveal his inability to halt his fearful downhill slide. Lavinia didn't drink much at all, and therefore she didn't believe that Claytor couldn't control *his* drinking. Claytor knew, though, that if Lavinia belittled what seemed to him a desperate, last-ditch effort to pull himself together, if he had to endure discouragement of any kind from anyone at all . . . Well, he already wavered on the precipice of believing that it was too late, that it was beyond him to regain some small bit of rational control of his own life, that he was inevitably bound to forfeit any happy possibilities left to him. It wouldn't take much to thoroughly convince him.

Milt had also offered the use of his own cabin, and it hadn't even occurred to Claytor that, since this was spring break at the public schools, it would seem downright strange not to take his wife and children to the lake, too. Lavinia *was* fairly astonished at his selfishness, at his not even thinking of taking his daughters, although, as it happened, there was almost nothing Lavinia would have less liked to do than spend a few days at a rustic cabin on an unlovely body of water.

And Claytor had explained again that he had been ordered to do nothing but rest. He could take a leisurely swim twice a day at the public beach if the water was warm enough, but no longer than twenty minutes or so, and not at all if no lifeguard was on duty. Every word he said to Lavinia was true; Milt had been worried about Claytor's health, but it was Milt's insistence on connecting Claytor's health to his personal life that Claytor could scarcely bear, and that he didn't mention to her. And besides, he said to Lavinia, there was nothing to do but go fishing or swimming, and the girls would be bored.

By the time Claytor was packed, Lavinia had been truly indifferent to his going, but the moment he drove out of the driveway, a bit of outrage took root in her imagination. Within a day or two she had nurtured it into despair, and inevitably it grew into anger as well.

And now that she was safely at Agnes's after Claytor had returned, and on her way to Charlottesville—or maybe Natchez—the next day, her thoughts were as ungovernable as a heavy rain. It occurred to her that not only did she need to buy an ironing board—which her mother refused to own on the grounds that no well-bred Southern woman did her own ironing—she also needed to get money out of the bank for the trip. She could do that first thing in the morning if Claytor hadn't frozen their account before she cashed a check. She couldn't come up with anything she liked about Claytor right now except that he loved their two cats much more than she did, and that he would never be unkind to the three dachshunds she had no choice but to leave behind.

During the first week Claytor was away, Lavinia had been listless and distracted, sleeping almost day and night, shut away in her bedroom. Now and then she made a foray into the rest of the house in an attempt to take care of her daughters, preparing fish sticks or a box of Kraft Macaroni & Cheese for dinner, or cooking liver or kidneys for the dogs and the two cats. Mostly, though, Julia and Mary Alcorn fended for themselves, fed the animals canned food to avoid the horrible smell of simmering kidneys or liver, and slowly began to believe in and enjoy the sudden peacefulness of their household.

No one else in the family knew that Claytor had gone to Milt Bass's cabin; the story was that he was in Chicago at a convention, but it was all fairly vague, and no one had thought about it much one way or another. Agnes and Trudy and Lily assumed that Lavinia would telephone or come into town if there was anything she needed, and Howard and Betty dropped by twice, but both times they arrived, Mary Alcorn answered the door and explained that her mother had a terrible cold. Betts was so busy with her three boys that she didn't even know Claytor was away. But the two girls relaxed. Years later Mary Alcorn and Julia would each separately remember that first week in April as a remarkable idyll in an otherwise exhausting stretch of time.

Mary Alcorn lazed in bed for two whole days reading *Advise and Consent* without her mother knowing and probably disapproving. Lavinia was no fan of much popular fiction, and there was no one whose disapproval could crush Mary Alcorn as much as her mother's could. When Lavinia criticized Mary Alcorn's carefully teased hairstyle, or a dress she had chosen that her mother said was cheap-looking—"Good Lord. You look like a prostitute! And that lipstick!"—afterwards, and in spite of herself, Mary Alcorn was self-conscious and unhappy wherever she went. And furious, too. She was privately convinced that her mother really did have an exquisite—if eccentric—sense of style.

Julia, on the other hand, spent most of the days outside with friends in the neighborhood, coming home in the afternoon in time to watch television with Mary Alcorn. They both sank wholeheartedly into *Leave It to Beaver, Father Knows Best,* and any show where small misunderstandings within a family caused confusion but were resolved within half an hour and summed up by the newly enlightened characters with self-deprecatory but fond laughter. Even *Lassie*. Especially *Lassie*, because Mary Alcorn and Julia had watched as small children, and both of them found they still did love that beautiful collie.

They were amused, though, that they hadn't noticed earlier in their lives that poor Lassie was saddled with looking out for a family of outright idiots. The Martin family repeatedly failed to realize that their barn was burning down, or that their kittens were drowning, or that once again Timmy had fallen off a cliff and was hanging on by the tips of his fingers—and most of this happened right outside their window as they sat primly at the kitchen table of their old farmhouse, passing dishes of peas or lima beans.

This time around, too, Mary Alcorn thought that Timmy's adoptive mother, whom she had once thought beautiful, looked like she might suffer from thyroid disease. *Something* about the way she looked wasn't quite right, at any rate, and Julia and Mary Alcorn regressed to the days when these subjects were serious matters of consideration and discussion.

The second week of Claytor's absence, however, Lavinia became restless and agitated. One morning she leaned around the frame of Mary Alcorn's door to say that after dinner there was something she wanted to talk to Mary Alcorn about. Lavinia always announced these upcoming confrontations early in the morning, with a recognizable edge in her voice, and the whole day was ruined for Mary Alcorn. She knew that during the ongoing hours of the day her mother would enlarge upon her concerns over whatever had first set her off—Mary Alcorn's character, or grades, or choice of friends, or whomever Mary Alcorn might be dating.

That particular day, with Claytor out of town, however, Lavinia had become more and more agitated, and had forgotten about whatever it was that she had meant to get to the bottom of with Mary Alcorn. Lavinia paced through the chaotic household obsessively—a sort of repetitive circle. And that afternoon she was all at once convinced that it was imperative to redecorate entirely before Claytor got home. It would be such a surprise for him, and she began hauling all their furniture out to the garage. The Scandinavian sofa, the tiled side tables, the bed frames, the lamps and pictures—everything went. The three of them had to retrieve their mattresses that night, and one lamp each, so they could find their way through the house, so they could read, and so they would have a place to sleep.

Mary Alcorn refused to help them remove the furniture in the first place. "Oh, my God! What are you doing?" she asked when she came upon her mother and sister on stepladders in the bathroom, which was sour with the smell of paste, and where crinkled, soggy ribbons of flowered paper covered the floor. "Mama, *please* don't do this! You'll never finish in time! *Please* stop! Everything will be ruined. Daddy'll be so mad! Let's get all the furniture back inside!"

"We need a new start, Mary Alcorn," Lavinia said, looking toward her older daughter with an expression that was almost plaintive. But Mary Alcorn didn't return her gaze with even the tiniest bit of mercy. Lavinia looked away and spritzed another section of wallpaper with a spray bottle. "I know I can always count on you to disapprove," she said in what her daughters referred to as her "Queen of England" voice, which was shot through with a steely thread of warning. "But even you won't be sorry to get rid of this wallpaper," Lavinia said, although her expression was still bewildered in the face of Mary Alcorn's discouragement.

"It's all right, Mama," Julia said. "I think we can get it done. We just have to get it *finished!* But we *do* have to bring the furniture back in the house, because we won't have time—"

"Oh, I don't think so. It's time for a new palette. A new idea," Lavinia answered. "This all" — and she swept her arm to indicate the empty rooms — "it was all so stale."

Mary Alcorn was beside herself with dread. As Julia and her mother spent three days dampening and scraping off all the wallpaper, revealing beneath it a meshed plaster surface that had become flaky and damp, and that couldn't possibly simply be painted over, she couldn't contain herself. Their three-way argument continued hour after hour and grew more heated every day.

"Julia, *please* don't help with all this. Mother! Stop all this! This is crazy! Don't you see that Julia just feels sorry for you?"

"That's not true!" Julia protested. "Why don't you ever just mind your own business? If you don't like what we're doing, then leave us *alone!* You just make trouble for everyone. Just go away! We'll be okay if you just leave us alone."

Mary Alcorn had almost forgotten her real life during the time she had spent with Julia over that lazy first week of passive inactivity; she had given herself over to the feeling that they would only ever be dependent on the other as company. But Mary Alcorn's nascent idea, the renewal of her hope that maybe everything would work out this time—it was all shattered in the moment Julia urged her so desperately to leave them alone. Mary Alcorn gave voice to a furious shout of protest.

"No! It won't! No, it won't, Julia. How come you never get it? It'll *never* be okay. Daddy will have a fit when he discovers this mess. We don't even have enough money for this! He said not to buy *anything* we don't *really, really* need. We can't just throw away all of our *furniture!*" This was so apparent to Mary Alcorn that her frustration turned into furious tears.

Lavinia turned on Mary Alcorn. "Stop it! Stop it! Leave your sister alone. You're the most self-centered girl I've ever known! You weren't so worried about spending money that you didn't charge that suede coat at Goldrings. You never say a nice thing to anybody unless you're trying to impress them. Oh, and *then* butter wouldn't melt in your mouth! I swear to God, Mary Alcorn! I wish I'd never had you at all! You ruin everything—"

"Don't *say* that, Mama!" Julia shouted at her mother while simultaneously covering her own ears. "Don't *say* that! She doesn't even mean that, Mary Alcorn! Tell her you don't mean that, Mama!"

And Lavinia didn't mean it, in fact, except in the very moment of saying it. But she was baffled and deeply wounded by Mary Alcorn's searing and relentless condemnation, and she didn't say a word; she just got back to work.

Late that afternoon, when her father returned, Mary Alcorn didn't have a single triumphant moment of being proved right about his reaction. In fact, as usual, she sided with Lavinia in all her mother's dashed hopefulness and disillusionment when faced down by Claytor, who had walked right out of the house as soon as he took account of its still-denuded rooms.

"Oh, my God! Lavinia! Oh, my God!" He walked into the rest of the house beyond the living room and came back again, looking around for a moment and then turning without saying another word, leaving without even greeting his daughters. By the time he finally came home, Julia and Mary Alcorn were asleep on their still frameless mattresses, which were laid down directly on the floor. Mary Alcorn and Julia woke up to the familiar sound of slamming doors and threats shouted back and forth.

"...we'd all be better off dead! You could never survive on your own! The girls...My God! What would happen to them? I should just kill every one of us!" their father said. "What's the use...What's the use of doing anything else? I'm trying to stop drinking...trying to pay all these bills. But you spend and spend...and you don't *help* me, no matter what I ask...When I thought that if I got away to the lake where there's no alcohol—no temptation! Why did you pack *beer* in the car...?"

"Oh, for God's sake, Claytor! You said you were going away to *rest!* I didn't know you were trying to stop drinking. And that's so stupid, anyway! You don't have to *stop* drinking! It's just this idea that you have! You just have to stop drinking so *much*. A six-pack of beer! I thought it would be a nice surprise . . . And the bills—You could pay the bills anytime! You're a *doctor!* But you're never at the office anymore. . . . Don't think I haven't figured out that you're having an affair!"

It wasn't possible to have any kind of privacy in the little house on Fairway Lane, and Mary Alcorn got up out of bed and trailed behind them as their argument moved through all the rooms. "Mama! Be quiet! Both of you should go to bed! The neighbors' lights are all on! Everybody can hear you!" But that enraged both her parents, and her father turned on her with a furious scowl.

"So *what?* Why do you always worry about the neighbors? Especially those *idiots* next door . . . They're insipid. Ordinary! Lacey Gillman—*both* the Gillmans! They've never done us any favors. But then there's Lacey getting your mother to hem a dress for her . . . *Stop everything, Lavinia!* And when Julia was so sick . . . *Oh, no! Lavinia! I can't risk getting sick myself.*"

All at once Mary Alcorn was terrified, even though he wasn't aiming his fury at her mother now, but at the neighbors. Her father seemed to her deranged with fury. Seemed huge, seemed unhandsome, seemed not to be a person she had ever known. She couldn't save her mother, and she couldn't save herself.

In the small second-floor bedroom at Agnes's house, just down the hall from her mother, Mary Alcorn was nauseated and at the very same time she was ravenous. But she was pinned exactly where she had first lain down by the realization of the responsibility she had suddenly taken hold of. She had hidden her father's hunting rifle behind the hot-water heater in the tiny closet in the kitchen; she had packed clothes for the three of them while her parents stormed through the house. She had seen the Gillmans' lights flick on, since there was nothing she could do to keep her parents' voices down, although she had closed all the windows. She even saw Mr. Gillman come out into his driveway, wearing his robe and slippers. He stood watching their house, moving tentatively forward and then retreating.

Mary Alcorn had finally found Julia tucked away in the alcove next to the clothes closet, and she had tried to tell Julia everything would be all right, that they were leaving, but Julia looked at her in a blank fury and told her to just shut up! And finally Mary Alcorn had slipped outside as silently as possible and opened the hood of the car. She replaced the missing distributor cap with one that her mother had bought at an auto supply shop, since Lavinia had suspected that Claytor might resort once again to removing it so his family could not leave him alone again, could not leave him all by himself, could not abandon him once more. The past two years or so, Lavinia and her daughters had taken to driving far out into the Ohio countryside when Claytor became menacing, when he began to change into some other person altogether. But before this spring night in April, they had always come home near dawn, when Claytor had inevitably been asleep—had been very nearly unconscious. Not one of them wanted to attract the possible judgment of the rest of the Scofield family on any one in their separate household. The Claytor Scofield family closed ranks against outsiders in order to retain their privacy, and because each of them harbored a kernel of shame, and also because each one of them loved the other three.

❧ ❧

This first time they had fled to Agnes's house the night wore on and on and on. Agnes lay awake pondering her choices. She didn't know what had happened; she wasn't certain even now that her son's marriage had reached a state of collapse, but it was unbearable to think of Claytor having caused all this sad and ruinous upheaval. Claytor had been the most soft-hearted of all the children she had raised; he had never been a boy who could cavalierly cause any creature to suffer. He had never for a moment—even all the years he was growing up—lacked a sometimes crippling empathy.

When they're ages six to, oh, about thirteen years old, you're apt to find almost any little boy—a few girls, as well—dissolving a snail in salt, say, or dropping a cat from a second-story window to see if cats do, in fact, always land on their feet. But Claytor had ended up in fistfights, attempting to stop any of his friends from trying pranks like that. In fact, even as a grown man during one year at Johns Hopkins, he had come home midyear resolved not to return because he was working in a lab that was using rats and guinea pigs for experimental testing of some sort. Agnes had never been clear about what bothered him so much, because he wouldn't say, but he couldn't abide the cruelty impersonally inflicted on the animals.

During that long night Agnes, too, found herself in tears. She was mourning the seeming obliteration of the person her beautiful and beloved son had been. She knew, of course, that it was because of Claytor that Lavinia and her daughters had fled their house in the middle of the night. And Agnes was much like Lavinia in her opinion of alcoholism. Agnes had never, ever, in her life, longed to reach — or to sustain — a state of mind by having just one more drink. She couldn't believe, therefore, that it wasn't simply some sort of character flaw to give in to the decision to drink too much. To get drunk. To lose touch with the innate governing device that regulates one's rational actions.

Without the ability to imagine such a state, Agnes was unable to feel empathy for her son, and all her efforts to understand him resolved in grief. She wondered if she should go out to Cardinal Hills in the morning and talk to Claytor about all this. After all, now that his family had sought refuge at his own mother's house, Claytor could hardly tell her that his life was none of her business.

On the other hand, Agnes knew so much was at stake if she interfered: Lavinia's and Claytor's pride, their privacy, the formality that would ensue between all of them if Agnes gave voice to her concerns — if she was forced to take one side or the other. All couples have problems. God knows she and War-ren had had plenty, and it had always seemed to her that any outside interference was never more than a dreadful humilia-tion. Agnes wished desperately that Sam was home right now. He always either knew exactly what to do or believed that he did, which pretty much amounted to the same thing.

When Agnes woke up in the morning, she was nauseated and lay in bed without moving, experiencing again an unnerv-ing flutter in her chest. She had become accustomed to its occasional return and had learned that the best way to handle it was to stay still and breathe slowly. Usually it would stop within a few minutes, and she had decided that it was only a symptom of anxiety. Besides, there were some questions she wasn't in any hurry to have answered—about her own health and, this morning, about Lavinia and Claytor.

Gradually that flutter abated, and the nausea receded. When finally she turned to look at the time, she realized that she hadn't thought to set her alarm clock. She had meant to be up and dressed, ready to offer Lavinia, Mary Alcorn, and Julia breakfast whenever they came downstairs. But now it was almost ten o'clock in the morning. She got out of bed in a rush and got dressed without fussing over her hair or anything else. But by the time she came down the back stairs, there was Claytor, sitting at the kitchen table across from Lavinia with the huge unabridged *Webster's Dictionary* open between them, working a crossword puzzle, while Julia and Mary Alcorn washed dishes from a breakfast someone had fixed.

Chapter Eleven

IN 1963, Harcourt Lees College was hosting an elaborate three-day symposium and celebration to honor Robert Butler on the occasion of his seventy-fifth birthday, which was September 15. So many of the distinguished guests were academics of one kind or another, however, that the celebration was scheduled to take place on the weekend after Thanksgiving, from November 29 through December 1, when teaching schedules wouldn't interfere.

Both Lily and Robert appeared to be pleased, and Robert, particularly, would be delighted to see many of his old friends and former students. But Robert, too, was beginning to lose his hearing, and the effort required to follow the thread of earnest and lengthy discussions and debates left him drained. He would have preferred a gathering in his living room, which would hold the charm of easy and rambling musings among good friends as opposed to what would amount to a performance. Neither Robert nor Lily admitted to the other that he or she was actually dreading it.

Agnes and Sam Holloway, and a very few other family and local friends of Robert Butler's, were invited as well and had accepted, but none of them was looking forward to it any more than Robert and Lily were. In fact, Agnes was unusually irascible in her otherwise polite note of acceptance addressed to the president of Harcourt Lees:

Dear President Wooden,

I am delighted to accept your invitation to celebrate the birthday, as well as the life and work, of my dear friend Robert Butler. I feel certain that the occasion will be enlightening as well as festive.

I wonder, however, why you have not included a celebration of his wife, Lily Scofield Butler's, birthday as well. The two were born here in Washburn, Ohio, on the very same day in 1888. Surely her contribution over the years to the Harcourt Lees community has been invaluable and should be recognized accordingly.

I do hope you will consider a small tribute to Mrs. Butler.

Yours sincerely,
Agnes Scofield Holloway

Agnes never received a response from President Wooden. At first she was only vaguely annoyed that Lily, who would turn seventy-five on September 15 of 1963 — just as Agnes's first husband, Warren Scofield, would have as well had he lived long enough — would be consigned yet again to the role of being nothing more than Robert's wife. Agnes knew that it wouldn't matter two cents to Lily, who was only dreading having to deal with Allen Tate and his new wife, Isabella, who were staying at the Butlers' during those three days. Lily was relieved not to have to deal with Caroline Tate, Allen's first—and his second—wife, but Lily hadn't met Isabella Gardner. She didn't know what to expect. But she was looking forward to seeing Robert Penn Warren and especially Peter and Eleanor Taylor, Robert Lowell, and even Randall Jarrell.

Agnes, though, became downright indignant that once again Lily would go unrecognized as the one person who had made possible Robert's intellectual life and pursuits, perhaps at the expense of her own ambitions.

When those three children had been born on September 15 in 1888, it had caused a sensation in Washburn, Ohio. The morning of September 16, 1888, the news had taken up the entire front page of the *Washburn Observer*. Leo Scofield, Lily's father, had made much of the fact that good luck followed any children born on the ides of the month, and perhaps that was the case. But Leo believed—as almost everyone who reads Shakespeare does—that the ides refer to the fifteenth day of every month, when, in fact, the ides of each month except March, May, July, and October fall on the thirteenth day. In his enthusiasm and off-the-cuff enhancement of the coincidence of those three births' occurring on the same day, Leo had unwittingly set forth a misconception that caused all sorts of tensions, hurt feelings, and unattractive gloating as the family enlarged through the generations.

Robert Butler had been the first to look up *ides* in the dictionary, and now and then he had tried to put the notion to rest; he had pointed out that the ides of September was, in fact, the thirteenth. "You might even say," he tried to explain on his seventeenth birthday, "that the coincidence really is

that the three of us *weren't* born on the ides of September."
But no one paid attention, since it was more interesting the
other way around.

In any case, very few people still alive knew anything about
it, and after the formal symposium and celebration at Harcourt Lees, the *New York Times* correspondent declared that
Robert Butler's birthday fell on November 30, and so it was
settled and declared eventually even in his obituary.

Agnes loved Robert Butler—never in any way romanti-
cally but because of his deep courtesy and subtle kindnesses,
among many other reasons—but she was determined that
Lily be celebrated as well.

Her determination seemed peculiar even to Agnes herself.
She wasn't generally observant of, or even interested in, celebrations of any kind. With so many birthdays in the family
these days, she concentrated only on giving the annual Scofield Christmas Eve dinner, but in the case of Lily's birthday
she made an exception. She didn't begrudge Robert one bit
of appreciative recognition of his work, nor of his standing in
the community of letters, but it annoyed Agnes time and again
to observe Lily's graciousness—faux or otherwise—simply
taken for granted by any number of posturing intellectuals
and literary lions. Taken for granted even by those who didn't
posture at all but believed that domestic concerns were incon-
sequential. If Robert had any fault at all that Agnes might
hold against him, it was that he didn't seem to notice that his
colleagues had no idea—weren't even curious about—
whatever Lily might think about anything at all.

In Washburn, Ohio, however, as Robert and Warren and Lily
had grown up, always in one another's company, it had become
clear to everyone in town that it was Lily who was the cleverest

of the three, not that they all weren't as bright as buttons. But certainly it was Lily who was most ambitious—not to achieve anything in particular, but just in a general way. And it was Lily who eventually was cherished by both men, but who everyone agreed had fallen in love with Warren Scofield, despite the complication of their being first cousins twice over.

Agnes Claytor had been an eighteen-year-old schoolgirl in 1917 when she fell yearningly in love with Warren Scofield. She had met him a few times, and then only in conjunction with her father's political career. But Agnes had been bitterly envious of Lily Scofield, even admitting to her eighteen-year-old self, in fact, that she would not have been sorry if someone came along one day and told her that Lily Scofield had suddenly died. Some swift death that hadn't caused any pain or suffering. It wasn't Lily, personally, whom she had hated; it was the version of Lily whom Agnes assumed existed in the mind of Warren Scofield.

Agnes didn't believe she had given any overt sign of her antipathy, but the memory of the strength of her former loathing—even some forty years later—was sometimes overwhelming. Indeed, whenever she felt even slightly irritated by something Lily said or did, Agnes offered excessive gestures of mystifying apology—baking a cake for Lily and Robert or perhaps a plate of assorted cookies, or she came by to see if Lily needed a hem shortened in any new dress she might have bought as well as possibly needing the sleeves shortened. Agnes could do alterations so deftly that the garment looked as though it had sprung into existence of its own accord, that no modifications had been necessary, and she was equally talented at tailoring Robert's suits.

As far as Lily was concerned, she looked back at the situation of herself and Robert and Warren and knew she had been greedy about their affections; she had wanted neither man ever to find any woman as interesting to him as she was. It was all vanity, not particularly unusual, and fueled further by the pretty girls at Mount Holyoke, many of whom were eager to catch the attention of either Robert or Warren when they met them through Lily. Even after Lily and Robert had been married for over five years, Lily had been offended and jealous when Warren fell for a local girl out of the blue. A girl from a perfectly nice family, but someone, nevertheless, just out of Linus Gilchrest School for Girls, while Warren was a grown man; he was almost thirty years old.

But by the time the two couples were settled permanently in Washburn, each with young children, and Agnes and Lily began playing bridge together, Lily was amazed that she had initially thought of Agnes as nothing more than a frivolous, pretty, unsophisticated girl whom Warren was eventually bound to find boring. Lily was a grand master at bridge and had even played with Goren, but she immediately recognized that Agnes had the ability to be a better player than Lily was herself, and there was nothing Lily admired more than a worthy competitor.

In any case, Agnes and Sam returned from Maine in mid-August of 1963, some three months earlier than usual, so that Agnes could plan and supervise birthday festivities aimed primarily at celebrating Lily. The party would certainly celebrate Robert as well, of course, and even serve as a commemoration of Warren Scofield. Agnes didn't believe in surprise parties; it seemed to her that the person who was being surprised nearly always felt foolish and even guilty at being the cause of too much forced cheer. Agnes simply phoned Lily and invited the Butlers to a late-afternoon picnic to celebrate their birth-days, which fell conveniently on a Sunday of that year.

Lily rarely came into town these days, and she and Robert knew nothing at all about the preparations; they were expect-ing a family gathering with a handful of other guests, and one of Agnes's famous birthday cakes for dessert—possibly two cakes in order to have enough to serve everyone. Robert and Lily were, in fact, expecting an afternoon much like the party that Trudy and Dwight had given five years earlier to mark their seventieth birthdays.

They had enjoyed themselves and been touched by Trudy's effort, but they had gone home exhausted about eight o'clock and gone straight to bed. All those small children had required so much more attention than Lily believed any children should need, and they were everywhere, particularly inter-ested in winning favor from her and Robert, who had relo-cated to Enfield by then.

Lily and Robert anticipated another afternoon much like that as Robert came in from his garden to shower and get dressed that Sunday the fifteenth for the party, and as Lily prepared herself by indulging in a long, hot bath.

Agnes had been taken aback by the eagerness with which the family had greeted her proposal for a birthday party. Dwight, for instance, had responded, oddly enough, with a reaction of relief. "That's perfect, Mother! That's *exactly* what we should do. That's just the right thing!" And even Trudy had been enthusiastic, as though perhaps she would get one more chance to overcome her now tiresome and habitual cynicism, to get over the grudge she'd held against family life in Washburn since she'd returned from New York after the war. Washburn was her definition of provincial. Unfortunately Trudy hadn't lived in New York long enough to discover that these days it was far more provincial and self-congratulatory than any other place in the world.

Over a hundred guests were invited, and the Eola Arms Hotel catered the formal picnic. Their staff covered the folding tables with white tablecloths that draped to the grassy, flat shared lawn between Agnes's and Dwight and Trudy's houses.

Betts had offered to help her mother decorate the tables, and the morning of the party, she and Agnes centered a large, thriving pot of ivy on each table so that the vines cascaded over the tablecloths gracefully and in abundance. Among their dark green leaves Agnes arranged lilies that she had cut at the last minute and plunged into rubber-topped, water-filled green glass florist's tubes, which kept the flowers from wilting but which were invisible among the profusion of ivy. The illusion was of a sumptuous, exotic, and appropriately lily-bearing plant.

The whole family had lent a hand. Claytor and Dwight had spent the first Sunday of September ambling around the property, chatting amiably and without any competitive edge cropping up between them. They agreed in every instance about what needed to be done in order to return the grounds shared by the three houses to good shape. They replaced sod, trimmed back dead branches, and removed the scraggly bushes that had grown up along the verges, among a host of other chores.

Trudy volunteered to take over the responsibility of coordinating everything, at which she was exceedingly capable. She never seemed a bit unnerved if the caterers were running late, or if the band was missing a member. She was not tactless but simply direct, and she plowed ahead, insisting that the food and the band appear in the right order, and since she was so certain that her expectations were justified, everyone involved snapped to, and events moved right along just as they should.

Howard and Sam put together a spectacular fireworks show, and Lavinia had thrown herself full force into the project of arranging the presentation of the family's gift to Robert and Lily, which was a croquet set Sam had commissioned from a talented woodworker he knew in Coshocton.

Sam asked Lavinia to plan the presentation of the gift. She was always relied upon to come up with an amusing tribute or a fitting toast in the manner of *The New Yorker*'s annual poem "Greetings Friends!" by Frank Sullivan. In fact, Lavinia had been wrestling with limericks, introductions, greetings, and poems for so long and for so many occasions that her older daughter, Mary Alcorn's, one grand ambition was to be included one day among the notable names in that annual *New Yorker* New Year's poem.

Lavinia's enthusiasm was thoroughly caught up in the project. She was talented at anything she turned her hand to, but no interest sustained her for very long. She was swept up in intense bursts of creativity that eventually wore her into a state of apathy. As a result, though, her frenzied looting of the artists' supply store in Columbus to find what she needed was entirely successful. Her determination was at a state in which if one thing wouldn't work, she was quick to adapt her concept to whatever else was at hand.

With Claytor's help, Lavinia built and decorated two elaborate and gleaming gold-glittered plywood thrones, with purple-velvet satin-tasseled cushions and a fleurs-de-lis painted in deep purple on each of the high jigsawed curlicued backs.

She spent hours figuring out how to weave two crowns from laurel branches, into which she wired clusters of faux red berries. For the final touch she wound the wreaths around with loops of undulating wired gold-mesh ribbon.

Lily and Robert were ushered to their thrones as soon as they arrived, and the two of them were resplendent in their crowns of laurel and their hastily run-up purple-velvet robes edged with what appeared to be ermine but which was, in fact, the silky fake fur from which Julia's life-size stuffed Steiff snow leopard had been made. The moment it had caught Lavinia's eye, it had struck her as a wonderfully coincidental find, but as the party picked up steam, she began to consider that Julia was not yet aware that her leopard had been sacrificed for this cause. On the other hand, Lavinia thought, Julia was sixteen years old, after all, and maybe she wouldn't even realize that it was missing.

But the hours Lavinia had spent and the leopard she had skinned seemed entirely worth it when Robert Butler was so pleased by the whimsy of the thrones that he asked her if she would be willing to let him buy them from her. She refused, of course, and said they were meant to be a gift to him and to Lily. It hadn't occurred to Lavinia that Lily and Robert would have any use for those thrones after the party was over, and she was delighted to overhear Robert asking Sam if—whenever he had the time—he would put them in his truck and deliver them to Robert and Lily's house in Enfield.

For years and years Lily and Robert sat in them comfortably at their own dining-room table, rarely remembering after a while that those surprisingly comfortable thrones varied in any way from the other chairs in the dining room, a situation that now and then baffled some journalist or other visitor. For

Lavinia the incident was a heady triumph; it remained the highlight of her life among the Scofields.

Lily's granddaughters—Amelia and Martha Claytor's—generation of Scofields had always been impressed by the feats their grandmother could perform, and Betts's youngest son, Danny, begrudged Martha her bragging rights and at first hadn't been certain that he wasn't entitled to them as well.

"Isn't Lily my grandmother, too?" Danny had finally asked Martha, at the table where he was eating supper at the party. Immediately he had been corrected by his older brother Douglas. "No, she's not," Douglas said. "*Agnes* is your grandmother!"

"Agnes *and* Lily," Danny insisted.

"No, just Agnes," said Douglas. "You know that, Danny!"

Martha was nearly sixteen years old, and she hadn't even meant to make a proprietary claim; she'd been asked to entertain her youngest cousins, which really meant only Daniel Dameron, who was ten. "It's all really confusing, Danny," she said. "There're so many of us. But Lily is really your cousin. Robert is too, I guess."

Danny didn't say any more. At home everyone in his family referred to them as Aunt Lily and Uncle Robert, and he was satisfied to find that he was in some way associated with Lily Butler, because it was she who had taught him how to balance a dime on his cocked elbow and then snap his arm forward so quickly that he caught that same dime in the palm of his hand. And if she challenged any one of her family to a game of Ping-Pong—even now that she was in her seventies—most of them insisted she handicap herself by using a book instead of a paddle because her reflexes were as sharp as ever. But the younger grandchildren had never entirely believed her when she claimed she could ride a bicycle backwards.

"I'm not promising that I can still do it now that I'm an old lady," she protested when Martha Claytor brought her bike to Lily and propped it on its kickstand next to her grandmother's throne.

"Lily, I don't think…," Robert said. "Martha, that's not a good idea! Your grandmother could hurt herself. We're too old—"

"Ha!" Lily was suddenly gleeful. "Speak for yourself, Robert!"

Lily had been a natural athlete all her life, far more gifted and a much better games strategist than either Robert Butler or Warren Scofield had ever been. For five years in her midthirties Lily had maintained the title of Women's State Golf Champion, and she was up for any challenge. She untied her purple robe and handed it over to Danny for safekeeping. Then she climbed waveringly onto the bicycle, sitting backwards, extending her arms behind her to hold on to the handlebars, and off she went over the grass. "Tell me if I'm going to hit a tree," she called to her grandchildren and the crowd of friends who cheered her on. When she dismounted, Danny seized the bicycle, and over the following two or three perilous hours he mastered the feat himself.

The croquet set was duly admired and then, when the tables were folded away, set up for a game on the level grassy area. Since Lily almost always won at croquet, she enjoyed herself immensely, although she never minded for more than about three minutes if she lost a game. Her children had grown up playing croquet, and Sam was always a formidable opponent, absolutely ruthless on the court as opposed to his nature in real life. They gave her a run for her money.

The following Thursday, when Agnes picked Lily up to go to bridge, Lily elaborated on the thank-you note she had already written and mailed to Agnes. "To tell you the truth, Agnes, I was dreading that birthday party," Lily said. "I was expecting a long afternoon of sticky children. But they've all grown up so much."

"That's about what I was expecting myself," Agnes said. "But I had a wonderful time. And you... Weren't *you* the Queen of the May! The whole family helped. Really, it wasn't even much work at all for me.... It reminded me of the parties we used to have at Scofields," Agnes added. "At the drop of a hat. Even when Warren and I were first married. And then afterwards, too, with children all over the place—"

Lily interrupted, "Oh, Agnes! I was thinking last night... Do you remember when Betts was about... oh... maybe three years old and came racing out of the house without a stitch of clothes on? It must have been the Fourth of July. The whole town was there... or at least it must have been a party during summertime—"

"Betts was *always* racing out the door as soon as she got her clothes off," Agnes said. "It used to drive me wild. There were so many of them in the house. Children, I mean. It was hard to keep track... I wonder if Betts still *does* that? Runs into the yard as soon as she takes off her clothes? I'll have to ask her..."

It was a pleasant fall in Washburn, at least for the assorted Scofields, because the birthday party had set a certain tone within the extended family. They had become for a season who they had been told—and had believed—they once had been. They had reestablished a singular connection that overrode their various differences. And the place itself, the Scofields compound, even as it sat among drugstores and dry cleaners and assorted doctors' and dentists' offices, seemed to the family to be all of a piece once more, to be sturdily unassailable and therefore still an accurate representation of the family in all its permutations.

Lily had decided that when she turned seventy-five she would give up driving except during the daytime, and even then only within the little village of Enfield. Therefore, on November 21, Agnes had driven to Enfield to pick Lily up for their regular Thursday bridge night—the last one before Thanksgiving intervened. She had arrived in plenty of time to have a drink, and to visit with Robert while Lily got dressed. But just as she had settled back comfortably with a manhattan, which she wasn't particularly fond of but which Robert delighted in mixing, the phone rang.

Lily was coming down the hallway from her room, buttoning her navy linen dress, and she picked up the phone where it sat in the tiny entry hall. She had been unable, though, to understand whatever was being said, and she handed the receiver over to Agnes. "You take this, Agnes! My hearing aid needs new batteries. I'd better change them. It sounded to me like someone speaking underwater."

Agnes put the phone to her ear and found herself trying to understand Julia, whose voice sounded frantic and who was drowned out, in any case, by an alarming, unrecognizable sort of moaning in the background.

"…heard him as soon as we got inside your house," Julia repeated.

Agnes listened for a moment more, and then she was overtaken by alarm. Sam was at a city council meeting, and when she had left to pick up Lily, no one else had been in the house.

"In town, you mean?" Agnes said. "In Washburn? *My* house?"

"... Mama told me to try to reach you before you left for bridge. He's making a horrible noise. I don't know what's the matter..."

Agnes simply hung up the phone and walked right out the front door. She couldn't imagine what was going on—Well, that wasn't true. Finally she gave in and admitted to herself that she could, at least, *imagine* what might be going on. Although she had tried her best not to dwell on it, her first thought was that Lavinia and Julia had fled their own house on Fairway Lane once again, and that this time Claytor had followed them. That he was drinking; that he was enraged; that he might be dangerous. But he was her own son; she loved him in spite of anything else; she knew him so well and pitied him so much! And since September everything between Claytor and Lavinia had been fine as far as she knew.

She drove away from Lily's house without remembering to explain to Lily, without remembering to say good-bye to Robert, without even remembering to close the front door behind her.

By the time Agnes had parked the car and hurried into her house, Claytor and Lavinia were crouched over Abel, who was stretched out on his side on the kitchen floor between them, and Claytor didn't look up while he concentrated on threading a tube down Abel's throat. "I didn't have anything but sodium amytal. I had to guess at a veterinary dose. But he's not in pain, Mother," Claytor said in a distracted but authoritative voice. If he *had* been drinking, there was no indication of it in his speech. Lavinia looked at him with an appraising glance. She didn't relax her hold on Abel, however, although she bent her head to swipe her cheek against the shoulder of her blouse, which was streaked with a yellowish foam.

The kitchen smelled of wet dog, which always reminded Agnes of steaming rice, but overpowering that scent was a high, dank stench that was unlike anything she had ever smelled, and something about that odor made her go stiff all over with alarm. Julia had come into the room, but she hung back beside the doorway.

"It's bloat," Claytor said matter-of-factly. "I don't think there's anything else I can do." He glanced over his shoulder and thought that his mother seemed to be struck dumb; she seemed to be in shock, which surprised him. He had never seen her so much as flinch as she dealt with any number of childhood catastrophes and injuries. After the bone was set, the gash was stitched, the fever broke, and they were tucked into bed, finally able to feel sorry for themselves, Agnes had become briskly efficient, and each one of them had felt—at one time or another—a little neglected by the lack in their lives of motherly cosseting. Although maybe, Claytor thought, she had only been trying to keep everyone around her calm and had later given in to delayed panic. He didn't know. He couldn't remember.

"I just came by to talk to Lavinia," he explained. "We were in the front room when Julia called us from upstairs." He was not only trying to calm his mother but to explain himself as well. The last time he and Lavinia had been in his mother's house at Scofields together, Sam had suggested to him that it was too much for his mother. That perhaps he and Lavinia could meet somewhere else. Claytor had endured a sudden clutch in his chest of pure outrage, to be spoken to by someone who wasn't even a member of the family. Spoken to as though he were some sort of wayward teenager. But then he reminded himself that it was just Sam, after all, who never judged anyone and was simply telling Claytor a truth he already knew anyway.

But now, seeing his mother standing frozen in her own kitchen, Claytor knew also from his experience with the families of his human patients that it helped them to be told exactly what was happening when an unexpected medical emergency overwhelmed them. "Abel was pacing. He was in a lot of pain. And moaning... Well, he was making a sound more like a cow makes. At first when I heard him, I thought it *was* a cow—outside somewhere. It took a minute to make sense... He wanted help, but he didn't want Julia to touch him. He was salivating—trying to retch, drooling foam. I've seen bloat in other animals... I'm sorry, Mama... but I couldn't stand it. Seeing him in that kind of pain. And I just didn't think there was time to wait until I reached you. But he's not feeling any pain right now, Mother. I think I've decompressed his stomach. And turned it. Sometimes their stomachs will suddenly flip—or *twist*. The way a lemon drop is wrapped. It closes the stomach off. Gas builds up... But I think he's stable, now."

Agnes didn't hear what Claytor was saying as much as she picked up on the tone of his straightforward account, and she looked at Abel, entirely helpless but not suffering at the moment. "But what will happen to him?" she asked, speaking as deliberately as possible.

"He could be all right for a while if he comes out of anesthesia okay. For days. For weeks, even. It may *never* recur. He looked to be about four years old when you first got him. I'd guess he's in his teens. He's an old dog, Mama. Given his size, I think it'll happen again, and it's an awful way to die. But I can get in touch with Ohio State and get another opinion. Not until tomorrow, though..."

Agnes moved forward and sank to her knees in front of Abel. She laid her head against Abel's sour, foam-slimed muzzle; she pushed her forehead firmly against his, and her graying hair fell across his brow, so that strands of hair and fur intermingled. "Oh, no, Abel," she said. "Oh, no. Oh, no. You are a *good* boy. You are the *best* dog! My beautiful boy. *Such* a good boy. And I won't let you suffer. None of us... We won't let you suffer anymore." She held his head between her palms, resting her lips briefly against the hard shell of his skull, and then she sat back on her heels, peering at him over her hands, which she had brought to her face instinctively as she watched him. Finally she dropped her hands and gave a forlornly helpless gesture, opening her palms out widely in front of her and toward Abel, which was clearly a signal to let him go.

"I can't stay here, Claytor. I can't watch him die. Will he know if I'm not here?"

Claytor looked at his mother and simply could not lie to her. "I don't know, Mama. I don't think so. But I just don't know."

Agnes moved forward again immediately, sitting down and sliding under Abel as he lay unconscious, lifting him as gently as she could so that his head rested on her lap, and Abel gave a single thump of his tail against the black linoleum kitchen floor. It may have been no more than an autonomic reaction, a last muscular spasm as Claytor administered a lethal dose of anesthesia. But the sound of that last thwack of Abel's sweeping, upward-arching tail in possible acknowledgment of their mutually deep and singular connection stayed in Agnes's memory, and she hoped he had not been alert enough to contemplate his own death, to feel pain or fear, but she also hoped that he had known she was right there.

Sam got home long after Agnes had gone to bed, but Claytor had stayed at his mother's house, waiting to explain about Abel's death to him, and also swabbing down the kitchen as he would if he had been sanitizing an operating room. Lavinia and Claytor had used a blanket from the trunk of Claytor's car to move Abel into the back shed, and then Lavinia had taken Julia home without giving any thought to the state she and her daughter had been in as they had left their house earlier in the evening. She forgot entirely that she and Claytor had begun arguing about money almost as soon as Claytor had come in the door.

All week Claytor had received calls at his office from various bill collectors about loans he had taken out and on which he had recently failed to pay interest. If he happened to be with a patient, most of those callers simply relayed the information to his secretary, who was then miserably uncomfortable passing the information along to Dr. Scofield.

"You could make as much money as you wanted to, Claytor," Lavinia had protested angrily when she understood that somehow Claytor was blaming her for the financial mess they were in. "I don't know why you always blame me for these things. Dr. Eberhardt just bought one of those huge houses—"

"God*damn it!* Lavinia! I've *told* you...I'm not anything like Jim Eberhardt! I'm not ordering tests for patients who can't afford them. Who don't need them! Jim also owns a third of an interest in Marshal Labs and Imaging!" Claytor opened the refrigerator and retrieved a glass of Scotch from the night before, in which the ice had melted, but Scotch was expensive, too, and he topped off his glass with the little that remained in the bottle.

"Oh, *well!* You are the vainest man I've ever known about your ridiculous integrity...Not even taking the GI home deduction because you hadn't served overseas. So noble of you...But who suffers because of that?"

Claytor suddenly grasped Lavinia by the forearm and dragged her toward the refrigerator, where he threw open the door once again and held her in front of him, forcing her to look at the contents. "That deduction! That deduction that you've gone on and on about ever since we bought this house! It wouldn't even pay for half of what you spend on food for one month. You manage to spend over five hundred dollars a month! But it's not like we ever sit down for a meal—"

"You think it's *my* fault that you're out with God knows who almost every night? I used to think it was a woman, but now...You come home at three in the morning with men you've met in bars I've never heard of! You think it's *my* fault that you'd rather drink your dinner. God knows what you're doing, Claytor, but this is a small town! I can't imagine what people must think—"

Had Mary Alcorn not been away at college, she and Lavinia and Julia would have been out of that house in one more minute—not that Lavinia would be pleased about that; she would have turned her rage on Mary Alcorn. But Julia's only strategy was to withdraw completely. Eventually when her mother rushed into Julia's room and locked the door, however, the two of them left through the sliding glass doors that opened from Julia's room onto the small enclosed patio. When Claytor realized they had gone, he drove his own car into Washburn, since he imagined they were at his mother's house once more.

But later that night when Claytor and Lavinia and Julia got home, he was exhausted and sad and didn't even remember the argument he and Lavinia had had earlier. He climbed into bed and slowly and cautiously and appeasingly made love to his wife.

Chapter Twelve

THAT FRIDAY MORNING in November following Abel's death the previous night, Agnes got out of bed as soon as it was light outside. She had come wide awake and had known it would be impossible for her to go back to sleep. She was barefoot and so quiet coming down the back stairs that Sam didn't know she was even in the kitchen until he turned from the stove and was startled to see that she was sitting at her regular place at the kitchen table.

He put the cup of coffee he had just poured for himself in front of her and turned back to pour another cup, which he put down at his own place at the table. He adroitly split the breakfast he was cooking for himself into two portions, settled a plate with a fried egg, bacon, and toast before her, and also put down a plate for himself. He didn't sit down, though. He walked around the table and loosely embraced Agnes from behind, resting his chin on the top of her head.

"I'm so sorry about Abel," he said. "I know it doesn't do much good to say so. But I've never in my life known a dog to be so devoted to any one person as he was to you. I've *read* about it...Do you remember that they put up a statue of that dog? Somewhere in Germany, I think. His owner died, but the dog still went to the train station every evening at the same time. He waited for his master to come home on the train every day, year after year. And there was another story I read somewhere. A lot like that—"

"But Sam...Abel wasn't...he wasn't really that kind of dog at all. He was always so *worried*...He knew he was supposed to be in charge, but he wasn't any good at it!" Agnes's voice broke and she was in tears.

"That's true," Sam agreed. "Abel always had to weigh both sides of things. He was as smart as a whip. That dog who waited at the train was a *loyal* dog. But he was clearly a slow learner," Sam said.

"Oh, Sam, I know it's not true—I can even *remember* other times much worse—but it seems to me that I've never been this sad before in my life. But, my God! Abel was just my dog! He wasn't a *person*. He was just an old dog. You see, though, I just wasn't *expecting* to be without him..." She swiped at the tears running down her face and motioned for Sam to sit down at the table and eat his breakfast.

"It takes a long time to get over losing a dog like Abel," Sam agreed. "Well, I'm not sure anyone ever does get over it. Or at least I wouldn't trust anyone who did. Would you?"

Agnes thought about that for a moment; she had been deeply ashamed of harboring such grief simply over a dog. She hadn't thought of her sorrow as anything but self-indulgence, but Sam seemed to be implying that it was a mark of good character. She looked across the table at him. "No," she said with a slight note of surprise. "No. I hadn't ever thought about that. No. I wouldn't much like any person who didn't grieve over the death of his dog. Well, but I didn't feel as bad about Shirley . . . I was *sorry,* of course . . ."

"I knew in my bones this whole week that something like this—some sort of bad news—was going to happen," Sam said. "I knew we were due to be sad. I'm like that sometimes," he announced unhurriedly while carefully repositioning his fried egg on top of his piece of buttered toast and then concentrating on dividing the combination into nine equal squares. "Some days the things that I imagine will happen . . . you know, when I'm just getting out of bed, still not quite awake, going over my plans for that day—an idea will pop into my head out of nowhere."

Sam had noticed, of course, that Agnes was trying to regain control of herself, and what he said was true, but he was only trying to give her a little time, he was mostly just putting events together as he went along.

"Take yesterday, for instance," he continued. "I suddenly wanted just . . . Well, even just a *taste* of homemade peach ice cream. Just one more taste. My sister and I used to take turns cranking the dasher whenever my father had found peaches he thought were worth the effort. My God! I've never had anything better than that ice cream. And, sure enough, I was going over some blueprints with Nell and Artie Blanchard late yesterday afternoon. They asked me to stay for supper. You had bridge. And Artie and Nell and I were going to have to go to the council meeting to present the plans for their house. Anyway, what do you think they served for dessert?"

Agnes smiled for the first time since she had come into the kitchen. "It's just a wild guess, Sam, but I imagine they had some wonderful homemade peach ice cream," she said.

"Oh . . . Well, no. It wasn't homemade. And it wasn't peach. But they had that new French vanilla. Nell had picked fresh strawberries . . ."

Agnes took a bite of bacon, and her smile at Sam across the table was genuine. "Oh, Sam!"

She knew that he really believed it had been a remarkable coincidence — his wanting homemade peach ice cream when he woke up in the morning and being served store-bought French vanilla in the evening. It would be the fresh strawberries that sealed the connection. Sam knew how to make all the events of his life interesting to recall, and Agnes thought that might be at least part of the secret of the overall happiness of his life.

In Tangipahoa Parish, north of New Orleans, the school year had begun as usual in July, to accommodate the need to harvest the strawberries during the spring months when the fruit ripened. Most of the students were needed to help with the work, and therefore the schools closed for the year at the end of March.

On that Friday, November 22, of 1963, the parish schools were almost halfway through their academic year as well as their football schedule, and in Hammond, Louisiana, Moulton High's biggest game of the season was scheduled for that same Friday night. David Broussard, the vice principal of Moulton High School, came on the public address system just as the students were drifting into their first afternoon classes after lunch.

"Attention, please! May I have your attention, please? The football game tonight against Catholic High School will begin an hour later than planned. Please don't arrive until eight o'clock at La Grange Stadium. The parking lot will be closed until then. Kickoff is at eight-thirty, so those who want to can attend an evening mass being held at St. Helena's at six o'clock this evening.

"I've been asked to inform the students of Moulton High that John Kennedy has been fatally shot in Dallas, Texas. Governor Connelly of Texas has been injured as well. His condition is unknown at this time.

"As usual, pep squad voodoo dolls for tonight's game are on sale all day in the cafeteria or in Miss Patterson's office in the gym. All proceeds go toward expenses the pep squad incurs while traveling to cheer on our football team. Let's see a big Marauders victory for Moulton High tonight!"

Vice principal Broussard turned off the PA system and remained in his office in a simmering rage. He hated John F. Kennedy with a passion so sweeping that he couldn't bring himself ever to refer to him as *President* Kennedy. He despised what he felt sure was Kennedy's sense of superiority. His rich background. His championing of the Negro race when you could bet he'd never met a nigger in his life. Mr. Broussard's resentment of the changes in the society in which he had lived for fifty-eight years had become the essence of who he was. His every thought was beset with the reverberations of a tautly drawn strand of fury—like some electric impulse over which he had no control. More bitter to David Broussard than Kennedy's election was the fact that now John F. Kennedy would become a martyr!

❧ ❧

Wernher von Braun was up early on Friday, November 22, at the Regency Hotel in Washington, DC, where he faced a morning of testimony on Capitol Hill before yet another congressional committee, and his mood was mixed. In the third year of the Kennedy presidency, the administration was divided and troubled by the huge expenditure of money required to maintain a viable space program. A program that was losing traction in the imagination of the American people.

John F. Kennedy's election in 1960 had seemed to bode well for the space program after Eisenhower's penny-pinching, but almost immediately Wernher had come up against the intense opposition to manned space flight from Kennedy's science advisor, Jerome Wiesner, among others. The case Wernher needed to make to the committee that November morning of 1963 was that nothing less than a manned lunar landing would serve as the ultimate victory over the Soviet Union in the ongoing cold war.

"I sometimes feel like a traveling salesman!" Wernher had complained to his wife, Maria, while he was packing for the trip to Washington. "Maybe I should make up little rocket models and carry them around in a flimsy case! Like pairs of scissors and dish brushes and cleaning powder," he said in a mood of grandiose self-pity.

Earlier that month, however, Wernher had personally briefed the president at the Saturn I Complex at Cape Canaveral, where SA-5 was sitting imposingly on its pad with the first functional S-IV liquid-hydrogen stage in place. Wernher had come away once again deeply impressed by Kennedy's shrewd mastery of all that a successful launch would achieve and imply.

By the time Wernher went into breakfast at the hotel he was looking forward to the meal and determined not to appear impatient before the committee; he would remain as genial and expansive as need be. He would give a measured reply to every question asked, no matter how simplistic or foolish that question might be.

It wasn't until he was on the flight home to Huntsville that the pilot advised the passengers that John F. Kennedy had been fatally shot in Dallas, Texas, on a beautiful sunny day while waving from his open car to the crowd who had gathered along the streets to watch his motorcade. Governor Connelly had also been shot, but his condition was still unknown.

Wernher von Braun was immediately assailed by grief and then, as well, by personal despondency. He knew that inevitably there were triumphs yet to be achieved in the space race, but at that moment, he thought he didn't have the wherewithal to start over once more from the bottom of the hill.

In Chicago, at lunchtime of that same Friday in November, Martyl Langsdorf met her husband at a little restaurant near the University of Chicago. She had come into the city to do some early holiday shopping, and she had found a beautiful pale yellow Villager sweater and matching wool skirt for one of her daughters, as well as the perfect gift for her mother. Besides, the serene but quite spare house they lived in, designed and built by the architect R. Paul Schweikher, didn't lend itself to spontaneous decorations of any kind, and Martyl savored downtown Chicago in all its sentimental Christmas glory. The day was overcast and cold, but the atmosphere was exactly right for the season, with thousands of lights decorating everything in sight. She was in wonderful spirits and looking forward to meeting her husband, Alex, for a pleasant meal. But she found him in a distracted mood. He and a few of his colleagues had still been debating the wisdom of having set the hands of the Doomsday Clock—the clock that Martyl herself had designed—back to twelve minutes to midnight only a few weeks earlier.

"After all," he told her, recounting a conversation he had had just that morning, "it was based only on *opinions* about the general state of the world. There was no real reason... We moved the hands from two minutes until midnight, back to the original seven minutes in nineteen sixty. But look what happened during the Cuban missile crisis just last year! We've probably never been closer to nuclear war than we were then, but we were caught flat-footed and didn't have time even to consider moving the hands of the clock before the whole thing was over! So why now? It hasn't even been a year since then."

She was annoyed that Alex brought it up. "I want your opinion about a Christmas present for Suzanne, Alex. I don't want to talk about that Doomsday Clock!"

He looked across the table at her, perplexed.

"You do know, Alex! You do remember that the only reason I put the minute hand at seven minutes to midnight in the first place was because it was the best design? I really don't think that anyone was wondering about the hands of that clock during the Cuban missile crisis!"

Midafternoon, on her drive home to Schaumburg, she was still angry at having lunch given over to even more discussion of the state of the world. She had wanted to relax and enjoy her husband's company. She was growing weary of arriving home from a dinner party only to have Alex go straight to his study to write down some idea that had occurred to him during the meal. She was too often fatigued by being the only one of the two of them engaged in the real life they led as opposed to the protection or destruction of its existence.

Finally she turned on the radio to distract herself, and it was then that she heard the announcement of the assassination of President Kennedy. She was so shaken that she pulled off the highway in Rosemont so she could listen to exactly what was being said. When she glanced into the rearview mirror, she realized that a number of cars had turned on their headlights and were slowly pulling up right behind her, parking along the side of the road, the drivers and passengers leaning intently forward, listening to the news. Oh, my God, she thought, what will this mean? How could this happen? Would the position of the hands of that goddamned clock ever be settled in her lifetime?

When Sam Holloway heard about the Kennedy assassination, he had just buried his wife's dog. Agnes had followed his pickup truck in her own car out to property she still owned near the Dameron house, on a wooded hill. Will Dameron had sent two of his workmen out early that morning to dig Abel's grave, and neither Sam nor Agnes pretended indifference as they lowered Abel's blanket-wrapped corpse into that damp brown cavity of earth.

They were each silently teary-eyed as Sam filled in the grave, but they didn't have anything much to say to each other before they drove away separately, Agnes in her car, followed by Sam, who was meeting a builder at a site in Mount Vernon. Just as they reached the Coshocton-Washburn intersection, though, Agnes pulled into the Dairy Queen parking lot, and Sam pulled in right behind her.

Sam jumped down from the cab of his truck and went to

the driver's-side window, where Agnes sat, letting the car idle so she could leave the radio on. "Sam! They're saying that Kennedy's been shot—"

"I just heard it myself," he said. "God knows! God only knows what'll happen now...Are you okay driving home?"

"Yes. I'm fine," Agnes said. "I just wanted to be sure I'd heard what they said...I'll see you this evening. I don't know...I don't know how long it'll take for me to believe this has happened."

⁓◎ ◎⁓

Whenever Sam heard someone reminiscing about the 1950s, he assumed that person was referring to the years between, say, 1957, when Sputnik captured the world's imagination, and August of 1963, when the March on Washington and Martin Luther King's remarkable speech vindicated—for a few heady weeks—Sam's hard-fought devotion to optimism.

But he believed that the 1950s came to an end at ten A.M., or thereabouts, on Sunday, September 15, 1963, when Denise McNair, who was eleven years old, as well as Addie Mae Collins and Cynthia Wesley and Carole Robertson, each of whom was fourteen, were killed in the bombing of the Sixteenth Street Baptist Church in Birmingham, Alabama.

Those four girls were killed and many others badly injured when the bomb planted by Ku Klux Klan member Robert Chambliss blew up and collapsed the building during Sunday school. Robert Chambliss was found not guilty of murder, although he was fined one hundred dollars and served a six-month jail term for possession of dynamite. Even before Sam heard the news of the Kennedy assassination a little over a month later, he had begun to disengage from hopefulness on a universal scale. He was nearly sixty years old before he finally learned too much to be able to indulge himself any longer in the notion that the reason and goodness and decency of mankind would eventually overcome the consequences of fear and hatred and paranoia. In fact, Sam began to disengage even from the *idea* of goodness and decency except in the way he defined it in his own life.

After 1963, the decade of the sixties seemed to telescope, encompassing tragedy after tragedy: the murder of Martin Luther King, of Bobby Kennedy. The implementation of Lyndon Johnson's remarkably progressive domestic policies was overshadowed by his disastrous mishandling of the Vietnam War. His presidency became little more, at the time, than a national and personal humiliation.

And in 1968, five years after her husband's death, Jacqueline Kennedy married Aristotle Onassis, an event that was at such odds with her iconic image that the myth of Camelot, cultivated during John Kennedy's presidency, began to be derided. After all, not only did Aristotle Onassis appear to have negotiated for and then bought his bride, but he wasn't at all handsome; he wasn't even as tall as she was!

But, of course, the everyday lives of all the separate people on earth continued in all their profound, mundane, and intimate details, shifting as need be to accommodate the natural and human events that constituted the atmosphere in which they lived. Some endured starvation, endless thirst, and brutality; others were lucky enough to worry about cancer and heart disease and their children's futures. And some were aware, but most were not, that the particulars of every instant in the lives they led was all that they could ever own. Sam had always understood that, and he paid attention to every moment of his life.

Agnes and Sam spent more and more of their time in Maine, staying at Sam's house during the winter when Agnes's cottage was impossible to keep comfortably warm. Finally Agnes had begun leaving a key to her house at Scofields with Lavinia, and often when she and Sam returned to Washburn they found signs of her inhabitance if she and Julia weren't, in fact, in residence when Sam and Agnes arrived.

One year Agnes and Sam got into Washburn early in the afternoon, and the house was locked and empty, which relieved Agnes. For all sorts of reasons she had hoped not to find Lavinia and Julia in the house, but primarily, on that particular afternoon, it was because she was tired and didn't want to do anything but take a nap. When she passed through the second-floor hallway, however, she was astounded to find that above the doorway of the bedroom where Julia generally slept when she and her mother stayed at Agnes's house was an elaborately painted crescent of vividly exotic, fantastic flowers and twining ribbons and vines encompassing the beautifully articulated script of the name: *JULIA*. It was a lovely piece of work, clearly done by Lavinia, but it was startling to see the glossy oil paint applied directly to the creamy plaster walls and the bull's-eye-carved post-and-lintel door frame.

Agnes's distress silenced her where she stood on the second floor; she was astonished at such a liberty taken by Lavinia without as much as a note requesting permission. Agnes was nearly sick with surprise as she absorbed the fact of Lavinia's familiarity and what it might signify for the future. But Sam had gone out, and Agnes went slowly up the stairs toward her own room on the third floor, deciding to take a nap and address the problem later. But there above her own door — in remarkable shades of silver, red, and black—was a slightly less exotic but very elegant decoration around the calligraphed words: *SAM & AGNES.*

She and Sam were only staying for five days, and the one time during that visit when she saw Lavinia, Agnes was unable to bring anything up to her about those surprising and unnerving decorations she had imposed upon Agnes's household. Sam merely admired them and assumed that Agnes had known all about their appearance, and Lavinia never mentioned them at all.

In June of 1969, Julia Scofield graduated with the first class at Harcourt Lees College to include women, and her cousin Martha Claytor graduated simultaneously from Oberlin. Sam and Agnes came home from Maine, of course, and those two houses at Scofields—Agnes's and Dwight and Trudy Claytor's across the way—became the headquarters for the family's celebrations. Mary Alcorn was there with her boyfriend, Peter Hovel. They stayed at Agnes's house along with Lavinia and Julia, and Claytor was in and out of the house every day.

Amelia Claytor and her fiancé were at Dwight and Trudy's, and because of separate graduation schedules, everyone attended both Julia Scofield's and Martha Claytor's graduations. Even Lily and Robert attended both ceremonies, although Robert had to fly off immediately after Julia's graduation in order to accept an honorary degree from the University of Texas.

Julia had moved out of her dorm room before Sam and Agnes arrived, and after Agnes had taken a long bath, she went downstairs and found Mary Alcorn and Julia arranging supper for whoever might be around. They had put in an order for four large pizzas from Dan Emmet's pizza shop, and Mary Alcorn was making a vinaigrette dressing as well as a homemade blue cheese dressing, while Julia was slicing cabbage for coleslaw, which everyone in the family still preferred made with Marzetti's dressing. For years they had had to bring their own containers and buy it from Marzetti's restaurant in Columbus, but it was now sold all over the country. Generally a mild debate broke out about whether or not the dressing tasted the same or had acquired a sulfurous commercial taint.

Agnes decided that she would set the table in order to get out of the way, but when she went into the dining room she discovered a jungle of stringy potted plants in hideous macramé slings hanging from the ceiling where someone had installed hooks.

"Julia," she called out with more urgency than she intended, "what's *happened* in here...?"

Julia came to the doorway to see what was the matter. "Oh, Agnes, I hope you don't mind. I had to find a place for my plants that got enough sunshine. The bay window in here—"

"I *do* mind, though, Julia. I mind very much finding out you've put holes in that plaster ceiling. And there's water on the floor—"

"It won't be a problem," Sam said as he joined them in the dining room. "This ceiling needed repair, anyway. But Julia, I think a better place to hang these plants would be from the wooden ceiling on the screened porch. I'll ask Bernie to stop in this week and be sure you have the right kind of screws..."

Agnes left the room abruptly and retreated upstairs to her bedroom, and Sam came in about a half an hour later. "I'm sorry," he said, "but Julia was about to start crying, and it'll be so easy to fix."

"But it's *my* house! Why in the world would she do such a

thing? I don't mind when they stay here... No, that's not even true. I *hate* it that Lavinia and Claytor... They're like magnets! They either attract or repel each other, and I'm just so tired of it..."

She bent her head and cupped her forehead in her hands in a familiar gesture that usually signaled the beginning of a headache, and Sam gave her some aspirin and suggested she lie down until she felt better. "This won't last forever, Agnes. It's bound to resolve itself one way or another when Julia's plans take her away from Washburn."

Agnes fell sound asleep when the aspirin began to work, and when she woke up she felt terrible about her earlier behavior. Julia was probably her favorite grandchild, and Julia had had such a hard time already, without Agnes begrudging her a place she could safely consider her own. Dinner was over by the time Agnes joined everyone else downstairs, but she hadn't wanted to eat pizza, anyway.

"Agnes," Julia said, "I wasn't thinking—"

"I'm so sorry I snapped at you, Julia. I've been so tired this summer, and the flight from Portland was delayed. For good-ness' sake, leave your plants wherever you want to!" The two of them apologized simultaneously, and Julia smiled with relief.

Lavinia came downstairs with a shiny, wrapped present for Agnes that looked to be a record album, and Agnes guessed that it was bound to contain a recording of Doris Day singing "Que Sera, Sera," which Agnes had liked so much for a while that she had set it on replay one day in the winter while she was making soup. The record player was in the dining room, and Agnes only owned the song on a 45. It had played well over twenty-five times before Lavinia — who had arrived late the night before and whom Agnes had forgotten was in the house — had come into the kitchen nearly in tears.

"Oh, please," she said to Agnes, "it's not that I don't like Doris Day...I *do* like Doris Day, but maybe I could find a different song..." And even then Agnes had laughed.

"Oh, turn it off! Lavinia, I forgot you were upstairs. I'm probably the only person in the world who wouldn't go crazy hearing that song over and over. I had forgotten it was still playing."

So when Lavinia handed her the package, Agnes smiled at her, meaning to acknowledge that small incident between them, but when the wrapping was removed, the gift from Lavinia turned out not to be a record after all. It was a matted and framed postcard of a painting. A portrait of a young man in what Agnes guessed was the impressionist style.

Lavinia was smiling with a delighted expression that Agnes had rarely seen before. "Isn't that amazing?" Lavinia exulted. "I couldn't find a print for sale anywhere. It's a self-portrait of Edgar Degas. A friend sent it to me sometime or other, but I just happened to turn it up again last week. You see how Degas looks exactly like Abel? See? His eyes are a little too high. Just like Abel's. And the same long, narrow face. I still miss Abel. He was the most interesting dog I've ever known. I think it was the first time I realized that dogs could be neurotic. He *worried* so much. Sometimes when I'm staying here, I wake up in the morning and think he'll be there. I think he'll be on the landing worrying that he might miss something. Something he needs to know. I'm always disappointed when I remember that he's not there."

"I still miss him, too," said Agnes, seeing that there was, in fact, a strong resemblance between the self-portrait of Edgar Degas and poor Abel, especially if Abel had been a person — or if Degas had been a German shepherd.

Agnes's house seemed to inhale and exhale people during those two weeks in June. Claytor and Lavinia were often out on the porch playing chess, although neither of them knew the game well. Peter Hovel, though, Mary Alcorn's boyfriend, loved the game and had played it all his life, and the sessions on the porch became small tutorials in chess strategy.

Amelia and her fiancé — a pleasant man, Bob Rachal, who had graduated from Oberlin the year before Amelia — were considering spending a year traveling everywhere they could. All over the world, because Bob might be drafted at any time. He didn't believe in the reasons for fighting the Vietnam War, however, and intended to relocate to Canada if need be. They were almost always at Agnes's house, since Amelia's father, Dwight, considered Bob's plan outrageous and cowardly.

"It seems to me it would be far more honorable to declare yourself a conscientious objector," Dwight weighed in. The problem seemed to be that Bob wasn't certain that he would be unwilling to fight in a war he *did* consider justified.

Children were all over the place. Lily Butler didn't even try to keep them straight; she just started with a possibility and ran through the list of all the children's names she could remember until the child she was addressing signified that Lily had finally hit upon the one that belonged to him or her.

Agnes and Sam enjoyed themselves at all the numerous occasions and celebrations, but both of them were relieved when they finally were back in Maine, making the turn onto Route 131, which ran the entire length of the St. George Peninsula and took them to the turnoff to Martinsville.

The extended Scofield family was back and forth to Maine during every summer, but Agnes visited Washburn, Ohio, only once or twice a year, and she never stayed longer than two weeks. Privately she considered Lavinia to be, essentially, the chatelaine of what had originally been John and Lillian Scofield's house in Washburn, inherited by their only child, Warren, and now, by default more or less, belonging to Warren's older son, Claytor, and his wife, Lavinia. That house in the center of the Scofield compound seemed to be the salvation of Claytor and Lavinia's marriage, for better or worse. It was the only place that the two of them could manage now and then to coexist peacefully, although officially they still lived out in Cardinal Hills at 2 Fairway Lane. And Agnes had long ago given up any objection to Lavinia's sudden arrivals and departures, but it did mean that the house in Washburn no longer seemed to Agnes to be her own home.

One of those warm but not hot August days in Maine, when tourists remember why they're visiting, and residents remember why they stay where they are, Sam packed a picnic for himself and Agnes, who had twisted her ankle the day before, and they simply took a leisurely drive, stopping wherever they wanted, but not too often. Agnes's ankle and heel were stiffly taped, and she wasn't yet comfortable on her pair of crutches.

They stopped for lunch in Camden, which was considered the loveliest village in midcoast Maine, but which Agnes and Sam decided wasn't a patch on the working harbor of Port Clyde. But the public park on the harbor was a shady, pretty place to eat lunch, and Sam spread a blanket in front of one of the park benches near the water. Agnes didn't want to attempt sitting on the ground, but Sam sat by the picnic basket, leaning back on his elbows and idly eating an egg salad sandwich. Out of nowhere, though, a German shepherd came skidding to a halt beside Sam with his eye on that very sandwich, and Sam froze, although the dog didn't seem particularly aggressive, and, in fact, he collapsed on all fours and groveled his way forward toward Sam in a frenzy of belated ingratiation when his owner shouted "No!" to him from up the hill.

Agnes and Sam both laughed, and Sam gave the dog half of the sandwich. "I'm old enough to know better," he called to the tall, spare man who was coming down the hill toward them rapidly, "but also old enough to spoil them if I want to."

"At a show that dog's a dream to handle, but otherwise ...," the owner said in apology. "Leon's good at persuading me to let him off leash ... and I buy it every time. Then there he goes. He's got me well trained."

Sam and Agnes offered lunch to Leon's owner, who introduced himself as Cary Priest. Sam and Agnes recognized the name, because he was well known in midcoast Maine for his champion German shepherds. And in the end, Agnes and Sam bought a gangly four-month-old puppy from Cary the following weekend.

The dog had already begun training and was named Jasper, which was a relief to Agnes on both counts. He was thoroughly housebroken, and it had always seemed to Agnes presumptuous to name a dog who had already become himself. She didn't feel the same about naming a baby—depending on the choice of name—but, then, a baby is a human being. If the dog's *mother* could name him ... well, that would be fine.

Jasper turned out to be a glorious dog! Really, Agnes thought, the most beautiful dog she had ever seen in her life.

And he was a wonderful companion, happy and self-assured, and protective to a degree but not randomly aggressive. Everyone who visited in the summer adored him, and he figured out within seconds if a person was welcome or not, and then he never forgot. A year later he would instantly recognize a child he had only seen a year before, when that child had looked like an entirely different species. A baby's transition to a toddler never surprised him even if he hadn't been around when it happened. Cary Priest became a close friend of both Agnes's and Sam's, and within three years the Scofields' extended family owned nine German shepherds from his kennel, two of them fathered by Jasper.

Each temperate afternoon Agnes and Sam developed a habit of going on a long walk with Jasper, taking books along with them so they could spend an hour or so reading while Jasper lay nearby. Cindy and Yvonne, the two cats who lived at Agnes's cottage in the summer and moved with her to Sam's in the winter, would finally give up the pretense of just happening to have followed along, and curl up on the blanket in the sun.

In the kitchen of the cottage, Agnes hung the framed picture of Edgar Degas on the wall above Jasper's dog bowl, which had been Abel's as well, although Edgar Degas and Jasper bore absolutely no resemblance to each other. If you imagined Jasper as a human being, he was much better-looking than Edgar Degas. Agnes never told anyone that Jasper reminded her of both Clark Gable and Cary Grant with a little Henry Fonda thrown in, and she was delighted to have Jasper live in her household. She was aware, though, that Jasper had everything going for him; he had a glorious existence.

He wasn't in need of the fierce devotion and advocacy she had been required and delighted to provide for Abel.

❧ ❧

The summer guests had all come and gone by the first of September in 1973, and Agnes was at loose ends, although she was also, as always, a little relieved to have her time entirely back to herself. She spent several days sorting pillows, blankets, towels, and whatever household goods needed to be redistributed within the house now that only she and Sam would be at home. She always put aside a box of the things Sam wouldn't be likely to have at his house, as well, which she took along when she stayed there during the most frigid months of the year. But finally on a warm day midweek, she abandoned her indoor chores and decided to prune the plants around the house and the rugosa roses that rimmed the yard but had made the various paths to the rocks, and the tiny strip of sand at low tide, nearly impassable.

She hated gardening, which had been considered odd of her when she was in Washburn, but which was considered downright heresy in Maine, where the growing season was so short. But she wanted to get away from the seduction of the rebroadcast of the Watergate hearings, which she hadn't been able to watch consistently with all the summer visitors in and out of the house. The hearings had ended August 7, but the Public Broadcasting System had garnered such high ratings during their coverage that the station had decided to rerun them after the summer people had gone home. Agnes watched off and on all day, and then watched again in the evening with Sam, when they were shown once more for people who had been away at work all day.

She took her clippers to the roses first, although she didn't have the slightest idea of how they should be cut back. It seemed impossible to kill them, however. She was beginning to attract bugs, as she always did, even when no one had spotted an insect of any kind for days. All at once some sort of fly managed to penetrate her still thick, curly gray hair and flew into her right ear.

She shook her head vigorously in an attempt to dislodge it, and when that didn't work she took some time to clean the pair of clippers with turpentine to remove the sap, thinking that if she didn't let it bother her, the bug would no doubt find its way out. The sound in her ear became increasingly annoying, however, and she went inside and tried using a Q-tip to remove it, and then tried flushing her ear with water, and finally mineral oil, but nothing worked. By the time Sam arrived to pick her up to go to dinner at the little café in Thomaston, she was in a terrible state and nearly in tears of frustration.

"I can't bother a doctor about something as stupid as a bug in my ear. All their offices will be closed by now!"

"But, Agnes, if it's bothering you that much . . ."

"*Bothering* me? It sounds to me like I have ball bearings rolling around in my brain!" she said. "I had no idea anything this minor—this . . . *silly,* might actually make me lose my mind."

Sam drove her to the small clinic in St. George, where there was always a nurse on duty, and when the nurse efficiently removed what turned out to be a tiny gnat from Agnes's ear, Agnes almost embraced her with gratitude.

"That's why I'm here," the woman replied. Her name tag said *Margaret.* She was considering Agnes carefully, however. "But, you know, I'm sure it's just a reaction to the irritation—

anything around your head is a lot of stress—but Dr. Hill is going to want to see you after he reads your chart. He's on duty tomorrow morning. But he comes so early that I really think you should stay overnight. Your blood pressure is elevated. I think you ought to let him check you over. There're no other patients right now. You'd have the room to yourself, and it's very quiet."

"Oh, I can just come back in the morning. I don't really think that's necessary." But Agnes lay on the examining table and realized she was drooping with fatigue, that even the thought of lifting her legs off the table and putting her feet on the floor distressed her. "Well, maybe you've got a point," she said finally, and Sam put his arm firmly around her waist to help her off the table.

"If you want to go home," he said, "we can go to whichever one of our houses you'd like. I'd be right there..."

"But I still would have to come back here early—or go into Rockland if I could get an appointment. This seems like the best idea, Sam."

"Do you need anything from home?" he asked.

"Not really. But Sam, you swing by and get Cary to go to dinner at the café. It's almost impossible to get reservations there now that they're keeping winter hours."

"I'd much rather have your company," he said.

"I'm serious, Sam. Don't let that reservation go to waste."

Sam smiled and nodded and bent over to give her a quick kiss before he went on his way.

As soon as the nurse had given her a glass of juice, offered some crackers that Agnes didn't want, and gotten the sheets and the blanket carefully settled, Agnes fell asleep almost immediately.

The nurse, Margaret Brayton, looked in on her once again and removed the juice glass, and then settled at the reception desk with the book she was reading. After a while she got up and moved to one of the two upholstered chairs intended for patients, putting her feet carefully on one of the magazines arranged across the glass coffee table.

Some hours later Agnes woke suddenly into an unfamiliar, watery darkness. It took her a moment to realize that she must have forgotten to turn off the downstairs light in the back hall. She lay still, trying to think what had awakened her, and then she realized she had been dreaming that she was gnashing her teeth. But she wasn't gnashing her teeth; instead her jaw seemed to have locked into some unusual position that caused a sharp pain across her cheekbone, under her chin, down the side of her neck, and across her shoulder.

Perhaps she should call Sam. But then she remembered he was at a convention in Boston. Well, maybe she should call the hospital. But then they would tell her to come in and see someone, and she knew she shouldn't try to drive there in the dark, especially feeling the way she did. They might send an ambulance. But that would be miserably embarrassing...

And, besides, she had forgotten about Abel, who slept on the landing every night in a watchful state of anxiety, sometimes falling asleep and whimpering until he woke himself up with a proactive bark. He would never let anyone into the house at this time of night. In fact, he might attack anyone who tried to get by him, and they might assume that this was enough of an emergency that they would shoot him. And, anyway, she simply wasn't that alarmed.

The pain was steady but certainly not unbearable, and she was so sleepy again, all of a sudden. If this is it, she thought, ruefully making fun of herself as that melodramatic idea flashed through her mind, well, she'd had a pretty good run. All the people she loved knew that she loved them, and many of the people she should love had no idea that she didn't. But the main thing was that she wasn't at all frightened. She let herself relax fully into the pillow beneath her head. All in all, she was relatively comfortable, and she fell back into a deep sleep.

When Margaret Brayton came by to check on Mrs. Holloway, that's exactly what crossed Margaret's mind as she leaned her head around the doorway. Mrs. Holloway looked so comfortable that Margaret decided not to disturb her and went back to reception, tidied the magazines, and put everything away before she went off duty.

She spoke briefly to Rose Dimmit, who arrived at five-thirty to take over from Margaret on the morning shift. Margaret briefed Rose on Mrs. Holloway and told Rose that Mrs. Holloway should be looked in on and her chart updated at six. "And she's bound to want breakfast. She hadn't had anything to eat when she came in last night."

Rose checked the clock. She had a little while to get her things put away and to change from her good shoes to her crepe-soled nurses' lace-up pair, which were essential on the tiles if the floor was wet. Otherwise it was too easy to fall.

She assembled a breakfast tray of juice and an individual serving of Corn Flakes along with a small paper carton of milk and some packets of sugar. If Mrs. Holloway wanted more than that, it would be easy enough to get it, but generally people simply weren't hungry after a night at the clinic.

She placed the tray on the bedside table and reached forward to take Mrs. Holloway's pulse when suddenly Mrs.

Holloway's eyes flew open. "Watch out!" she said. "Watch out for the dog!" And in spite of herself Rose glanced toward the door, although she knew quite well that there was no dog in the building.

"Mrs. Holloway!" she said. "I'm sorry! I didn't mean to surprise you."

Agnes carefully studied the woman leaning over her. She was a pleasant-looking brown-haired woman whom Agnes had never met before in her life.

"Mrs. *Scofield,*" Agnes said, still not completely beyond her dream, which was also fading, leaving her in a temporary quandary. But a worried look of doubt crossed the woman's face, and Agnes forced herself a little further into the morning. "No, no," she amended. "I'm so sorry. You're right. I *am* Mrs. Holloway. I used to be Mrs. Scofield." But the woman still seemed concerned and kept her eyes on the meter as she took Agnes's blood pressure.

"Well," Agnes said, making an effort to wrench her thoughts into context, "and before that I was Agnes *Claytor,*" she added, trying for a jaunty tone. "By the time you're my age, you get all your husbands completely confused with each other," she added. "And your children, too."

The nurse smiled at her at last. "I do that already," she said, "and I'm just forty-two."

Dr. Hill showed up at six-thirty, and by then Agnes was dressed and feeling fine. She was ready to go home as soon as Sam arrived, but she did pause a moment when Dr. Hill asked her if her health was generally good.

"As far as I know," Agnes answered. "But, Dr. Hill . . . Well. This may sound ridiculous, but I either dreamed last night that I wasn't well, or I really did have a terrible pain in my jaw and all down my shoulder. Is it even possible to *dream* pain? It was gone when I woke up."

"Do you have a regular doctor here in Maine?" Dr. Hill asked deliberately, looking over her chart. "I can give you a list of doctors I would recommend. You seem to be here more often than in Ohio. But I think what happened—whether it was a dream or not—was a reaction to having had something in your ear. We get that pretty often in the summer.

"People never realize that something actually buzzing in your ear causes all sorts of alarms to go off. And almost always someone who's had something in their ear will have ground their teeth. It's a defensive reaction to the irritation of the noise. I had a patient who had been two days out sailing and didn't come in until he docked. He had ground the surface of his teeth almost totally smooth. I couldn't believe none of them had broken. You might feel the same thing off and on for a few days. But I do want you to make an appointment with one of these doctors and set up regular checkups. Your blood pressure's still too high. But I think you're fine right now."

Agnes sat in one of the upholstered chairs in the reception area to wait for Sam. She hadn't been able to reach him, and she had left a message with Cary and also around town. She wasn't really in a hurry, though, and she chatted amiably with Rose.

Agnes was a woman in whom other people confided even if they were complete strangers, and she listened absentmindedly to the problems Rose was having with her oldest daughter, who thought she was in love. And Rose's husband—her second husband, who, after all, was only her daughter's stepfather—he was no help at all.

Agnes murmured appropriately now and then, looking

past Rose and through the window where a local restaurant sat on the cove, swaying slightly as the tide came in, since it was built partly on pilings over water. It was a good place to come for lobster.

She was over seventy years old. The thought astonished her. And as she pondered that fact, she supposed this had been only a dress rehearsal. Just a dry run this time, she thought to herself. And what a lucky way to die that would have been. She didn't imagine the real thing would be so easy; death was so often prolonged, as well as being emotionally and physically untidy. And she was too old to put the thought out of her head, as she had done for years and years in order not to distract her from whatever happened day by day. But she decided to take a leaf from Sam's book and enjoy herself. After all, lots of people didn't die every day.

About the Author

Robb Forman Dew was born in Mount Vernon, Ohio, and grew up in Baton Rouge, Louisiana. For the past thirty years, she has lived in Williamstown, Massachusetts, with her husband, who is a professor of history at Williams College. The recipient of a Guggenheim Fellowship, Dew is the author of the novels *Dale Loves Sophie to Death,* for which she received the National Book Award, *The Time of Her Life, Fortunate Lives, The Evidence Against Her,* and, most recently, *The Truth of the Matter,* as well as a memoir, *The Family Heart.*